James Calbraith is a Poland-born writer, foodie and traveller, currently residing in South London. His debut historical fantasy novel, "The Shadow of Black Wings", has reached ABNA semi-finals. It was published in July 2012 and hit the Historical Fantasy and Alternate History bestsellers list on Amazon US and UK.

Praise for *The Shadow of Black Wings*

"Fast paced and full of energy."
— Adrian Tchaikovsky,
author of the *Shadows of the Apt*

"This manuscript is full of highly crafted detail that will make readers shiver at times with fear and delight...a familiar yet highly original fantasy that is a worthwhile read."
— Publishers Weekly

"The real-world cultures are incredibly well-researched and truthful, and yet well-balanced with the fantasy elements. An intriguing and impressive series."
— Ben Galley,
author of the *Emaneska Series*

P·F·V·S

By James Calbraith

THE YEAR OF THE DRAGON
Book One: The Shadow of Black Wings
Book Two: The Warrior's Soul
Book Three: The Islands in the Mist
Book Four: The Rising Tide
The Year of the Dragon Books 1-4 Delux Edition

Transmission
Dragonbone Chest

Visit James Calbraith's official website at
jamescalbraith.com
for the latest news, book details, and other information
Or sign up for the newsletter at:
tinyletter.com/jcalbraith

The Islands in the Mist

Book Three of
The Year of the Dragon

James Calbraith

FLYING
SQUID

Published July 2012 by Flying Squid

ISBN-13: 978-83-935529-5-5

Cover Illustration: Daniel Kordek
Map Illustrations: Jared Blando and Flying Squid
Cover Design: Flying Squid

TABLE OF CONTENTS

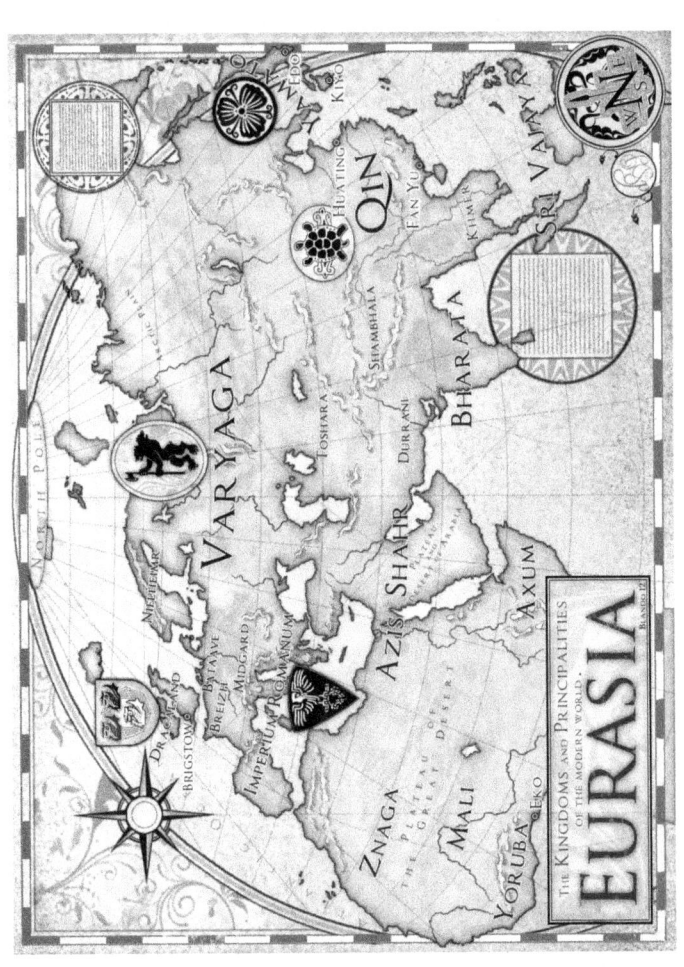

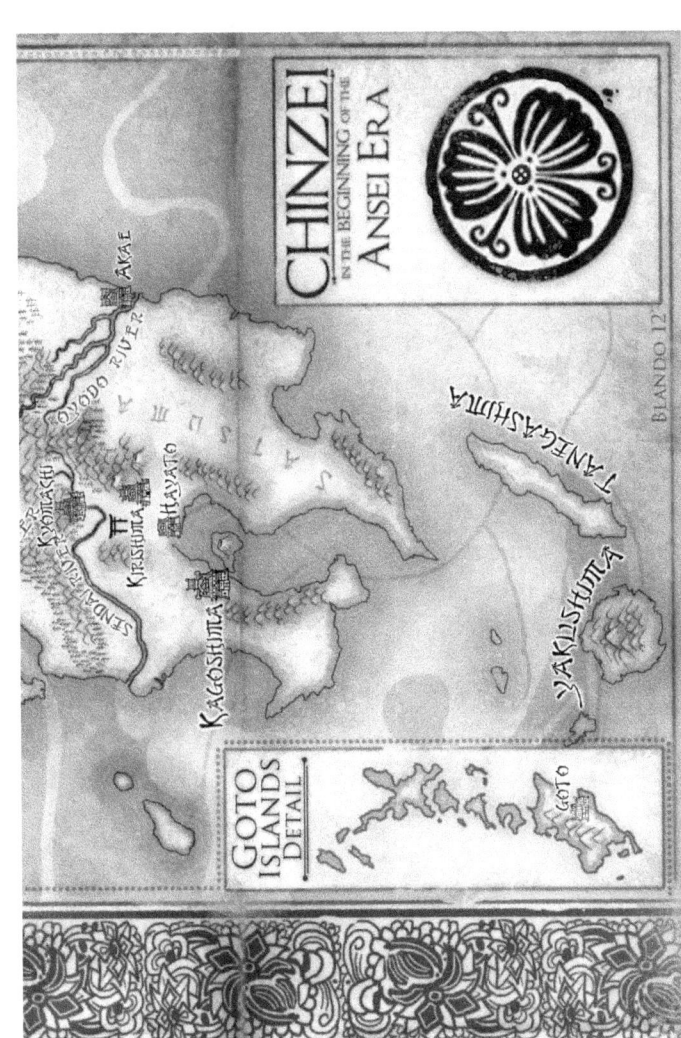

CHINZEI
IN THE BEGINNING OF THE
ANSEI ERA

BLANDO.12

AKAE

ŌYODO RIVER

KYOMACHI

KIRISHIMA
HAYATO

SENDAI RIVER

KAGOSHIMA

TANEGASHIMA

YAKUSHIMA

GOTO
ISLANDS
DETAIL

GOTO

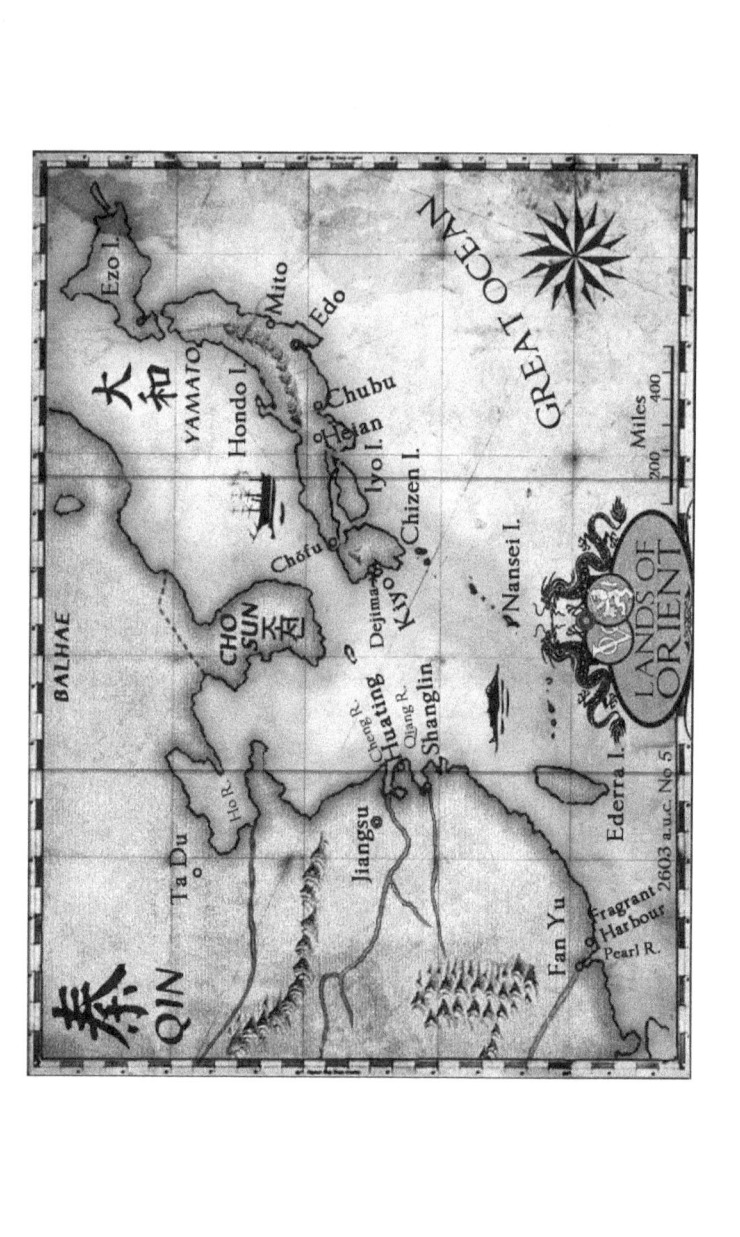

The spring is a dawn. The vast sky turns pale, the peaks of the mountains brighten gently. In the purple glow, the thin clouds linger towards the horizon.

The Pillow Book

PROLOGUE

The white silk of his robe was stained with the blood of his brethren.

Wet sand squeaked under his bare feet. At the break of dawn the sea was silent, cold and dark like the swords which slaughtered the priests at the Mekari. His brothers had thrown themselves against the blades to protect him and that which he carried away.

The Jewel was not for human hands to hold. The orb of white crystal burned his skin and flesh like a glowing ember. He bit his lips and endured.

The black line of gnarled, twisted pines moved closer with his every breath. He dared not look back; he knew the grey-clad assassins were near. He hoped to lose them in the dark forest growing on the windswept seaward slopes of the nearby dune ridge. If he could only make it to those trees…

Out of the corner of his eye he glimpsed the falling blade and instinctively raised his hand to shield himself. The sword clanged harmlessly. The white sleeve of his robe fell, revealing an arm covered with black scales, glinting in the first rays of the rising sun.

THE ISLANDS IN THE MIST

He grasped the blade and snapped it in two. The swordsman stared incredulously at his broken weapon, then at the long, sharp claws reaching for his eyes.

He left the howling assassin to bleed out onto the sand and kept on running. The trees were now less than fifty paces away, their safe shadows beckoning him invitingly. The others were now so close behind he could hear the shuffling of their feet. He stumbled, losing precious seconds. Thirty paces. Twenty. His aching calves cried for him to stop, but he ignored the pain. His heart pounded as if trying to break free from the ribcage. Just a little more effort. Just a few more steps.

He glimpsed them standing among the trees, swords drawn, and realised all was lost. He slowed down and stopped. The men behind him stopped too, waiting, patient. He turned around. There were three of them, all in the same grey, unmarked uniforms, solemn faces without a trace of emotion. Two more approached unhurriedly from the forest.

They could see the Jewel clearly, shining like a beacon through his right hand and the white silk sleeve, but, for the moment, were more concerned with the left hand, armed with its deadly claws. Wary of the fate of their comrade, the swordsmen bid their time until, at last, the first one leapt towards him with the weapon raised. There was no war cry, not even a hastening of breath.

The sun rising over the dunes painted the sea as crimson as the blood of the five men lying in the sand and the robe of the long-haired, gaunt faced man standing before him.

"I'm impressed," the man said, grinning to show his sharp, black teeth. His eyes glinted like nuggets of pure gold. In his right hand he was holding a giant sword, almost four feet in length. "So, this is how the last of the Sea Dragons fights."

The priest said nothing, saving his strength. Two of his claws were broken, his left eye gouged, his stomach and chest cut with many deep wounds but, somehow, he was still standing. He no longer felt any pain, only weariness.

The man in the crimson robe drew his sword and threw away the plain wooden sheath.

"This is where you should say something poignant," he remarked and raised the weapon horizontally above his head. The priest wondered if it was too late to pray to the great Watatsumi for help.

With a sudden roar he lunged forwards. The man in the crimson robe stepped back and brought the sword down. The blade struck the priest's right shoulder, slicing the arm cleanly off his body, but the claws pierced deep into the enemy's chest. No blood pulsed in the swordsman's veins; no heart beat inside the ribcage.

The demon laughed and pushed the priest away. He reached down and wrestled the Jewel, clutched in the hand, though the arm was cut clean off. A frown marred its pale face as the gem's white light burned through the parchment-thin skin.

"That's not right," he murmured to himself. The priest tried to crawl away, slipping and stumbling, but the demon grabbed him by the folds of the white silk robe, turned effortlessly and, with a swift stab, pierced his chest.

With dying eyes, the priest watched as his own blood stained red the Jewel of the Ebbs, turning the stone from a white diamond into the purest of rubies.

CHAPTER I

Slender fingers picked the polished piece of white clamshell up from the wooden bowl and dropped it onto the intersection between the straight black lines with a soft tap.

Atsuko straightened and looked up from the board. Her eyes met those of Komatsu and she smiled encouragingly. He lowered his gaze immediately and pretended to focus on the setup of the black and white stones on the rectangle of golden *kaya* wood.

The boy is very silent today, she thought. *No, not the boy. Komatsu is a man already.* They were both the same age after all. With his top-knot perfectly straight and his black kimono lined on his shoulders without a crease, he seemed very presentable. Any woman he chose for a bride could deem herself fortuitous.

The stone of black slate clicked on the board. Komatsu nodded, acknowledging his move.

"I am to travel to Edo," she said, picking up a white stone and studying its surface carefully. Komatsu looked at her, startled, but composed himself in an instant.

"I know," he replied.

"Ah?"

"Tadayuki-*sama* told me."

"I see."

Tap. The white stone joined four others in a group which seemed hopelessly trapped in a ladder pattern.

"I may never return."

Komatsu swallowed loudly before answering.

"If such be the will of Nariakira-*dono*…"

His fingers reached for another stone.

"I'm leaving in two days."

The black stone dropped back into the bowl with a clatter.

"Two days…? But I thought…"

"Father's request. The auguries for a later date proved inauspicious. Everything is ready for my departure."

"*Hime*…"

He closed his mouth, straightened his back and nodded again.

"I wish you all the best."

"Thank you."

The black stone tapped louder than the others.

"You broke the ladder, Komatsu-*kun*," she noticed, "you haven't got any better since we last played. Have my lessons been so bad?"

"I'm sorry, *hime*. I am a poor student. And your skills at *igo* are unmatched."

8

"Nonsense," she said sharply, "I can see your mind is elsewhere today."

"I'm sorry," he repeated.

A black kite screeched in the sky. They were sitting in an open room in the summer house overlooking Nariakira Shimazu's famed garden. She could see the summit of the great Sakurajima above the treetops, a thin plume of white ash rising from the tip straight into the sky – or was it the smoke from her father's elemental processing plants?

She looked to the corner of the room where a Bataavian wind machine of brass and polished wood stood, placed there to please the guests with a cooling breeze. Lord Nariakira was very proud of the invention and had one installed in every building in the garden, but she didn't like the clackety sound the device made. She unfolded her paper fan and started to cool herself the traditional way.

"The air is still today," she remarked, "it feels like summer already."

"Yes, *hime.*"

"Oh, stop being so formal, Komatsu-*kun.* You act as if we hadn't known each other since childhood."

He looked her straight in the eyes. His face tensed.

"You weren't a princess then, Atsuko."

"No, I suppose not." She sighed. "We all must carry our burdens without complaint."

"Is being the daughter of a *daimyo* really such a burden?"

Atsuko twisted her mouth in a wry smile. She smiled a lot, knowing that her wide, slightly pouty mouth was not one of her best features; smiling helped a little.

"Father has great expectations of my mission to Edo."

Komatsu nodded.

"Nariakira-*dono* is greatly preoccupied with the matters of state."

She touched the stones in the bowl, enjoying their smooth coolness.

"Do you know why I have learned to play *igo* so well?"

"I have often wondered. It is an unusual pastime for a woman."

"It is perhaps because I am a woman."

"Ah?"

"In *shōgi* every piece has a rank and a role. Even the golden general can only move in one way. But in *igo* all stones are equal and their fates are never determined. Depending on the player's actions, an *igo* piece may die a pointless death, or change the fate of the entire battle."

"Like the ladder breaker," he said and smirked. "Are you a ladder breaker, *hime*… Atsuko?"

"I am but a humble woman," she replied softly, "and my fate is what the player wishes it to be."

She heard the tinkling of bells and the whirring of wheels squeaking across the floor of the verandah. Her chaperon automaton was returning to escort her back to the female quarters.

10

"Promise me," she said, standing up, "that we will finish this game one day."

"Y… yes, *hime*."

Komatsu also stood up and bowed deeply. She felt tears welling up in her throat.

"Thank you. Goodbye, Komatsu-*kun*."

"Goodbye, Atsuko."

The palanquin standing on the slate pavement was the most ornate she had ever seen. *Fit for a princess indeed*, she thought bitterly. Covered entirely in black lacquer and gold leaf ornaments, with the great cross-in-circle emblem of the Shimazu clan on the sides and red silk-covered roof, it was so large and heavy that six of Satsuma's strongest porters only managed to carry it with great difficulty. A brass spout in the shape of a dragon protruded from its roof – the exhaust pipe of a small wind machine. Lord Nariakira spared no expenses to make her portable home as comfortable as he could. After all, she was to spend the next few months inside.

A soft breeze picked up from the sea, scattering the browned petals of the last of the azaleas. The long procession of servants, porters, scribes and retainers waited for her in a rigid line. An unusually large oxcart with an iron studded box stood before the garden gates, surrounded by armed guards. She recognised a few of her father's wizards standing beside it in silence.

A girl approached her with a parasol and gestured towards the palanquin.

"My lady," she said with a slightly trembling voice.

"Are you so eager to get rid of me?" Atsuko asked. The girl gasped and dropped to her hands and knees, apologizing for the rudeness. Atsuko recognised her – the youngest daughter of one of the lowest retainers of the Shimazu clan, destined for eternal servitude to her superiors unless a higher ranking samurai decided to adopt her.

"I'm sorry," Atsuko said, "please, stand up. You're Shosuke-*sama*'s sister, aren't you?"

"Yes, *hime*."

"Is he well?"

"Yes, *hime*."

"Did his facial hair succumb to the barber's knife at last?"

The girl giggled, covering her mouth politely.

"No, *hime*. It still grows in unruly patches."

"I wish he could be here to see me off. And Saigō-*sama*. And Komatsu-*kun*." Her voice trailed off wistfully.

"*Hime?*"

"Oh, nothing. Very well, no point keeping everyone waiting. Are you part of the procession?"

"Only to Akae, *hime*."

"I will be glad of your company."

The girl bowed and then, seeing something behind Atsuko's back, she bowed again.

Atsuko turned around to face her father. Lord Nariakira grimaced in a pretend smile, but she could see sadness in his eyes and was grateful to share this glimpse into his heart.

"Father-*sama*," she nodded.

"Are you ready, child? This will be the longest journey you will ever undertake."

"I am prepared well, Father-*sama*."

"Good."

"Father-*sama*, are you sure this oxcart will fit on a ship?"

"Do not concern yourself with it, Atsuko. It will only go as far as Kirishima."

"But what is it?"

The *daimyo*'s smile was now real and broad.

"A gift from the Gods, some might say. Something *almost* as important for my plans as you."

She remembered something. "Does it have something to do with that fishing village you had destroyed two weeks ago?"

Lord Nariakira's eyes narrowed. "Where did you hear about that?"

She smiled and lowered her gaze in pretend coyness. "The paper walls of the palace are thin and the narrow corridors carry the voices far… I know how you despise killing peasants, Father-*sama*. Something extraordinary must have happened."

The *daimyo* scowled. "You're right. The peasants are the lifeblood of the province, and I wouldn't waste any of them if I didn't have to. Forget about what you've heard, Daughter, and forget about the oxcart. I'll make sure the walls of my palace are reinforced and the voices in the corridors *stifled*."

She shuddered under his angry stare. Lord Nariakira was a man who did not hesitate to strike, even at his own family, if it meant protecting his secrets. She turned towards the palanquin when she felt a gentle shudder under her feet. She swayed and Lord Nariakira caught her arm to assist her.

"Sakurajima is restless today," she said.

"She's saying her goodbyes. From now on, another mountain's shadow will be watching over you – the great Fujisan."

She put her foot into the black and golden box and turned her head one last time towards the garden and the mansion. She wiped her eyes with the sleeve of her kimono.

"You will forget all your woes in Edo," her father reassured her. He was smiling again.

How quickly he changes his mood.

"There're too many distractions to worry about the past."

"Yes, Father-*sama*."

"I will join you in a few months, once I deal with all my matters in Satsuma."

14

"I shall await you eagerly, Father-*sama*."

She stepped inside the palanquin at last and sat herself down as comfortably as she could among the black silk pillows, scented with plum blossom. She lowered the golden grate, enclosing herself in the darkness. The wind machine attached to the ceiling began to whirr and clack rhythmically.

A cross-shaped shadow passed over his face, waking him from slumber; another albatross far above the clouds. The majestic birds were the only diversions in the featureless azure sky. Even clouds were scarce. The sea and sky were remarkably calm, almost boringly so.

Samuel reached for the barrel and poured the last few drops of fresh water into a tin cup. The raft hobbled dangerously as he let slide the now empty barrel into the sea.

There could be no other way to describe what had happened to him other than a miracle. The old nameless God of his ancestors must have looked upon him with a sympathetic eye on that terrible night.

He still could not remember how he had found himself, soaked and battered, on the piece of wooden decking floating on the dark waves. The *Ladon* burned and sank on the horizon. Screams of the dying carried over the sea for miles and he could do nothing to help them, struggling himself to survive.

When he woke again it was high noon. He was still not far from where the ship had gone down – this was another miracle. A vessel the size of *Ladon* never sinks without a trace – there was an ocean of buoyant debris strewn all around him. Using a wide board as a paddle, Samuel sailed among these riches, trying to gather as much as he could onto his little makeshift raft – barrels of freshwater, crates of rusk, sacks of dried meat. With careful use his finds could have lasted him for weeks.

And then his luck – or Providence's favour – had run out. A storm raged, not strong enough to drown him, but devious enough to destroy all the meticulously prepared provisions. By the time the wind passed and waters calmed, he was left with one crate of hardtacks and a single barrel.

To make matters worse, looking at the stars, Samuel realised he had drifted to the north-east of his original position, into the open sea, far away from any known land.

In his grandmother's fairy tales, which he read from a big old tattered book written in strange letters, the unnamed God was often trying his people. One particular story had always terrified Samuel. As the result of a wager with one of his servants, the God tormented some poor human in increasingly horrendous ways, just to prove his point. Samuel had never learned the end of the story – his mother saw him crying and forbade him to ever read from the book again.

Is this unnamed God now testing me?

The raft bobbed up and down ceaselessly as the current carried him ever farther away into the vast ocean. He had lost count of the days. Food and water had run out a long time ago, and with them – hope. His skin, burned by the sun, was peeling off and covered in painful blisters, his mouth and throat parched, his eyelids stuck together with dust. He lay still, motionless, waiting for death.

A shape appeared in the water, long, vertical and black, like the fin of some strange fish. The sea water bubbled and foamed. A black form emerged slowly out of the waves, larger than the greatest whale. Samuel gathered the last of his strength to raise himself on one elbow and observe the mysterious phenomenon. *So this is how my life will end ...eaten by a monster in the middle of an empty ocean...*

Metal fittings glinted in the sun as the strange object halted just a few yards from the raft. It was no fish – it was a machine! A round hatch screeched and began to unscrew at the top. Samuel waited patiently. As his raft drifted alongside of the vessel, he saw an easily- recognisable crest painted on the black steel hull; a two-headed bear, rampant, holding an axe. The Varyaga Khaganate. What were the Northern people doing in these waters, and what kind of a ship was this?

The hatch unscrewed at last and a bearded sailor emerged, wearing a blue and white uniform and a white flat cap. He shouted something in the stiff, harsh tongue of the Varyaga and reached down to pull out a kisbie ring tied to a rope. The ring-shaped buoy landed with a splash a few feet from Samuel, but he was already too weary to keep hold of it. Seeing this, the sailor jumped into the water and, holding on to the kisbie ring with one hand and to Samuel's raft with the other, let himself be pulled in by another crew member. More curious sailors came out onto the narrow deck to watch the *Ladon's* doctor being brought up a rope ladder.

THE ISLANDS IN THE MIST

The inside of the cigar-shaped ship was dark and stuffy, smelling of oil, tar and sweat, filled with the buzzing hum of pumps and engines. Samuel coughed and heaved, but had nothing left to throw up. They carried him down a narrow corridor and laid him on a canvas bunk.

He allowed himself to drift off.

The walking machine waded across the muddy-brown river to the other side. A lonely shell fell into the water a dozen feet away with a whistle and a splash but no explosion – a dud.

The ground was pock-marked with craters and scorched with dragon flame. Remnants of tents, carts, kitchens and destroyed war machines were strewn all over the plain between the walls of the Huating Concession and the river bend. A few rear-guard marauders wandered about the field of battle, assessing what seemed like the complete rout and destruction of their army. The soldiers of Huating garrison wasted a few bullets chasing them off.

"That's the last of them," said Edern, lowering his binoculars.

"They'll be back," said Dylan. "They are merely regrouping. The delta is too important."

A strange clanking and hissing sound came from behind their backs.

"Here comes the Admiral," said Edern, turning. A white-haired, surprisingly lively man, short and stout, approached them from the pier where his cutter had moored. As he walked, steam puffed from a small brass box at his belt. A fetching young aide-de-camp followed, a few feet behind, carrying a large satchel and an old sword.

"*Rear* Admiral," said Dylan quietly and climbed down from the palisade to welcome the newcomer and to introduce himself.

"Ab Ifor?" the Admiral squinted, remembering something. "*Bore da!* I used to have a midshipman called Ifor. Good sailing stock, you Gwynedd folk."

He turned a spigot on the box at his side. The gears in his shoulder and elbow whirred and his hand reached out in a greeting. Dylan clasped it carefully, feeling the cold metal through the calfskin glove. *An automaton.* The Admiral's right arm and right leg were artificial, thaumaturgic devices made of steel rods, brass clockwork and leather straps. The contraptions were noisy and their moves were clumsy, but they seemed to be serving the Admiral well enough.

How could anyone outside the Royal Family afford something like this?

"We have sea in our blood, Sir. Or so my wife says."

"A sailor with a wife!" The Admiral laughed. "Ho! Now there's a dangerous combination. And what about you, Banneret? Is a Faer lass waiting for you back in your forest?"

Edern's eyes darted aside. "No, Sir."

The Admiral stopped laughing and turned back to Dylan.

"Take us to your war room. You have a war room prepared, Ardian?"

"I have requisitioned the council's building. This way, Admiral. Edern, will you take the Admiral's aide to the quartermaster. We need to figure out how to accommodate everyone. I predict we will have a lot more guests coming…"

The Tylwyth Teg looked at the handsome young man standing shyly behind the Rear Admiral and grinned.

Rear Admiral Broughton Reynolds leaned over the map, straightening out a rolling corner with his left hand. The metal arm hung limply along his right side, switched off – the noise and fumes would be too bothersome in the small enclosed space. The map was smudged with soot and blotched with ink and oil.

And I thought Fan Yu was bad, thought Dylan. The "war room" he had managed to procure on short notice was just a small chamber in the basement of the council hall, with a single table, an evertorch on the ceiling and a battered cabinet against the wall.

"And where are the Councillors, Ardian?" the Admiral asked, looking up from the map.

"They wanted to give the concession away to the rebels, so I had them locked up for treason."

Reynolds laughed with the hearty laugh that was beginning to grow on Dylan.

"Dracaland needs more men like you, ab Ifor. Do you know, there are folk back in Lundenburgh who think we should support *the rebels* instead of the rightful rulers?"

Dylan grimaced. "Their ideology can appeal to certain… elements in the Capital."

"Ah, yes. But, it's bad for business, right, lad? Changing regimes like that. Much better the old evil."

"I believe so."

"Politics! Pah," the Admiral snorted. "All I know is that I have my orders to keep this place safe from any barbarians, no matter what side they're on. War! Let's get back to that. What can you tell me about our situation, Ardian?"

Dylan briefly described what his scouts had been reporting. Once the Rear Admiral's flotilla steamed up the Wusung River and removed the immediate threat of the rebel siege, the riders of the Second Dragoons were able to fly once more and the information started trickling again to Dylan's headquarters. The Heavenly Army had indeed captured the old Qin capital of Jiankang and managed to reduce all government-held cities along the great Chang River delta. Huating was the last fortress standing between them and the sea.

"The rivers are the key to all war in this land," Dylan explained. "We must control both riverbanks if we are to even think of successful defence."

"Rivers? I'm not a pike, Ardian, I'm a shark."

"The rivers and canals of Qin are like the straits of the lesser seas, Sir. The Chang is fully navigable for a thousand miles, even for a flotilla like yours. I'm certain we'll be able to use the firepower that you have brought us, wherever the war takes us."

The Admiral scratched his side-burns in thought.

"Well. A man learns all his life – I may yet have to learn how to fight on a river. But what did you have in mind?"

Dylan put his finger on the map and winced, feeling the grease.

"A thirty-mile perimeter, all the way to the Tien-shan Lake here. We will need two thousand people."

"We have two hundred."

"I know. But we can train and arm the people of Huating. They have already requested it. I have the first hundred waiting outside the walls."

The Admiral's eyes widened and he started coughing violently.

"You wish to give *them* our weapons? Have you gone mad, man?"

"Anyone can be trained to use a rifle, Admiral. They are eager to learn."

"I bet they are."

"They are just townsfolk who want to defend their land. The Qin army has abandoned them."

Reynolds squinted one eye.

"What's your history with this place, Ardian? I'm sensing this isn't your first time here."

"I have fought in our previous war with Qin."

"Ah, the *Coronet* affair…"

22

"There was a bit more to that. It lasted three years."

"I was stationed in Bharata back then. Recovering from this," he said, patting his iron thigh. "Never paid much attention to the issues of the Orient until I got this assignment."

Dylan said nothing. The Admiral seemed a clever enough person.

Let him figure it out.

"They will need to swear allegiance to the Crown if we're to command them."

"That… may cause problems in the long run."

The Admiral sighed.

"Then we will need to wait for the Emperor's permission."

"Do we have that much time, Sir?"

"How do you think the Qin government will react to us arming their citizens willy-nilly? I may not know these particular people, but politics works the same everywhere. There must be *some* semblance of order."

There were fast steps on the stairs outside and a rapid knock on the door.

"Come in, Banneret."

"Sir, there are dragons coming from the north."

"An attack?" the Admiral asked before Dylan opened his mouth.

"I don't think so. There are only three of them, and the beasts are all yellow."

"What does that mean?" Reynolds turned to Dylan.

"Yellow is the Imperial colour. I believe our wait may be much shorter than we had expected."

The beasts coiled on the landing glade, surrounded by curious soldiers, many of whom had not seen a Qin dragon up close, on the ground. They were smaller and slimmer than the mounts of the Marines, their yellow scales smooth, more like those of a fish than a snake. Their horns branched like deer antlers, and their ends were rounded, not sharp. And of course there was only a vestige of wings in the middle of the long, serpentine body. But there was no doubt of the kinship between the *long* and their Western cousins. The same wise eyes shone above the many-teethed maws, the same sharp claws glistened at the ends of the muscular legs, and the same commanding dread surrounded the creatures. Perhaps even more so; the Qin dragons, especially the Imperial Yellows, spread among their admirers not a primitive, wild fear, but an inspiring awe.

Dylan could see this awe in his men. None dared approach the beasts closer than a few yards. The troops formed a tight circle around the landing glade, murmuring and pointing with respect.

The man who climbed down from the largest of the beasts looked around and smirked with arrogance. "Narrow" was the only word Dylan could come up with to describe this strange person: tall, slim and angular in face and movements. He took off the overcoat, revealing the many-buttoned jacket of yellow silk underneath – sign of the Emperor's favour – and handed it to one of his men. While a servant hastily combed his pointy beard, he put a round blue cloth cap on his bald head, straightened the creases on his clothes and marched proudly towards Dylan and the Admiral.

He barked a few sentences. His words sounded as angular and sharp as he looked.

"The Bohan is taking over the command of this city and all troops within," spoke the interpreter. He was an opposite of his master in every way: crescent-shaped eyebrows and crescent-shaped moustache in a round face. Instead of the rich court robes, he wore a simple dark blue coat with snow-white cuffs. The Dracalish words flew smooth and round from his mouth, with only a hint of an accent.

"Bohan?" whispered the Admiral, "is that the man's name or his title?"

"Both, I would guess."

"The *Bohan* is not on Qin territory," the Admiral said loudly. "Or do I need to remind you of the treaties between our Empires? His troops are over there – ," he added, pointing towards the walls of Huating, " – what's left of them."

"I hear you have been arming the Emperor's subjects. This is a violation of the treaties and reason enough to revoke your concession."

How did he learn about it so fast? How do they always know about everything?

"No Imperial subject has yet been given a weapon from our stock," answered Dylan. "We had merely received their request and have been pondering an answer when you arrived."

The two men consulted briefly.

"Whose request was that?"

Not a chance.

"Some of the townsfolk – I do not know their names."

The man called Bohan eyed Dylan suspiciously and barked some more words, pointing at the Ardian and the Admiral.

"Which one of you is the Commander of this place?"

"That will be Ardian ab Ifor," replied Reynolds, "I am merely the commander of the flotilla you see stationed on the river."

The Qinese followed the Admiral's hand and opened his eyes wide, as if only now noticing the imposing line of warships, their guns aimed at Huating and beyond. At last, he nodded.

"You will refrain from answering the petition and from any contact with the civilian populace outside these walls," the Bohan ordered. "This rebellion is an inner matter of Qin. We are grateful for your assistance, but no more will be required at this moment."

With that, he turned back towards the yellow dragons.

"*The Qin army's skills of camouflage are next to none,*" Dylan said quietly in Qin. The Bohan turned again.

"*What did you say?*"

"Admiral, did our scouts spot any Imperial troops coming in Huating's direction?" Dylan asked, pretending to ignore the question.

"Only what seemed like groups of marauders, wandering to and fro north of the river."

"And yet the Bohan here assures us that our assistance will no longer be required. What can he possibly mean?"

"Perhaps his armies are moving underground!" replied the Admiral and they both laughed.

The Bohan's face turned purple.

"The invincible Imperial Army is needed elsewhere," the interpreter said, his calm delivery belying his master's rage. "We do not need to concern ourselves with every stockade in the middle of a cholera-ridden marsh."

"Oh, that's a relief. When the Heavenly Army returns, we can just stand back and watch the city fall for the second time."

The Bohan gnashed his teeth. He spat out his last sentence and marched back to the dragons.

"You will have your answer tomorrow," the interpreter said before joining his master.

THE ISLANDS IN THE MIST

CHAPTER II

A gust of wind shook the ferns and the thin branches of the cypress trees surrounding the glade. The mist parted revealing a samurai, tall and heavily-built, wearing a gaudy, colourful kimono of yellow and blue, and a purple hooded cape. A number of small canvas pouches and wooden *inro* containers hung off his *obi* sash. He shook the blood off his twin swords and started to wipe the blades with a piece of paper.

Bran recognised the round, slightly bulging eyes and the whisker above the narrow lips, that were twisted in a strange, disconcerting smile.

"You're the man from the inn!"

"So I am," the samurai replied. He bowed in a greeting as if only now noticing the three travellers. "And you're the boy who can drink like a seasoned warrior," he grinned.

"What are you doing here?"

"Saving your lives," the stranger said. Satisfied with the state of his swords he sheathed them into the plain black scabbards. He said nothing else.

"Did…did Yokoi-*dono* sent you?" asked Satō, lowering her weapon. Bran looked at her sharply. Her hands were trembling, she could barely stand. Nagomi propped her up by the shoulder. Her skin was pale, her lips trembled, her eyes lacked focus. They all badly needed rest, but Nagomi seemed to be in the worst shape.

The samurai looked at her and blinked once before answering.

"Yes, I have been sent by Yokoi-*dono*. I should have introduced myself yesterday; perhaps we could have avoided this… debacle." He nodded at the dead bodies.

Satō let her sword slip to the ground and leaned her back against the earthen wall of the mound.

"You have our gratitude…"

"You may call me Dōraku." The samurai bowed again. "I left food and water by the side of the road. By your leave…"

Samurai disappeared into the forest.

"What luck," the wizardess sighed, collapsing to the ground, "Yokoi-*sama* made good of his promise."

"I'm not so certain," said Bran. He walked up to the dead bandits. The *onmyōji's* headless corpse was covered in blood that was quickly drying; the others seemed as if they had been dead for a long time; their faces had now returned to human form. He still could not detect any magic. *Does my True Sight simply not work on Yamato spells?*

"What do you mean?" asked Satō.

"How do we know he's telling the truth?"

"He did save our lives."

"This could have just been a ruse."

"Why bother? He could have killed us in a blink of an eye."

"There are fates worse than death," said Nagomi quietly.

"Not you too!" Satō raised her hands in exasperation.

"I just think we should be cautious, that's all."

The samurai returned noisily with a large bundle of luggage. He took out a large *bento* box.

"It's not much but you can have it all," he said. "I have already eaten today."

He then presented a dusty sword. "I found this on the road," he said. "I see your sheath is empty." He pointed to Bran's waist.

"This is my weapon. You have my thanks."

"Interesting blade. I have not seen a design like this… for a long time."

Bran bowed stiffly, sheathing the sword without a comment.

Satō looked to the sky. "I suppose we're staying here for the night."

Bran turned to Dōraku.

"Will you not come and sit with us… Dōraku-*sama*?"

The samurai hesitated. He glanced at Nagomi for a moment so brief only Bran managed to notice. "There doesn't seem to be enough room inside. I don't mind the rain and the air is nice and fresh."

"Except for the smell of the dead."

"They do not smell yet," the samurai replied, smirking. "If you need me, I'll be over there," he said, pointing to the remnants of an old wooden shed, half-buried in the ferns and ivy.

By the light of Bran's flamespark, Satō unpacked the *bento* box, reached for the rice ball and started munching it as eagerly as her manners allowed. Nagomi gingerly picked up a piece of broiled eel.

"Aren't you going to eat, Bran?" asked Satō, swallowing the rice loudly.

"I'm fine."

"It's not poisoned."

"I'll have some later."

He did not wish to argue but he couldn't shake the feeling that there was something odd about the whiskered samurai.

"You said wearing two swords was just for show," he said.

She thought for a moment before answering.

"I have never seen anyone *fight* with two blades. I will need to ask Dōraku-*sama* about his technique."

We will need to ask him about many things, Bran thought but decided to keep his doubts to himself. Feeling his strength slowly coming back as he rested, he charged the flamespark a little more. The light, until now the equivalent of a faint, small candle, illuminated the cave like a bright chandelier, revealing the limestone walls around them. He looked up and opened his mouth in silent astonishment.

Nagomi followed Bran's finger with her eyes and, in the flickering light of his magic flame, gazed at the white limestone wall over their heads. It was covered with carvings, etched painstakingly into the soft rock from the top to the bottom of the chamber.

They were primitive drawings, made only of thin straight lines, but they were strangely compelling and seemed to be brimming with ancient primeval power. She could feel their energy. Bran was pointing to a group engraved in the middle of the wall some four feet from the ground. It showed several human beings, stick figures with dots for heads; some of them had horns, others wings. All were gathered around an outline of a circle and inside it, a few specks of bright blue enamel were still stuck to the limestone. The figures were kneeling before the circle. Above the scene were engraved serpent-like creatures, coiling zigzag-like in the air, with bony wings spread wide. The largest of them all, in the most prominent position, had eight long necks ending with eight large heads.

Even she knew at once what they were. *Dorako. Dragons.*

"What is it...?" Bran managed to finally find his words.

"The Ancients," said Nagomi, "they must have carved it while building this tomb."

Bran leaned over to examine the roughly hewn carvings.

"What do you think that round thing is? The Sun? The Moon?"

"I have no idea," Satō said, shrugging. She joined Bran by the wall but pretended not to care much about the discovery. "Nobody really knows anything about the Ancients."

"It's blue," he said, tracing the outline of the circle with the fingers of his left hand, "look, there are still bits of colour left. A blue... stone."

He looked at his hand as if remembering something. Nagomi remembered too. *What through tide stone can you see?*

"I... I have something to tell you," she spoke softly. They turned to her in surprise and all the carefully prepared sentences evaporated.

"Well?" Satō urged her.

With a breaking voice she recollected what she had seen in the Waters of Scrying all those months ago: the red, blue and green stones, the man in the red robe, the sea monster and the ray of jade green light.

"There was more," she added. "Kazuko-*hime* showed me an old scroll with black dragons drawn on it: the rest of the Prophecy. It spoke of the coming of monsters, the Storm God and an eight-headed serpent..."

They stared at her for a long time in silence.

"So you think my grandfather's ring – the blue stone – is somehow involved in all this?" Bran said. "And the eight-headed serpent is this one, here?" he asked, nodding at the largest of the carvings.

"That's an ancient legend," said Satō, "Orochi, the eight-headed dragon, was the father of all the *ryū*. It is said it was slain thousands of years ago. But why haven't you told us all of this before?" she asked Nagomi.

"Kazuko-*hime* believed the Prophecy foretold the… fall of the *Taikun*. She asked me to keep it a secret."

"*Fall of the…!*" Satō gasped.

"Then why are you telling us this now?" asked Bran.

"Because…" Nagomi took a deep breath, "it doesn't matter anymore. The damage is done. The High Priestess is dead."

Satō's face turned grey. Bran narrowed his eyes and then slowly nodded.

"How do you know?" the wizardess asked.

"I saw her in a vision in Hitoyoshi and then in a dream, last night…"

"So you're not certain – "

"I am!" she protested. "The vision was very clear."

"I don't know much about these things," Bran interjected. "You speak of visions, prophecies – is it anything like geomancy?"

"I don't know what – " Nagomi started, but Satō interrupted her.

35

"It's just as vague and enigmatic. There are many interpretations – "

"Not this time," said Nagomi. "I know what I saw!" she started coughing. Exhausted, she leaned back against the wall and could not speak for a while.

"I don't doubt that," the wizardess said, "But what if you saw something in the future, not the present?"

"I know…what…I saw," Nagomi repeated. She reached for the water flask and both Bran and Satō rushed to help her; the boy was faster, pressing the bottle's mouth to her lips.

"How did she die?" asked Bran when she finished drinking.

"Executed by the Magistrate."

Only when she spoke those words did she understand and accept their meaning. Her heart was surprisingly calm.

"It's my fault," the boy said.

"Everything she did was of her own accord," she said. "I'm sure she wouldn't have helped you if she didn't believe it was important…"

"Important? Why? I'm just a castaway. You should have left me on that beach."

"Haven't you been listening?" she protested, "the Prophecy…"

"Even if my ring *is* somehow involved, it's not like *I* have anything to do with it. I just carry it around."

"What about the other two stones?" asked Satō, "what of the blood stone and the jade?"

Bran's eyes glinted in the light of the flamespark and Nagomi thought of her own interpretation of the Prophecy, the one she hadn't even shared with the High Priestess.

"I don't know… those remain a mystery."

"All my ring ever does is light up whenever I contact my dragon," the boy said.

"You've never mentioned it before," Satō eyed Bran's hand.

"It never occurred to me that it was important. I thought it was just some magireactive mineral, like Carmot."

"And yet the *onmyōji* attacked us because of your ring. I wonder how he knew?"

"I bet that man outside knows about it too," Bran said, nodding towards the tomb's entrance. "I noticed him glancing at my hand a few times."

"That doesn't mean anything. People in Yamato don't wear rings, so it's natural he was curious."

"You seem very eager to trust him."

"Dōraku-*sama* saved us all. I just think he deserves a little more confidence."

"We don't know *anything* about this swordsman. We don't know anything about those bandits. All that happened today could have been an elaborate trap. How did you even manage to find this tomb?"

Satō's hand, holding a pickled plum, stopped halfway between the box and her open mouth. She turned to Nagomi.

"That's a good question – how *dia* we get here? I was following your lead."

"I… I had another vision yesterday," Nagomi admitted and told them about the third of Aoi Aso Shrine's revelations. The first one, concerning her and Bran, she chose to keep to herself. She finished by recounting the last message she had received from Lady Kazuko's spirit.

"Do you think she meant Dōraku-*sama*?" Satō said, biting her lip in doubt.

"Who else?" Bran shook his head in exasperation. "But what was she trying to tell us? 'You must…' what? Trust him? Follow him? Fear him? *Kill him?*"

"I don't know. I'm sorry," Nagomi replied.

"You don't have to apologise," said Satō, "we're all stumbling aimlessly in the dark."

In the silence that filled the tomb they heard the pitter-patter of the rain upon the wooden door frame and the rustling of the cypress trees in the wind. Nagomi raised a hand to cover her mouth.

"We should go to sleep," said Satō, packing the *bento* box and stowing it away in the corner of the chamber, underneath the ancient carvings. "We've learned much today, but we need to think it through in the morning. My father always says there are two things one shouldn't do in excess before night: eating and thinking."

The girls soon fell asleep, despite having to lie on the packed dirt floor without so much as cloaks to cover themselves. Everything they had, except what they carried on them, was lost somewhere on the road.

Bran sat with his back against the limestone wall, his hands wrapped around the hilt of his sword. He was wide awake. The rain poured outside, and the water found its way through the earthen mound and a crack in the stone, dripping rhythmically into a small puddle on the floor. A thunder clapped in the distance.

"*Well, well, so the old witch is dead at last,*" the spirit in his head spoke suddenly.

"What do you care? You didn't know her."

"*On the contrary, boy,*" Shigemasa replied, "*you're forgetting I was one of the Scrying spirits of Suwa. I've known her since she first came down to perform her divinations.*"

"What was she like?"

"*Very noble, I suppose,*" the General admitted with some reluctance, "*and with great insight. She was the only one who could read straight through me whenever I tried to play with the visions too much.*"

"You liked her!" Bran realised with surprise. He got used to thinking of Shigemasa only as a malevolent presence in his head. Now for the first time he had to consider him a real human being.

"*She knew she would die because of what she had been doing – I foretold it myself – but had no fear of death. I respected that.*"

The general fell silent for a while, and when he spoke again, he picked a new subject.

"*Your beast… it is asleep all the time.*"

"How do you know that?"

"*I can see it snoring in front of the gates of your Innermost Keep. I could walk past it now without a problem.*"

Innermost Keep…? The red-eye tower!

"Don't you dare try anything!"

The general laughed bitterly. "*If I wanted to, you couldn't stop me. I can see the walls of your castle crumble all around me. I know how the battle must have exhausted you.*"

"Then why – ?"

"*I am now intrigued with you, Barbarian. This talk of prophecies tonight… I know how they work. I've been there. If what the red-hair says is true… I have waited so long, I can wait a little more …*"

"That's… a relief, I suppose. Of sorts."

"*Make no mistake, it's not because I'm growing soft on you or anything.*"

"I'll remember that."

He wanted to ask about their new companion, but the spirit had already slid away into the dark silence, leaving Bran alone with his thoughts.

He flicked a weak light and directed it towards the carvings on the wall. Their strange inner power continued to intrigue him. He took out his pencil and notepad and copied the drawings as well as he could. *No Westerner has seen these things before me,* he realised. *I'm an explorer, like Cook or Brendan. I should have been noting everything all along.*

Some of the human silhouettes had wings drawn in the same way as the dragons above them. What did it mean? Were they shamans disguised as dragons, or was there some greater mystery behind it?

He touched his ring and it lit up lightly. Satō was right, nobody in Yamato wore this kind of jewellery. Obviously it had been drawing everyone's attention. How could he have missed it? His entire disguise could have been ruined by the tiny trinket. He slipped the ring off his finger and put it inside the black lacquer box. It was safer that way.

The blue stone and the dragons – he had dismissed the connection as coincidence earlier, but now he wasn't so sure any more. All the questions that had made him embark on the sea adventure in the first place were now coming back. What secret had his grandfather bestowed upon him? Who was the Yamato beauty, the beloved Omon? He dared not think yet of Nagomi's divinations. Satō had said so herself, the prophecies were often vague...

He turned away from the wall and looked at the girls, sleeping on the naked floor in their travelling clothes, their silhouettes faintly illuminated by the flamespark. The apprentice lay still, on her back, her dark red hair, with traces of henna washed off by rain, spread on the floor. She seemed barely alive, like some enchanted princess in a fairy-tale. Satō kept moving about, changing position, unable to keep still even in her sleep. She had uneasy dreams.

THE ISLANDS IN THE MIST

He needed to stay awake, to protect them from whatever lurked outside. With his father so often absent, he had felt it his duty to protect their small family from whatever dangers he had imagined. And right now, he realised, Satō and Nagomi were the closest he had to a family in this strange land. *I can't let any of them get hurt*, he thought. *I owe it to them.* The brave wizardess who had lost her father because of him, and the copper-haired girl who had performed what amounted in his eyes to a miracle – and yet remained so humble about it all; these were debts that were difficult to repay.

The girl was a *healer* – and apparently, one of the many in Yamato. His mother, being a Cunning Folk, knew how to brew restorative poultices and soothing concoctions and he had heard of some experiments in using strong, precise thaumaturgy for medical uses, but the conflicting Potentials of the patient and physician made it an expensive and difficult matter. The ability to heal a broken arm within mere minutes remained the stuff of dreams and legends.

His thoughts raced back to his father and the Marines. What would the army of the Dracaland do with the power of healing the wounded on a battlefield? The first modern nation to get its hands on this magic could easily bid for mastery of the whole world. It was a good thing the Yamato were so isolated after all. The Bataavians in Dejima must have known about this, but they chose not to share the news with anyone. The small republic could never defend itself or the Yamato from the likes of Dracaland, Breizh or Midgard, if any of these powers discovered there was something worth fighting for here.

He could not even begin to grasp the rules of the native magic. What good was his knowledge of Potentials, Willpower, Energy Equivalence or Conduits if the spirits of the dead themselves were able to come from beyond the veil to assist the caster? The spirits of the Yamato dead – the *kami*, as Nagomi called them – seemed to simply bypass all the barriers, disregard the laws of nature; and that mage – shattering his *tarian*, fed with Bran's own life energy, with a piece of paper… Summoning demons to aid him… None of this made any sense. How could he try to protect the girls if his magic proved so powerless? Perhaps they did need a bodyguard after all…

The night passed slowly – or so he guessed, unable to see the sky and the stars. The damp air inside the tomb induced a fit of coughing. Satō stirred, almost woken up.

He started quietly chanting the lullaby his mother used to sing, a long time ago on the long winter nights, when they waited for Dylan's return:

> *Huna'n dawel, heno, huna,*
> *Huna'n fwyn, y tlws ei lun;*
> *Pam yr wyt yn awr yn gwenu,*
> *Gwenu'n dirion yn dy hun?*

He remembered Rhian's face by the bed, the carved oaken frame and the cold white-washed walls of his bedroom, illuminated by a dancing fire fae trapped in a jar on the shelf.

43

THE ISLANDS IN THE MIST

Paia ag ofni, dim ona deilen

Gura, gura ar y ddôr-

There was a shrieking yelp and a brawling noise outside. Bran leapt to his feet at once, extinguishing the light. He looked through the slit in the door, but could not see anything in the darkness. He heard growling, which subsided to gurgling and then silence.

Carefully, he removed the door boards and peeked outside, but could see nothing in the darkness. He lit the flamespark again and walked out into the rain, sword in hand. He walked past the bodies of the bandits and further into the forest, crossing the circle of stones, towards a ruined shack, where the strange samurai was supposed to be sleeping.

How could he possibly sleep in this rain? The shed had barely any roof and only faint remains of walls. In the flickering light Bran glimpsed a large shadow to his right. With a heart beating feverishly, he turned towards it. There was a man-sized shape of a creature, sinister in the darkness, slouching, silent. Bran approached the mysterious figure, the grip of his sword now slippery with sweat and rain. Every step he took filled his heart with ever more dread. The night was filled with the smell of death and blood.

What am I doing? I should be running away. No, I should wake the girls and then we should run away.

"Halt, demon!" he cried out. The spectre turned around. For a blink of an eye, in a flash of lightning, the shadow twisted its face into an evil, hellish, inhuman mask, but in the next moment, Bran realised it was Dōraku.

The samurai sighed with relief and put a hand on his chest, jokingly.

"You've frightened me, boy! And not many managed that and lived to tell the tale."

"What… what are you doing?"

"What does it look like? I've been taking a night's piss!" the samurai replied, adjusting his *hakama*, "what are *you* doing in this cursed weather? Go back inside, you'll catch a cold."

"I… heard something… You haven't noticed anything strange?"

"Apart from seven corpses lying in front of an old shrine?" Dōraku grinned. "No, it's as peaceful as it gets tonight. You must have been dreaming."

Purple-green rays of a forest dawn penetrated the tomb, casting playful reflections on the limestone wall. The wind had chased the clouds and the mists away, the morning was bright and almost cheerful.

There was a knock on the door. Carefully, with sword in hand, Bran looked outside to see Dōraku holding a couple of sodden-through bundles of cloth in his arms. The samurai observed the boy for a while before speaking.

"I found your luggage on the road," he announced, presenting the bundles.

Bran did not respond, so the samurai laid them on the shrine's porch.

"And I believe I've discovered the source of your nightly fears. Please, come with me."

Reluctantly, Bran followed. Dōraku parted the ferns on the eastern side of the dale revealing the body of a wolf, with its throat gruesomely torn off.

"The wolves must have fought over the meat. Will you help me dispose of the corpses?"

"We do not have time to dig graves," Bran replied.

"I've dug a pit already. It would be unwise to leave the traces of battle out in the open."

The bodies were stiff, cold and heavy. Having grown up in the countryside, Bran had seen a few dead bodies in his life, but never handled any, certainly none as gruesome as the corpse of the *onmyōji*. Flies and woodland creepers had already started nibbling on the bloodied stump of the neck and the chest, blistered and charred by Bran's dragon flame. The samurai kicked the head unceremoniously into the grave before picking up the body by the shoulders. Bran lifted the *onmyōji*'s legs and together they hauled the rigid carcass across the glade.

"*Eeh*, would you look at that!"

Dōraku pointed to the *onmyōji's* chest. The pentacle tattoo was half-washed off with rain.

"What does it mean?" asked Bran. Looking at the headless body he could barely contain nausea.

"It means he wasn't an outlaw, only pretending to be one. He must have been licensed to work at the court."

"The *Taikun*…?"

"That's what I'm trying to find out," the samurai said, ruffling through what remained of the dead mage's clothes. Bran turned his eyes away.

"Ah, there it is. This will have the crest of his lord…"

Dōraku picked up what looked like a golden coin, covered in dried blood. He spat and cleaned it off. He then stared at the golden disc for a long time, scratching his beard.

"Well, what is it?"

"Most interesting. That's the crest of the Hosokawa," the samurai said, casting the coin over to Bran. It was decorated with the eight circles pattern he had seen everywhere in Kumamoto.

"Wait – isn't Yokoi-*dono* serving under the lord Hosokawa of Kumamoto Castle?"

"Last time I checked," the samurai replied, nodding. His bushy eyebrows moved closer together and his brow furrowed.

"Then I don't understand…"

Why are you showing me this? This proves you've been in league with those bandits.

"The *daimyo* has no need to consult all his moves with his retainers, and a retainer doesn't share all his secrets with his samurai. There are some very complex games being played, boy."

And I'm the prize, Bran realised.

CHAPTER III

He heard Satō call out to them. She was looking through the bundles brought by Dōraku.

"I found these all over the road," the samurai said, "I brought what I could."

The wizardess unpacked one of the lacquer boxes with delight. "That's the food I bought in Hitoyoshi! It's still dry. Nagomi, wake up!" she cried inside the tomb. "Karasu-*sama*, come, maybe you'll want to eat *this* one."

Bran glanced nervously at the samurai.

"Karasu-*sama*?" Dōraku said, bemused.

"Karasu of the Aoki clan," Bran murmured, bowing slightly.

"I see."

"Oh, I'm sorry," said the wizardess standing up, "we haven't been introduced properly." She bowed politely and, before Bran managed to stop her, said:

"Takashima Satō, heir of Takashima Shūhan."

He winced. She was being so careless in the presence of the samurai! Of course, if this Dōraku was really in Yokoi-

dono's service, he'd know about Satō already, but if he wasn't…

Nagomi clambered out of the mound, rubbing her eyes. Sleep did her well. Her skin had healthy colour, only her hair remained mousey and drab.

"Nagomi-*sama*, is it?" said Dōraku, "that will be Itō Keisuke-*sama*'s young daughter, isn't it?"

"Yes," the girl opened her eyes wide, "how did you know?"

"I have been quite recently to Kiyō. The city is full of rumours…and certain names are often repeated."

"You have news from Kiyō?" Satō looked at the samurai curiously, "have you heard anything of my father?"

"I've heard some say he's not as… *deaa* as the Magistrate thinks."

"And what of the High Priestess of Suwa? Is she really…" she stopped, glancing at Nagomi.

"When I left the city she was still in the Magistrate's prison. I'm sorry Nagomi-*sama*, as her apprentice, you must be – "

"She's dead," the red-haired girl said with confidence, reaching for the food. "And I'm a priestess, not an apprentice."

Bran and Satō stared at her in surprise.

"Kazuko-hime had me ordained as a priestess of Suwa before passing away," Nagomi said. "Are these our things?"

She started to unravel her bundle.

"Congratulations, priestess," Dōraku said, bowing. "The High Priestess must have held you in high esteem. Now, I'll scout the way ahead. We should be moving out soon."

"But you don't even know where we're going yet," protested Bran.

The samurai smirked.

"The road goes in only one direction. I'm sure I'll figure it out eventually."

They trudged through the dense woodland, Dōraku in front, cutting the trail along the animal paths and lumberjack tracks through the tall ferns and young, slender camphor trees. Bran followed close behind him, with the girls at the back. He preferred to keep an eye on their guide.

The samurai insisted they didn't follow the main road, wary of more unpleasant surprises waiting further on. He led them down the mountainside, avoiding the densest parts of the woods, bypassing the gullies and the windthrows. It was certainly a safer way than the road, but it meant they were moving at a much slower pace. By evening they were still in the deepest part of the forest. As the twilight grew around them, the trees seemed to grow closer, the green canopy above them tightened into an impenetrable roof. They walked now in a dark, humid tunnel, tripping over the roots and dodging the low-hanging branches. Bran mumbled curses under his nose directed towards their guide, but Satō and Nagomi said nothing.

At last they reached the side of a small babbling brook; a cascade of liquid ice shimmering in the starlight. The brook turned north here and its gentle bend formed a cosy, sandy cove, shaded by a large weeping *katsura* tree.

"We sleep here," decided Dōraku, dropping his luggage on the grass underneath a camphor tree.

"What, just like that?" Bran protested. "Shouldn't we at least start a fire?"

"Too risky," the samurai said, "it might draw more bandits or… other things."

"*Other things?*" Bran felt cold, remembering the warnings of the creature from the hot spring.

"It's an old forest."

"We'll be fine," said Satō, "it's not the first time we have had to sleep under the stars. Let's just be glad the weather turned out fine."

Bran looked up. The stars twinkled brightly in the sky; as far as he could tell, this meant no rain for at least one more day. The forest air was surprisingly warm.

Satō stepped up to him with a smile. "I too would have preferred a bed at an inn," she said, "but there is soft grass and thick moss here that should be enough of a mattress, considering the circumstances."

The mention of the inn and her closeness reminded him of the night in Hitoyoshi. *How much does she remember?* he wondered. She behaved as if nothing important had happened between them. *Maybe she's right. Maybe I'm just imagining something where there was nothing.*

A strange buzzing noise woke Satō up, as if a huge bumblebee droned among the trees. When she listened closer she also heard electric crackling and the sound of splintering wood .

She waited until her eyes adjusted to the dim starlight and sneaked carefully towards the sound. Soon she could see a white light flickering among the cedars and a blue streak of lightning jumping from tree to tree.

There was a round glade where a large tree had fallen not long ago and other plants had not yet grown over it. In the middle of the glade stood Bran, panting, holding in his hand a six-foot long shaft of solid blue light. A flamespark hovered above his head. All the tree trunks around the glade bore scorched scars.

He heard her come through the undergrowth and pointed one end of the shaft towards her.

"It's me, Satō."

The dragon rider breathed out and the blue light in his hands flickered and disappeared.

"What was that?"

"Soul Lance. A dragon rider's weapon. Did you not see me use it in battle yesterday?"

"I was busy enough with my own fight. How does it work?"

"It is part of my life energy. Instead of using it to power spells, like the wizards do, I use it to create this long, unbreakable piece of light... umm... crystal."

53

"Can anyone do that? Or only dragon riders?"

"Anyone with magic talent, I think. But it's really only good for dragon combat. It's the only weapon that is certain to withstand dragon flame and penetrate a fully grown dragon's armour. It's virtually unbreakable."

"But…?" she asked, sensing Bran was not telling her everything.

"It's only as strong as the rider that's wielding it. And it failed me yesterday."

"This is why you're here, training," she guessed.

He summoned the lance again with a buzz.

"A trained soldier's lance is nine feet long. My father's is at least twelve feet, the blade as broad as a glaive. This…" he said, giving the lance a shake. Air shimmered around the blade. "…this is pathetic. If we are to face a real enemy – one that is likely to be much more powerful than that *onmyōji* – I *need* to make it work."

"If we are to face an enemy, you need to be rested," she said, smiling.

"You're right." He opened his palm and the lance vanished with a flicker. He moved back towards the camp, but just as he was passing her, he stopped, turned and looked her straight in the eyes.

"What is it?"

"That song you sang in Hitoyoshi… what does it mean?"

"What song?" She looked away, feeling suddenly hot. "I sang many songs. So did everyone."

"*Now, now, now…*" he hummed.

"It's just a song," she lied, feeling her cheeks burn up. "It doesn't mean anything."

"I…was thinking about that night."

She looked back at him. Even though his Yamato face was familiar, she could not penetrate the stare of his alien, jade eyes.

What does he…

She held her breath, feeling his fingers on her cheek. She wanted to run, but made no move. All fell silent; she could only hear the thudding of her own heart. She closed her eyes and shivered.

"What was that?"

His touch vanished and she heard a buzz of summoned lance.

What?

She opened her eyes and saw him crouching defensively, pointing the lance towards the treetops.

"There's something up there. Look!"

A black shadow jumped from tree to tree noiselessly and disappeared into the darkness.

"Let's go back to the others," Satō said quickly. "Dōraku-*sama* might know what it was."

"Yes." He scowled at her mentioning the samurai's name. "*He* might."

They found Dōraku waiting for them under the *katsura* tree, trying to light his long bamboo pipe.

"The *tabako* got wet," he said. He gave up and hid the pipe away into the sleeve. "Do you still have trouble sleeping, Karasu-*sama?*"

"There is some... *thing* in the forest," Bran said quietly, careful not to wake Nagomi.

"I told you. It's an old forest. There are always *things*."

"Still, we thought it'd be best to keep watch," added Satō. "For the rest of the night."

The samurai nodded. "All right, I'll take the first shift."

"No," said Bran, "*I* will keep watch first. Then Satō. Then you."

Dōraku chuckled. "Very well. Have a good night." And with that, he got back to his bedding.

"What?" Bran asked. He could not see Satō's face clearly in the gloom, but he could sense her anger.

"That was extremely rude!" she fumed. "The way you spoke to Dōraku-*sama*, that mistrust in your voice..."

He raised his arms in exasperation. "He knows I don't trust him. Why should I pretend otherwise? Our lives are at stake. I grow tired of all these Yamato niceties!"

The last sentence came out as a shout. She stepped back.

"You... you may speak our language, but you still have a lot to learn about *us*!" she said and turned around in a huff, leaving him alone in the night.

Bran watched the silver-lined wisp of a cloud move slowly across the night sky. He put his fingers to his mouth, remembering the touch of Satō's skin.

I wonder if her lips taste different than Eithne's...

She hadn't run or shirked away from his touch. He no longer doubted – there had definitely been *something* between them. Except now he'd ruined it all.

He bit his lips and clenched his fist on the hilt of the sword.

I may not get another chance.

There was a change in the wind. The silver-lined cloud obscured the moon; the forest fell silent, shrouded in pitch blackness.

An army of bandits could sneak up on me in this darkness. He remembered his duty and summoned the power of True Sight to sweep the area around him.

Contrary to what many laymen thought, it wasn't a real "see-in-the-darkness" spell. What he saw were subtle differences in the layout of mystic energies and ley lines caused by physical objects around him – and, of course, any spells or magic objects. Since he wasn't a trained wizard, the True Sight always put a great strain on his eyes whenever he used it for more than a blink. After a few seconds of studying the forest his head started aching and he was forced to return to normal vision – but not before he spotted a brightly shining shape in the branches of a tree before him.

Things in the forest.

Slowly and quietly, he slid his sword from the sheath and lay it on his lap. Whatever the creature was, it did not make any attempt to attack them – it just sat on a branch, watching.

What is that?

"*Nothing worth losing sleep over,*" a voice spoke in his head. Bran jumped up.

"*Taishō!*"

The general chuckled. "*I see you're learning to refer properly to your superiors.*"

"Do you know what it is?"

"*I can't see with your magic eyes, boy. But I sense no malice in the creature. If I were you, I'd be more worried about your new companion than whatever lurks in these forests…*"

"Dōraku? Why?"

There was a long silence and Bran thought Shigemasa had once again wandered off, but the voice spoke again.

"*Be cautious. Listen, observe. Strangers you meet on the road are rarely what they at first seem.*"

Bran sensed the general retreating. "No, wait! You must tell me more!"

"I *must?*" the voice resounded with sudden anger. *"Child, you presume too much!"*

This time, the old spirit's voice vanished from his head for good.

Bran sighed. *Tonight I manage to annoy everyone I speak to.* He looked up at the tree before him. The watching creature was gone. The forest was so quiet that he could hear Satō and Nagomi breathe in their sleep. The wizardess muttered, suffering again from another nightmare. But there was a sound missing. The third breath.

Listen, observe. Bran rose softly and snuck up towards the massive dark frame of the sleeping samurai. His chest seemed to make no move under the silk kimono.

Is he dead?

Bran reached out to touch Dōraku's hand. Moonlight seeped through a gap in the cloud and fell on the samurai's face. He snored loudly and turned to the other side. An owl hooted. The wood came back to life with a myriad of night voices.

Bran shook his head and returned to his post.

Tiny fish danced around Nagomi's toes as the priestess stepped into the freezing stream to refresh herself before breakfast.

"This place is beautiful," she said, sighing. The sunlight danced on the babbling water. The spirits in this part of the forest were calm, joyful. The stream was too cold and shallow to bathe in, so she just washed her face and hands.

"It is pretty in the daylight," agreed Bran, taking a bite off a large, flat rice cracker, "but how long will it take us to get down from these mountains at this pace? Are we sleeping rough tonight again? We're running out of food."

The samurai puffed on his pipe.

"Don't worry, I know a safe place we can stay today," he said, "and tomorrow we should descend into the valleys."

"How long are you planning to accompany us?" Bran asked.

Satō gave him an angry look, but the dragon rider either failed to notice it or decided to ignore it.

What's up with these two again?

"As long as it's necessary to keep you safe," the samurai replied, "or do you wish me to leave you alone?"

"No!" Satō said hastily. "Please. We're glad to have a swordsman of your skill on our side, Dōraku-*sama*."

The samurai bowed politely.

"I have never seen anyone fight like you," the wizardess said. "Who was your teacher?"

"I had no teacher. I invented this style myself."

Satō gasped.

"*Impossible!*"

"You fared well yourself against those bandits, Takashima-*sama*. That mage was a difficult opponent for one so young."

The girl looked down in embarrassment.

"We would perish without your help."

"You're being too modest."

He's playing with her, Nagomi realized. *Why can I see it but she can't?*

Bran stood up abruptly, knocking over the water flask.

"Shouldn't we be moving on already?" he spoke through clenched teeth.

He noticed it too.

Dōraku smirked and reached for his bag.

"As you wish, Karasu-*sama*."

Dōraku led them for a few more hours down a slightly descending path, along the hollows and ravines, across cold streams and over the crags, until they reached a cliff-side, a sheer drop of rock barring their path. He pushed the ferns aside and gestured them to have a look.

Nagomi stood beside Bran, taking in a magnificent view spreading below. A vast, low-lying plain stretched all the way to the horizon, flooded by the mists, steams and vapours coming down from a jagged line of mighty cone-shaped peaks bordering the valley to the south. The fire mountains rose from the haze below like an archipelago of small islands rising over the ocean of mist, a few of them bellowing out thin wisps of grey, ashy smoke.

There was a town in the middle of the plain, crouched on both sides of a silver ribbon of a river among the fields of tall, pinkish grass, sweet potato farms, tea groves and citrus orchards.

Bran opened his satchel and put the spyglass to his eye, studying the landscape.

"This is Kyomachi on the Sendai River. Beyond that, *Ebi no Kogen*, the Highland of Shrimp Grass," explained Dōraku. "See how the grass turns pink in the sun? Like boiled shrimp."

"And those peaks on the horizon?" asked Bran.

"That's Kirishima, the Island in the Mist."

"*Kirishima...!*" Bran exclaimed, almost dropping the telescope. The samurai looked at him curiously.

"I... I've heard it has a magnificent shrine."

Where did he hear that? thought Nagomi.

"How do we get down there?" asked Satō, peering over the cliff.

"There's a gully further east we can use to descend," the samurai replied, "but that's not for today. We need to reach our lodgings before the night."

Bran raised an eyebrow.

"There is lodging, here, in this wilderness?"

"You'd be surprised. I know I was the first time I found it."

This was by far the greatest tree Nagomi had seen in these mountains: an enormous cedar shooting straight towards the clouds like a pillar supporting the heavens. The twisted maze of roots thicker than a man's thigh sprawled like veins and tendons of some ancient creature at its base. There was a well dug out among the roots, lined with round stones and covered with a bamboo mat, and a tiny box shrine nailed to the trunk. She bowed a quick greeting to the tree's ancient spirit, then looked around, searching for a dwelling. She found none.

"Who lives here?"

Samurai pointed upwards with a grin.

Half-way up the trunk was a rectangular platform of wooden planks with walls of bamboo and reed.

"Wait here," said Dōraku and approached the tree. Finding hidden leverages in the trunk, the samurai climbed up to the tree-house with the speed and deftness of a hungry bear.

A minute later a trap door opened and a rope ladder unrolled to the ground. Dōraku's head appeared in the opening.

"Come up. He's not here."

"He? Who's *he?*" asked Bran, grabbing the ladder and testing the strength of the ropes.

Nagomi scaled the ladder after him. The tree-house was neat and surprisingly spacious. A small clay stove stood in the middle with a cast iron pot on top, a bed of thickly packed straw by one of the walls, a small chest of heavy wood, darkened with age, and little else.

"Is this a *yamabushi*'s hut?" she asked.

"Of sorts," agreed Dōraku.

"Can we really stay here? Won't the host mind?"

"We'll have to wait and see. Sit down, I'll make some tea."

The pot bubbled merrily away on the stove. Nagomi tried to take as little place on the floor as possible, in case the mysterious owner of the tree-house returned. The samurai opened the wooden chest unceremoniously.

"There should be… ah, there they are."

He produced five tea cups and put each before one of the travellers, setting the fifth one aside. The cups were of superb quality, each a slightly different style, but they had all seen better days. Nagomi's vessel was burnt orange in colour, chipped and cracked in several places, with markings of some ancient master still discernible near the bottom.

"*Eeh*! These are worthy of a *daimyo*'s treasure" Satō said in admiration. Her bowl, black and metallic, was perfectly irregular, blotched with white glaze like snow clouds in the winter sky.

Bran paid little attention to his cup – red with silver streaks - absentmindedly contemplating the wall ahead.

Dōraku poured the hot brew into all five cups and raised one to his lips. Before taking a sip he turned towards the same wall that Bran stared at.

"Aren't you going to join us, Kabuto-*sama?*"

"Why are you bringing strangers to my house uninvited, Swordsman?" a disembodied voice croaked.

"Come now, Kabuto-*sama,* you know very well that would be impossible. You invited me here a long time ago."

For a moment nothing happened and then something started revealing itself in the corner, as if from under an invisible mantle. A humanoid creature, tall and slender, clad in the red robes of the mountain hermit. A single wing of black feathers twitched nervously over the creature's shoulder. In the middle of its red face, between two golden, eagle-like eyes, protruded a long sharp beak.

Nagomi cried out and jumped away in terror, reaching for her wand.

"A *tengu!*"

Satō drew her sword a few inches. Only Bran remained calm.

"You're one of the *kappa's* friends, aren't you?" the boy said matter-of-factly. "I saw you last night."

The bird-like creature's eagle eyes narrowed. "It takes a keen eye to spot a *tengu* in the darkness wearing its mantle."

"What are you talking about?" Satō leaned over to Bran "What *kappa?*"

"I met one in Hitoyoshi. In all the commotion since then I almost forgot about her."

"The old lady from the hot spring!"

Kappa? Tengu? All those fairy tale creatures were supposed to be extinct, hunted down by the *Taikun's* armies generations ago...

"If you're referring to Kuma-*hime*," the *tengu* croaked, "then yes, I have the honour to be her acquaintance."

Dōraku laughed heartily.

"You are full of surprises, Karasu-*sama*!"

"Karasu-*sama*?" the creature turned its head to one side, studying Bran with curiosity.

"That is my name. Aoki Karasu," the boy replied.

"What a coincidence. So is mine. Karasu Kabuto – Kabuto of the Crows."

The *tengu* bowed clumsily, spreading its wing in greeting.

"Your tea is getting cold, old friend," Dōraku noted, pointing to the cup.

"What cause do you have to disturb my isolation – again?" the *tengu* asked, lifting the tea bowl. It opened the beak, stretched out a long thin tongue like a woodpecker, and started slurping the drink loudly.

"We are simply passing through the mountains, trying to avoid the main road – again," the samurai answered, smirking.

"When last you had to hide you were alone, Swordsman, but now you have a priestess and two wizards for company. Have your enemies grown so strong since?"

"How did you know…" Satō asked.

The *tengu* let out a screeching sound which terrified Nagomi until she realized the creature was laughing.

"I am Kabuto of the Crows. It was I who conversed with Kobayakawa-*dono* on the summit of Mount Hiko. You think a fledgling like you can keep a secret from me?"

Satō hid her face inside the teacup.

"You are here because of the Great Magic, aren't you?"

"The Great –?" Bran started, but Dōraku interrupted him.

"We do not wish to burden you with our tale. Can you spare us a roof for the night?"

"As long as you promise to leave in the morning," the goblin replied, "there are blankets in the chest – as well you know."

"Excuse me," Satō spoke, her voice trembling, "but do you have any food to spare? We can pay…"

The *tengu* scoffed.

"Look around – what good is your gold for me? There's plenty of rice and bamboo shoots in the larder, but you'll have to go down among the roots to find it. You may wash yourselves while you're at it. What are *you* looking at, priestess?" the goblin said gruffly, turning towards Nagomi. She almost dropped her cup.

"I'm sorry!" she said and bowed deeply, her head touching the floor, "I was just wondering… about your other wing."

The *tengu*'s face turned sour – or so Nagomi guessed.

"Matsudaira Nobutsuna himself slashed it off with his great sword *Daihanya*. He wanted to make me a gift for the

Taikun – the last *tengu* of Chinzei. With only one wing I could no longer fly or use my magic… still I escaped."

A rattling sound made everyone turn their attention to Bran. The boy's cup lay overturned, his hand clenched around the hilt of his sword.

"Nobutsuna…" the dragon rider struggled to speak. His eyes darkened.

The Spirit! Nagomi realised. *What does he want now?*

"Matsudaira Nobutsuna led the *Taikun*'s armies to victory at Shimabara," explained Dōraku, observing the boy carefully. "He subdued this island all the way to Satsuma. Why does his name anger you so?"

Bran breathed in deeply and loosened his grip on the blade.

"It is his deed that angered me, that's all."

"You intrigue me, Aoki-*sama*," the *tengu* tilted its head from one side to another, "first you keep a *kappa's* secret, now you take pity on a goblin?"

"Didn't I tell you last time we met, Kabuto-*sama*," Dōraku said, grinning. "The Yamato is changing."

"So you did, Swordsman. Perhaps there is yet hope for the likes of us in this world."

CHAPTER IV

Torii Heishichi, the Arch Wizard of Satsuma, had no way of knowing whether the spell had worked. He had been designing the pattern ever since he had received Lord Nariakira's mysterious order, four days ago. Two more days it had taken himself and six of his best students to weave it into place, infusing the bars of the great iron cage with complex magic. He could only hope it was enough to hold the beast down.

It lay asleep peacefully in its cage, but it could have been a hunger and weariness-induced lethargy, rather than effects of his spellcraft. Heishichi knew enough of the *Rangaku* scientific method not to put too much trust in a simple correlation of facts. The Court zoologist had found records that seemed to confirm his fears — there were dragon-like creatures living in the rivers of Bharata which could survive for weeks without food in this dormant state... They could only wait and observe.

An old scholar who had once helped Lord Nariakira's father with his financial and agricultural reforms was now tasked with calculating how much a beast of this size would need to eat, and how often it should feed. It was all guesswork, based on old legends, ancient chronicles studied by Lord Hosokawa in Kumamoto, and secretly smuggled bits of Western knowledge. Was the *dorako's* metabolism more akin to that of an ox, or a wolf? Or maybe a giant snake? In the end, the scholar cautiously estimated that it should be fed a wild boar or a deer at least once every three days just to keep it alive.

This posed another difficulty. Should they wake the dragon to feed it? If they hadn't, would it perish of hunger in its sleep? He could only guess the extent of Lord Nariakira's wrath if the beast died through neglect of its keepers. Getting away with a disembowelment order would be lucky. The dragon's well-being was his own responsibility – whether the beast perished of hunger or ran away, his blame would be the same.

Heishichi hated the dragon and the new situation he had found himself in because of it. He held the post of a *Daisen,* the Arch Wizard, but now he had been turned from an academic to a farmer. As one of the few who had unlimited access to the beast, he had to take care of its needs. His hands reeked of raw meat. And he was running out of time.

They were scheduled to leave soon for Kirishima, where he hoped to utilise the power of the magic nexus to make the binding spell stronger and reduce the number of wizards needed to sustain it to a more manageable number. But to make it to Kirishima, the dragon had to feed.

"On a count of four, disrupt the channelling," Heishichi commanded and winced, seeing hesitation on the faces five of the wizards. Only Sugimoto, the young Earth Wizard, remained composed.

Four was an unlucky number, foreboding death. He had chosen it deliberately; there was nothing he disliked more than foolish superstition. His students were quick to learn of this particular quirk of his character, but old customs took long to get rid of.

A heap of untouched carcasses lay before the beast, its nauseating stench permeating the air. Days had passed uneventfully. The dragon did not wake of its own accord, so Heishichi decided to risk it and remove carefully the enchantments binding the beast inside the iron cage.

"...*four!*" he shouted.

The wizards broke their concentration and dispersed their energies, unravelling the enchantment – just by a fraction, to see what would happen. The beast did not move.

"Should we unravel the second coil?" asked Sugimoto.

"Yes, prepare to... no, wait."

The dragon stirred at last. Its nostrils flared. Picking up the scent of the meat, its eyes started opening slowly, narrow slits at first.

"Careful now."

Fast like a whip, the beast's head snapped forward. Teeth clenched on a wild boar's carcass and pulled back before anyone could react. Heishichi had never seen anything so big move so fast. He heard others whisper astonished prayers.

The dragon swallowed the boar in a few gulps, then reached for another carcass. It was then that it noticed the presence of the humans. Heishichi's eyes met the beast's gaze and his skin was covered with a cold sweat and his throat tightened. The *Daisen* felt for the first time the legendary fear gripping the soul to the core.

"Enough," he whispered what was supposed to be a sharp command.

The six wizards raised their arms and tightened the spell's pattern. The dragon shook its head from side to side, struggling with dizziness. Heishichi reached into his sleeve and pulled out a pouch of white powder. He blew it into the air around the dragon's maw. The beast succumbed, lowering its head to the ground and fell back into a heavy sleep.

The *Daisen* breathed a sigh of relief. The white powder, a strong concentrate of purest Cursed Weed smuggled from Qin at great expense, was his own invention. As with everything else regarding the *dorako*, this was also a never tried before experiment.

"Prepare it for transport," Heishichi commanded, fixing his horn-rimmed glasses.

The buzz of a lazy fly added to the monotonous drone of the priest's prayer. The small cemetery glade was surrounded by tall pine trees, cutting it off from the refreshing sea winds. In the stale air of a warm midday Heishichi struggled with lethargy.

He knew he had to at least show that he cared. This was, after all, the funeral of one of his students. The wizard's body lay on the funeral pyre covered with a white shroud so that the gathered would not have to see its terrible state.

72

The family would not be told of what had really happened, but they had accepted their fate a long time ago. A wizard's life in Lord Nariakira's service was never a long one. Ever pushed to the limits of their knowledge and power, the *Rangakusha* of Satsuma perished in their prime whenever an experiment went wrong or the forces unleashed proved too strong.

In his position as the Satsuma's *Daisen*, Heishichi had presided over many such funerals – too many to remember. This, however, was the first time he had to say farewell to the victim of a dragon.

He had been trying to figure out what went wrong all night; why did the *dorako* wake and snap like that? Was there an error in the holding spell, or did he mix up the proportions of the sleeping powder? In the end he had to concede he had not enough information. This worried him much more than the loss of a student. Men could be replaced. They only had one dragon.

Perhaps, perhaps… he lost the train of thought. He had a feeling the solution to the problem was within his grasp. If only he could focus. If only the priest stopped mumbling!

He became aware of the sudden silence. Everyone was staring at him.

Did I say that out loud?

"I'm sorry," he said with a bow.

"It's all right," the celebrant replied, "it must be difficult for you. You were his teacher, I am told."

"I was."

"I am finished with my prayers. The ceremony can proceed."

"You are aware of our custom, priest?"

"I have been made aware, yes," the celebrant replied, the polite smile disappearing momentarily from his lips.

"Step aside, then."

Heishichi and two other fire wizards approached the body of their slain comrade and put their hands on what remained of his chest. The *Daisen* summoned a white flame which started to devour the flesh from inside. Within seconds the corpse incinerated, leaving nothing but a pile of ash underneath the white shroud.

At Heishichi's signal, Sugimoto stepped up to the pyre and whispered a spell word: "*Aardse Nor.*" Earth parted beneath the pyre, burying it along with the shroud and the ashes.

"There will be no tombstone necessary," Heishichi announced.

"But the Spirit of the deceased must be…"

"None of my students has ever come back to haunt me. I doubt this one will."

"I cannot agree to this."

"You are free to argue your point with Nariakira-*dono*."

The priest made no answer, aware of the *Daisen's* elevated position at the Satsuma court.

"Good. You may clean this up. I must return to my duties, I have wasted enough time on these pointless rituals."

He turned on his heel and headed back towards the shrine. By the time he had passed the last of the stone grave marks, he had forgotten all about the deceased student of *Rangaku*.

Councillor Hotta Naosuke climbed the narrow road leading up the Shiba Hill, past the long row of thousands of little bodhisattvas wearing red bibs that marked the border of the Zojō Temple, along the stone walls of the Okubo Clan residence, through a small pine grove and further on, still upwards.

Near the top he stopped for a moment, catching his breath, took off the tall black cloth cap that indicated his status as a government official, and wiped his face with it. The sun was merciless. The road here wound westwards along the slope, and the glade where he chose to rest commanded a magnificent view in three directions. Naosuke looked north, back whence he came. From the hill he could see almost all of Edo, all the way to the *Taikun*'s Castle, rising in its many tiers like a mountain of white, dazzling in the sun. The city of wood, stone and noise sprawled around it in all directions endlessly, except to the East where the reclaimed land encroached on the uneasy ocean.

Southwards lay the marshlands and the rice fields of the Kantō Plain, the water in the muddy ponds glittering like mica dust. But the eye was quickly drawn away from these vistas to the only view truly worth seeing in all of Yamato: rising in a perfect cone, with its top forever hidden in the clouds, snow-covered slopes dazzling with golden light, at once majestic, beautiful and terrifying; the unparalleled Fujisan.

If we were to clear the hilltop and build a viewing tower, thousands would flock to this place, he reflected. *I should propose it on the next Council meeting.* He took one last look at the city and then gazed up, into the azure sky. A large black bird with a long tail and broad wings soared high above the sparse clouds.

On the northern slope of the hill there was a long deep dell, hidden in the shadows of tall silvery firs and black pine trees. Long before reaching the hollow, Naosuke smelled the heady odour of brimstone filling the forest and heard the strange hissing and gurgling sounds coming from beyond a rocky outcrop. But there were no volcanic fissures or hot springs in this part of Edo.

The Councillor climbed the sharp boulders, hid among the roots of an old pine tree and looked down. The hissing repeated, even louder now, followed by a screech and a cracking noise, as of tree branches being broken. On a narrow sward of grass nine tall men were sitting by the campfire, wearing hooded cloaks of dark grey cloth. Further down the valley, beyond a circle of white tents, coiled three monstrous creatures, resting. Each as big as a rice ship, their reptilian bodies, massive heads and long, spiked tails were covered with jet-black, glistening scales. The terrible jaws, dripping foul slobber, seemed capable of swallowing a human whole. Leathery, bat-like wings, folded along the sides, heaved up and down as the beasts breathed in and out.

The hissing was the sound of a plume of steam and smoke, wafting from the monstrous nostrils with every breath. The cracking sound was the bones of a deer – one of several piled in a nook of the dale – that one of the creatures devoured in a few snaps of giant teeth.

Naosuke observed the monsters with curiosity. He had read the reports and studied the legends, but he was little prepared for the sight of the black-winged monsters. He had not been in Edo when the dragons had arrived. The Council had been called immediately to deal with the threat, but still it had taken him a few days to reach the city from his summer house in the mountains. By the time he had arrived, a semblance of calm returned to the capital, although the city buzzed with rumours and tall tales. The invaders did not yet wish or dare to attack the *Taikun*'s castle, instead they had set up their camp on the slopes of the Shiba Hill, out of sight, and waited.

Not even the *Taikun*'s scouts dared get close to the barbarian encampment. Nobody knew what it was that they wanted or what they were waiting for in the shadowy vale. They had sent no envoys, they had made no threats, although their presence was enough to cast a dark shroud over the entire neighbourhood. Only the monks at Zojō remained steadfast, everyone else had moved out of the vicinity of Shiba. Looking at the resting dragons, Naosuke could not blame them. A primeval terror reaching deep into the soul gripped anyone

who got near to the three beasts.

Three? There should be one more... he gazed upwards once again and realised that what he took for a bird at first was in fact the fourth of the dragons – the largest one. The monster was circling above Edo slowly like a vulture, far beyond the range of muskets and arrows.

The Councillor decided he had seen enough and started climbing down from his lookout point. A small stone escaped from under his feet, triggering an abrupt avalanche. It would have been too quiet for any human to hear. But one of the grey cloaks stood up in an instant and turned towards Naosuke, searching the precipice for the intruder. The Councillor could not see the eyes under the hood's shadow, but he sensed their piercing power. One of the black monsters paused between gulping one deer carcass and the next and also looked up.

There was no point running away. He stood up straight and, with as much dignity as he could muster under the terrifying gaze of the beast's eyes, spoke loudly:

"I am Hotta Naosuke, son of Hotta Naonake, representative of the Council of Elders of Yamato. I came to hear you out."

The Councillor passed through the imposing Shōin-mon gate, nodding out of respect to the giant chrysanthemum crest made of pure gold, attached to the dark wooden beams.

The guard bowed deeply.

"Your weapon please, Hotta-*dono*."

He pulled out his ceremonial *wakizashi* and lay it on the guard's outstretched arms. None could enter the inner court with a sword, not even he, one of the five most important men in the country excepting the *Taikun*.

He tightened his sash and walked on, passing the paper lanterns marked with the sign of the mallow crest. The guard waited until he thought Naosuke was well out of sight, before speaking to the other.

"I don't know why, but I always get the chills when he walks by."

"I know what you mean. Makes my hair stand on end. There is something odd about this Councillor."

Naosuke chuckled as he walked through the pillared corridor of the Outer Palace of Edo Castle. His hearing was much better than the guards suspected, but he made nothing of their insolence. He had not got to where he was by having petty quarrels with commoners.

He passed the golden-walled reception chambers, where the *daimyo* waited for an audience, then the white room, where the *Taikun* met the imperial messenger on the rare occasion one was sent from the *Mikado*'s Palace. All this he was leaving behind. Long ago he would have been one of the lords in the inner room, hanging on to *Taikun*'s every word, bickering among themselves for the master's attention, quarrelling for every extra *koku* of rice given or taken on the Master's whim. Now he had access to the Naka-ōku, the Middle Palace, where the *Taikun* met with his closest advisers. Beyond it lay only the private rooms of the ruler's family and concubines.

He entered the Great Room. The paintings on its gilded panel walls showed the bay of Edo, surrounded by tall, snow-capped mountains, with merchant ships and fishing boats scattered on the waters. This reminded the council of what mattered most in the politics and survival of the island nation: the Sea.

Naosuke was the first to arrive. He prided himself in diligence and punctuality. Others could be "fashionably late", but not him. He sat down on a silk cushion, admiring the view to a small stone garden of the inner courtyard. The gleaming white gravel was spread before the verandah like a beautiful shingle beach in front of the sea painted on the walls. His dark brown eyes glittered and his waxen, pale skin wrinkled in a grin.

A servant slid open the door to the Great Room. Masahiro Abe peered carefully inside. Somebody was already there, sitting by the garden.

"Councillor Hotta. First as always."

The Councillor turned around to face him and bowed. "Chief Councillor. I wonder how long before others arrive?"

"I've seen old Tadamasa-*dono* on his way here. Ah, here he is."

An old man with a face wrinkled like a pickled *ume* plum appeared in the corridor. A staunch ally of Abe, he greeted the Chief Councillor with a light nod and sat on a cushion beside him before bowing to Hotta.

Next came young Kuze Hirochika. He was only a few months older than Abe. As such, he had had a chance to observe the Chief Councillor's rise to power first-hand. This made him admire Masahiro's abilities, but despise his conciliatory character. Master Kuze was a man of quick action and a few words, the hot-headed leader of the War Party. Lastly, the two Matsudairas entered the room. They were a confident pair, almost to the point of insolence, certain of their position in the Council as a decision could rarely be made without the consent of them both.

They had all come from various parts of the Empire, mostly the central provinces, except the Matsudairas, who had come the longest, from Izumi in the south.

"Please slide the screens behind you, Noriyasu-*dono*," Abe addressed the elder of the two cousins. The Councillor pulled the paper screens together, enclosing them all in an octagonal space.

"I shall be brief, for the matter is pressing. Councillor Hotta here claims he has news about the invaders that require our urgent attention."

The Councillors looked at Naosuke with vague interest.

"I hope you have found a way to drive them out of our sacred land," said young Hirochika.

Councillor Hotta smiled and bowed lightly.

"I'm afraid not."

"What is it then?"

"I have spoken to the barbarian commander."

They all gasped loudly, except Abe who had already heard the story. Now they paid more attention to what Naosuke had to say.

"They have an interpreter with them," the Councillor answered a silent question, "a man from Chūbu they found cast away on the Great Ocean some years ago."

"Traitor," murmured Hirochika.

"Who are they? What do they want?" asked the Matsudairas almost in unison. "Why did they attack the Uraga Harbour?"

Abe raised his hand and they fell silent.

"They come from a land across the Great Ocean, but they are of the Western race, as far as I could tell. Their language is strange to me. They hide their faces under the grey hoods so you never know which of the twelve you're looking at."

"There's only twelve of them?" Hirochika asked, "that's not even enough to bother the army. The city guards should be enough to deal with the Barbarians!"

Are there no limits to his stupidity? wondered Abe.

"As for Uraga, they did not attack it – although they might as well have," Naosuke continued, ignoring the interjection, "I have been to Uraga myself, to see the destruction up close. Only the forests on the cliffs were scorched by the dragon flame, as a show of strength. The fires in the city were caused by panicking crowds. Overturned braziers and kitchen fires, as is usually the case."

"You have not yet told us what the barbarians *want*," said the younger of the Matsudairas.

"At first their commander demanded to speak to... and I beg you to withhold your anger... His Imperial Excellency."

"*Preposterous!*"

"I told him that even if a thousand dragons descended on the Imperial Capital, the people would rather perish in fire than allow them to sully the *Mikado* with so much as their presence."

I'm sure you have.

"Well said!" Hirochika clapped his thigh.

"At length, I have convinced them to present their demands... *requests* in a missive to the Council. I have made five copies of the letter," Naosuke said, handing out the folded papers to the Councillors.

Abe waited until all of them finished reading. He observed their reactions carefully. Kuze Hirochika's hands trembled, his face turned purple with anger and by the end he tore the paper into pieces. Old Makino put the letter close to his nose, squinting to read Naosuke's squiggly characters. He harrumphed and put the missive away with a face grim and sour. The two Matsudairas exchanged whispered remarks and grunts full of meaning.

"It is this Council's task to decide what response – if any – we give to the enemy commander," Abe said at last.

"The barbarians are not deserving of our response. The missive is obviously aimed to insult us and provoke our anger," snorted Makino. He and Abe represented the conservative party, favouring the status quo. To him, there was no force under the Heavens strong enough to impose a change on the *Taikunate* and the *Mikado*.

"If that was their aim then they've certainly succeeded!" Hirochika banged his fist on the floor. "Send out the army to wipe the scum out and let's hear no more of it."

Naosuke scratched his long, crooked nose in a gesture he was famous for; this indicated an utter disdain to his interlocutor's proposition. He gazed at Kuze with his shallow set eyes.

"Unlike you, my dear Councillor, I have seen the Black Wings with my own eyes, up close. The commander of the Westerners demonstrated to me how little harm our arrows and muskets can do to these monsters. Obviously we're dealing with something far more dangerous than ever before."

"We must treat them as we treat all barbarians," Kuzo was adamant. "Make them suffer for what they have done. Landing on Imperial land without permission is an act of war."

"Makino-*dono*, you're the minister for capital defences," Abe said, turning to the old man, "How long, do you reckon before we can gather enough force to thwart the Black Wings?"

The minister wiped sweat off his forehead with a silk handkerchief and gathered his blue robe nervously. "The treasure is rather empty until the end of the year. We've only just started building the new forts to Bataavian design. We are yet to receive new canons, and we would have to call upon the *onmyōji* and warriors from the outer provinces..."

Well played. The two had been practising this exchange all morning.

"There you have it," Abe turned back to Kuze, "the Westerners are here to stay, at least for a while. And if you read the missive carefully, they warn of an even greater force awaiting their signal off-shore. We must negotiate."

"That would be regarded as a sign of weakness," Naosuke said, unexpectedly supporting the hawk party, "not only by the barbarians, but internally. The *tozama* clans would use it as proof of our failure to govern."

"There is virtue to be found in prudence," said the younger of the Matsudairas, "The *Taikun*'s rule would not spread over a unified Yamato if his divine ancestor had resorted to attacking overwhelming odds headfirst without preparation."

"What do you propose, Tadakata-*dono*?" inquired Abe.

"Open negotiations, agree to some of their initial demands, but no more. Give them access to the Kiyō corridor – they will be easier to contain there. You know my opinion on dealing with foreigners. It's high time to open our country up to their trade and science."

"Preposterous," replied Kuze, "the *Taikun* will never agree to this."

"And where *is* the *Taikun* at this hour of national emergency?" asked Councillor Hotta, raising his eyebrow.

"His Excellency is still indisposed," said Abe, annoyed at Naosuke for bringing this up. *You know very well where the Taikun is. In the Inner Palace, with his many concubines.* "Kuze-*sama*, may I remind you of the fate of the Qin Empire when it stood against the powers of the West without due preparation?"

"The downfall of Qin started with letting the barbarian ships too near their coast," snorted Hirochika, "they were weak in the face of the enemy."

"So are we!" Tadakata rose himself up from his cushion. "How do you propose to defend Edo from the Black Wings? With bow and arrow? Or with the primitive tricks of our court magicians?"

"With a strong will and iron heart, if you have them!" Hirochika stood up as well, his hand inadvertently reaching for where his sword would have been, had he not left it at the gate.

"Enough!" Abe clapped the floor. "Let us not forget who our real enemy is! Sit down, Councillors. Your shouting will disturb his Excellency's rest."

"The esteemed Tadakata-*dono* is right, but, in a way, so are you, Kuze-*sama*," he continued when both lords sat back down, "we cannot afford to antagonize the Westerners just yet, but we also need, as the *Taikun*'s government, to present a strong and unified front against the internal opposition. We know there are forces in the south that would too easily jump on the opportunity to exploit any weakness shown by this council."

And there are forces in Edo who would love nothing more than a hastily gathered army they could take control of, he thought, looking at Councillor Kuze. He couldn't say that out loud, but he hoped the majority of the Council understood that as well as he did.

"What we need is time. And only negotiations can give us enough time," said Naosuke. "Anything else would be invitation to a war we can't afford. But what if we run the negotiations covertly? The *daimyo*s need not know about anything. That way all sides would be appeased."

"Can we even do such a thing?" Tadakata straightened himself up in surprise. "How do you conceal four dragons from the public? Everyone knows they're here."

"The commander of the Westerners is willing to co-operate," said Naosuke and Abe couldn't help wondering what the Councillor had promised the barbarians in exchange for their co-operation. "He's agreed to fly the Black Wings away from Edo, in a pretend retreat. We just need to provide them with a place to hide, and enough meat so the dragons don't need to hunt in broad daylight. If we play our cards right, we might convince everyone that the Westerners have gone for good."

"It's a bold idea," said the older of the Matsudairas, "if the secret is revealed, the damage to our prestige might be irrevocable."

"If the secret *is* revealed, it will mean one of us failed to keep it."

Naosuke looked intently at Councillor Kuze.

"Are you suggesting I could betray the Council?"

Chief Councillor raised his hand to silence young Kuze from bursting out again in anger.

"We have ways of dealing with disagreements in the council. Now, please, everyone, calm down. The motion proposed by the esteemed Councillor Hotta is a valid one. I suggest we vote on it now. Should we open the clandestine negotiations with the invaders?"

He and Hotta Naosuke raised their hands. Kuze and Makino voted against the motion. This was a surprising development. The oldest of Councillors only very rarely disagreed with Abe. *What's he playing at? Surely it's not a sudden influx of patriotic feelings...*

The two Matsudairas looked at each other and smiled knowingly. Only one of them raised his hand; the other remained silent.

"Interesting," observed Abe, trying his best not to let annoyance show in his voice. *Tricks and ploys. Can't they see we're trying to decide the future of the entire nation?* "Seems like we have a stalemate. I adjourn the meeting until next week. Let us discuss the matter among our own advisers and then maybe we can provide the *Taikun* with a decision."

CHAPTER V

A soft singing woke up Bran. He looked down the entrance hatch. Nagomi was crouching by the square well, washing her hair, sparkling copper and gold in the morning sun, humming. Her travel clothes were folded neatly on a flat stone. She smiled brightly seeing him climb down the rope ladder.

"The tree spirit has taught me a new song," she said, "from the days when it was young."

"You… you really can *talk* to them…?"

"Not always... But this one is as old as Yamato and taught itself to speak to anyone who can listen. I'm sure if we'd spent some more time here you'd start hearing it too."

"And what does the tree… tell you?"

"Stories from days gone by. There used to be an entire village of the *tengu* here, a long time ago. And before that, a holy place of the Ancients…"

"It remembers the Ancients? Perhaps we could ask it – "

She shook her head. "It was just a sapling back then. The Ancients worshipped its parent tree, long since felled by the winds."

89

THE ISLANDS IN THE MIST

The forest reverberated with the sound of an axe. It was the samurai, chopping firewood in exchange for their host's generosity.

"I've noticed you share my concern about our new companion," Bran remarked.

"Dōraku-*sama*? I'm… not sure. He seems well-meaning, but there is something very strange about him. *Oh!*" She clasped her hand on her mouth. "Maybe he also has a Spirit within him, like you do!"

"Maybe that's what it is. I think Shigemasa… the *Taishō* knows something about him, but he's not telling."

Bran drew a bucket of icy cold water from the well and splashed it on his face. A pheasant cawed in the distance. The boy looked around and saw a large black silhouette perched on a thick branch of a nearby tree.

"Kabuto-*sama* is watching us again."

"I wonder if he had any family of his own, living in this village. Maybe we remind him of his children."

"Have there been many of his kind before the Yōkai War?"

"The forests in the old stories are full of them. They must have been at least as numerous as the *kappa*. Was the old lady really a water sprite?"

Bran nodded. "She even gave me a golden coin as a reward for not telling on her, but I must have lost it in all the running."

Nagomi washed off the last remnants of greyish lather off her hair and reached for the towel.

"I too have lost something in the running," she said, "I have only one portion of Kazuko-*hime's* black paint left."

"We're so far from Kiyō now – maybe you don't need it anymore?"

"Perhaps… I wonder how the people in the valley will react when they will see me. Maybe they will think *I'm* a goblin." She giggled.

"Everyone I've seen so far in Yamato and Qin has hair as black as raven's feathers," Bran said.

"I've never met anyone like me," she said.

"So how come yours is that colour – if you don't mind me asking?"

"Not at all – it's no big secret. It's because I'm a *Dejima daughter*."

"What does it mean?"

"It means my father was a Bataavian – a physician from Dejima. His hair was the colour of fire as well."

"Your father…? But I thought…"

"Itō Keisuke-*sama* was one of my father's disciples. He felt it his duty to take care of his master's family after the Bataavian was banished from Yamato."

"Banished?"

"He was accused of spying when a map of Yamato was found in his luggage. He was only using it for his research! That was some three years after Ine was born – she told me she still remembers saying farewell to him from the pier and Mother hiding her tears behind a paper fan…"

"So, what about you?"

"He managed to return to Dejima in secret ten years later, for one last meeting with my mother."

"And how did your stepfather react to that?"

"How should he react? He accepted me as his daughter also. It was the only honourable thing to do."

"He didn't mind that his wife had slept with another man?"

"There was never any passion between my parents, so there was no resentment," Nagomi answered, very matter-of-factly.

In Gwynedd a family like theirs would be the talk of the town…

"So you've never even seen your real father."

"Only in a picture. I don't even know his full name, other than *"Firippu"*, which was what my mother called him. The few letters she got from him were signed with just the initials, *P.F.V.S.*"

"P.F.V.S..." Bran repeated.

He was certain he had seen these four initials somewhere. Before he could remember, Satō called on them from the tree-house above.

"Rice is ready!"

The *tengu* followed them down the forest path, skipping from branch to branch, watching them with its large sad eyes in silence. At last they reached the cliff-side again and the path started to wind down the gully mentioned by Dōraku the day before. A large ship-shaped rock split the path in two. Before any of them managed to pass it by, Bran heard a loud crow. He looked back; it was Kabuto, with its head thrown back and the beak opened wide. Dōraku bade them stop.

"This is the limit of my domain, Swordsman."

"Till our next meeting, Kabuto-*sama*," Dōraku bowed.

"No," the *tengu* said, shaking its head.

"Oh?"

"I may have lost most of my magic but I still have a little of the Gift. One way or another, we shall never meet again."

"It saddens me greatly."

"We've lived long enough, Swordsman. I bid you fare well."

With that, the mysterious creature leapt away into the deep wood, leaving them to contemplate its ominous warning.

What did he mean, "we"? wondered Bran. *We, the tengu or we — me and the samurai?*

By noon the path led them back onto the main road. It was no longer an empty forest track but a lively thoroughfare, connecting the many farms and villages of the Sendai Valley with the shores of the meandering river.

THE ISLANDS IN THE MIST

"I hope we will reach Kyomachi tonight," the samurai said. "It's the last town before this road splits in different directions."

They marched into the crossroads town shortly before dinner time. It differed little from Hitoyoshi. There was another timber harbour here, another hot spring and a few inns serving those coming down from the mountains in the direction of Satsuma. Taking the matters of the lodging in her own hands this time, Satō managed to find the most expensive inn in the town, a large, three-storey white-plastered building on the outskirts, almost in the forest, with its own garden, dining hall and an outside bath sourced directly from the hot springs beaming underneath the town.

"This is the first decent guesthouse since Kumamoto," she said, her ears closed to Bran and Nagomi's pleas for caution. "I'm a samurai and I can afford a good room in some mountain backwater."

Without even stopping to unpack she went straight for the hot spring, while Dōraku sat down in the common room to try the various liquors available at the inn. It was up to Bran and Nagomi to go to the market to resupply for the onward journey.

A small vermillion *torii* gate marked the entrance to the shrine. So near the marketplace and the harbour, the shrine had to be dedicated to the *kami* of good trade and luck in fishing, Nagomi guessed. It didn't matter.

"Wait here a moment, please," she asked Bran.

She picked up a wooden ladle from the fountain at the entrance and splashed water on her hands and face. Passing by a bronze statue of a sitting cow – polished to brightness by countless pious hands – the priestess approached the modest, tile-roofed Prayer Hall.

The shrine was neither particularly ancient nor rich; the decorations were modest, unassuming. The humble townspeople prayed here for everyday blessings and protections. There was nothing unusual about the place.

This was a welcome change for Nagomi, a well needed respite from the overwhelming events of the past few days. She took a few deep, calm breaths, revelling in the tranquillity of her surroundings before approaching the altar. She started with the usual thanks to the *kami* and Ancestors for their protection and good will towards her and her friends and family, for being alive and healthy. But then her voice broke.

"Please," she started, feeling her eyes well up, "I have never asked for anything before. But now I… I just don't know what to do anymore. It's all just too much… I need guidance."

She pressed her hands together and closed her eyes.

"Kazuko-*hime*, please tell me what did you mean to say about Dōraku-*sama*. Sacchan trusts him but he scares me so… I can sense something's not right, but I can't tell what it is."

She clapped her hands twice and shook the bell rope.

THE ISLANDS IN THE MIST

"I feel so alone... You're gone forever, my family is far away... I have only Sacchan now, and... and..."

Bran's green eyes appeared in her mind. She remembered the warmth of his touch. Satō rarely touched her like that. *I suppose I'm still a child,* she thought, *and Satō's all grown up now. It's no longer proper.*

She shook her head and focused on her prayer. "It doesn't matter. I just need strength to carry on. But... if I only knew we were on the right track. That we're doing the right thing... Just a sign..."

She clapped one more time and opened her eyes. Nothing happened. Nothing would, of course. It was silly of her to hope otherwise. She sighed and turned away from the altar. Bran was waiting for her outside the shrine gates.

The sun was nearing the rooftops and the marketplace was closing down. Bran and Nagomi had to squeeze their way through surprising crowds of shoppers going the opposite way. They walked along the river bank, past the fishing boats lined on the pebble beach. As in every harbour, the vendors sold mostly fish from the river – fresh to locals, salted to travellers – but other produce drew Bran's attention, great stone jars of yellow *mikan* fruits, pickled from last winter, and sacks full of sweet potatoes prepared in every manner imaginable; fried, baked, boiled, and just plain raw.

Bran and Nagomi, their mouths sticky with sweet *mikan* juice, packed bags full of fruit, baked potatoes, pickles and freshly harvested bamboo shoots, first of the year, boiled to perfect softness.

"We either bought too much or too little," said Bran. "Either way, Satō will be mad at us."

"It's her own fault. She should have come with us, instead of moping about in the bath. Why is everyone looking at us?" she stopped.

"I think it's your hair – your hood is off..."

The girl quickly pulled the straw hood back over her amber hair, but it was too late. Some raised their fists in a gesture against evil, others clapped their hands in prayer but mostly they just seemed intrigued. A small crowd started gathering around Bran and Nagomi.

"Come," Bran grabbed the girl by the hand and pulled her out of the circle of people, out of the marketplace, leaving the curious crowd behind.

He was hoping the commotion would end once they got back to the inn, but it was a futile hope. The rumour overtook them; the townsfolk had already begun to gather at the inn, frightened and confused. The landlady watched the growing crowd for a while, and then approached the travellers with a concerned face.

"I'm sorry, but your rooms are... not fit for your esteemed persons."

"What do you mean?" Satō asked, rising from the floor.

"They, um, they are infested by lice."

She's not even trying.

"We'll take another room."

"All other rooms are full, *tono*. I'm very sorry. Perhaps another inn."

"We will pay more," Satō insisted, "isn't this the best place in town?"

"Your money will only turn to leaves in the morning!" the landlady blurted, unable to keep her fright beneath the mask of politeness anymore. She glanced at Nagomi, who tried, futilely, to keep her copper locks under the hood of her cloak.

Satō's face tensed. She reached for her sword, but Bran was faster. His blade was already drawn and pointed straight at the landlady's widened eyes.

"I have a good mind to slay thee for this insolence," he said, seething. The landlady stepped back, but still she refused to kneel. Bran looked around. The crowd fell quiet and anxious. Satō froze with her sword drawn half-way, staring at him in surprise.

He found Dōraku, observing the scene with some amusement. He was smoking his long pipe and sipping from a large bowl-like cup in silence. The locals gave his table a wide berth. He poured himself another cup and sipped it.

Their eyes met. The samurai frowned and stood up, in a few long steps came up to the anxious landlady and leaned towards her. He whispered something in her ear. The woman's face turned white. She quickly bowed before him and started placating the agitated crowd and removing them from the inn.

"It's all right now," Dōraku said after they were gone.

"What did you tell her?"

The samurai smiled vaguely. "I simply gave her a warning. You can put that away."

Bran looked at his own sword as if seeing it for the first time. He sheathed it with a clank. Dōraku smiled again and got back to his table.

"I'm sorry," he mumbled. *I really was ready to kill that woman,* he realised with a shudder.

"Sorry for what?" asked Satō. "She was asking to have her head cut off. I've never been so insulted in my life. I'm not sure if I want to stay here anymore."

Nagomi stood up. Her face was pale and her lips pursed together fiercely.

"I'm tired. I'll be in our room," she said.

"Wait!" Bran moved to follow her, but Satō gripped his arm. The priestess disappeared up the stairs without turning back.

"Will she be all right on her own?" he asked.

"She *wants* to be on her own now. She's learned to handle her... condition this way."

"Condition...?"

"She may not seem so to you, but to the people of Yamato she's a freak, an aberration. And it's worse here, in the countryside, among the commoners."

"Now I wish I hadn't convinced her..."

Satō shook her head.

"Don't worry. She's survived fifteen years of this, she'll manage."

Bran sat down and played with his chopstick in pensive silence for a while, then stuck them in the pile of rice in his bowl.

"Don't do that," said Satō sternly. "It brings bad luck."

"Sorry," he mumbled and put the chopsticks on the wooden rest.

So many things to remember.

"Look, I... I never apologised for that...outburst in the forest."

She looked at him, puzzled, then remembered. "It's Dōraku-*sama* you should apologise to, not me."

I couldn't care less about him.

"I ...will, but I wanted to talk with you, first."

She sighed. "It's all right. We were all stressed. Still are."

Tentatively, he reached out his hand to cover hers. She twitched, but didn't move it.

"I... " He struggled for words.

This would be so much easier if I knew at all what I wanted to say.

A bottle of saké appeared on the table with a soft clank. Satō immediately withdrew her hand.

The landlady bowed with an apologetic smile. "It's a flask of our finest," she said. "I hope you will forget this little… incident, client-*sama*."

"I'll go check on Nagomi," said Satō, standing up.

The inside of his satchel was filled with blue light.

Bran had opened the bag to take out the notepad and pencil. He wanted to make some notes to clear his mind, as he had been doing since the night in the tomb of the Ancients, but seeing the light seeping through the hinges of the black lacquer box made him forget all about the journal.

He took the ring out of the box and the brightness almost blinded him at first. He guessed quickly the reason for the jewel's dazzling radiance. Since they had descended into the valley, Bran had been feeling his connection with Emrys greatly increased. The dragon was really close now, the Farlink amplified. Even though the beast was still fast asleep, he could now sense the direction and distance precisely to where it was being kept. The blue stone must have been reacting to this proximity.

Now I definitely can't be wearing it in public, he thought with regret.

To fit the box and notepad neatly back into the satchel he first had to take out the dragon figurine. He had almost forgotten about it. He had seen so many other dragon sculptures and carvings all over the Yamato that the little statuette seemed no longer to hold any importance. He kept it out of sentiment – it reminded him of Samuel and the crew of MFS Ladon, of the birthday on board the great ship.

But if there ever came the need to discard any items from his luggage, the red dragon would have been among the first to go…

He was about to put it back and close the bag for the day, when the carved letters on the figurine's base caught his attention. He scratched his nose in thought.

There was a knock on the door. Nagomi quickly wiped her eyes.

"It's me," said the boy, "I… I brought some fruit."

She nodded at Satō to slide the door open. Bran sat down by Nagomi's *futon* with a reassuring smile.

"Here," he said, handing her the peeled fruit.

"Thank you."

She wasn't hungry, but was grateful for the gesture. The boy opened his satchel.

"That's not really what I came here for. I just remembered something."

He took out the red lacquer figurine of the dragon, the cheap and tacky Kiyō souvenir.

"You said your father – your real father – signed his letters to your mother with four letters."

"Yes."

"I thought it may have been a coincidence, but… I doubt there would be two men with such strange initials."

He showed her the figurine's base, scratched with four symbols.

"I... I can't read that."

Satō leaned over.

"Are these letters of some kind? I noticed these marks when you first showed us the statuette."

"These are Latin letters, the alphabet they use in Rome."

"What do they say?"

Nagomi's heart was beating furiously, as if after a long run, though she didn't know why.

"P – F – V – S."

"No!" she cried and turned away. The tears returned and started flowing down her cheeks uncontrollably. "That's a very bad joke."

"It's true. I promise."

"But how?" asked Satō, "how is this possible?"

"My father said he got it from a Bataavian physician. It must have been your – "

"It's too much of a coincidence," Nagomi said firmly, holding back the sobs. She could not help her tears and did not know how to stop them. "This... this must have been some other Bataavian. Maybe it's a common name."

"That's not what Kazuko-*hime* would have said," Bran replied.

She sniffed and turned back to him. She reached out her hand.

"Can I…"

"Of course," Bran replied, "it belongs to you."

It was smooth and warm, like Bran's hand when he had taken her away from the marketplace.

"Kazuko-*hime*…"

Is this your sign? Is this your response to my prayers?

Yellow sulphurous mist descended on the Sendai valley in the morning. The air was warm and thick with dew, making it difficult to breathe, not to mention walk. Dark clouds returned, coming from all directions like a besieging army.

She had on her straw hood, but decided not to dye her hair after all. Bran's miraculous discovery had cheered her up greatly and restored her fortitude.

They halted at the crossroad, on the outskirts of the town. Several bridleways were spreading from here, all leading roughly south.

"Which road do you wish to take?" asked Dōraku.

"Which one leads to *Kirishima*?" Bran replied with a question.

Why Kirishima? She looked at Satō, but the wizardess only shook her head and shrugged. *We might as well,* her eyes seemed to say.

"The town or the shrine?"

"Is there a difference?"

"The shrine is farther up. Closer to the fire mountains."

"The shrine, then."

The samurai nodded. "This way."

He stepped upon the path leading straight towards the tallest of the sharp mountaintops on the southern horizon.

"I hope you bought enough supplies."

"Why?"

"Because it will take us three days to reach the shrine and we're not stopping anywhere along the way."

"*Three days?* I can't wait that long," Bran whispered. The three of them marched a short distance behind their guide. The road was rarely used and badly in need of repairs.

"Why are you in such a hurry? What's in Kirishima?" asked Satō.

"My dragon," the boy replied and winced, "we need to hurry."

She drew her breath, a little too loud. Master Dōraku turned to them.

"Is something wrong?"

"No, it's fine. Is this the fastest route to the shrine?"

The samurai chuckled.

"You should already know you can't afford to follow the fast routes. Whoever your enemies are, they will be expecting you."

"He's leading us into a trap," Bran murmured.

"You said the same when he guided us to the *tengu*'s house, and then when we climbed down the mountains," she replied, "and he's right about the enemies – the Crimson Robe *would* expect us to take the main road."

"I thought we *wanted* the Crimson Robe to find us. How else are you going to find out what happened to your father?"

"I thought you might want to get your *dorako* first. We could use it in a fight."

He did not respond, picking up the pace instead.

We never discussed it before, she realised as the boy marched a few paces before her. *What if he doesn't want to help us? What if he only cares about his beast?*

Not everyone was as selfless as Master Dōraku, after all. The samurai guided them tirelessly through the towns and wilderness, just because Yōkoi-*dono* had asked him to. She was growing weary of Bran's suspicions. Even Nagomi seemed apprehensive towards their guide. Why couldn't they just let him be? He was as cheerful and open as the few men she had met. So what if he had secrets – who among them didn't have any?

He was following the Way of the Sword and, she was raised to believe, wielding the swords with utmost skill required a clear mind and a pure heart. She only had to remember that knave, Tokojirō – a coward and a traitor who managed to get himself disarmed by a confused Westerner.

And he *was* guiding them well. The volcanic peaks emerging from the mist seemed much closer by afternoon. The road started climbing upwards again. The villages and fields grew sparse, replaced by low growing, thin islands of forest in the sea of short, bright green grass growing over the ancient lava flows. The weather turned for the worse. It was the beginning of the rainy season in this southernmost corner of Yamato. The clouds, gathering since morning, finally released their waters in a torrential downpour, beating upon the travellers with a force of a mountain waterfall. Shivering under their straw raincoats, they climbed still upwards across the rocky, torn highland. The stinking brimstone vapours had been dispersed by the rain.

"At least now I know we won't suffocate – we'll drown," Bran remarked wryly.

In these conditions they managed to traverse a far shorter distance than she had expected before having to stop, exhausted. Master Dōraku led them to a small copse of thin, gnarled pine trees. He pulled out a large measure of tent cloth from the bag and wrapped it around the branches, forming a very rudimentary shelter from the elements.

"I'd prefer to face our enemies than this weather," said Bran, preparing his bedding on the wet soil.

Will his whining never stop?

Satō rolled her eyes.

And to think I almost let him kiss me. Again.

107

What was she thinking? And after she had *promised* herself…

"You'll be fine. We'll soon start a fire," said the samurai.

The bleak weather managed to turn even him grim and sullen. He picked up some wood from around the thicket, but it was all wet. Satō tried to help him light the campfire, but the firesticks got damp and could not produce even the tiniest of sparks.

"Or maybe not," Master Dōraku commented their efforts with a joyless smile.

"Oh by the Dragon's Breath…"

Bran reached out towards the pile of firewood and flicked his fingers. A wide tongue of flame spewed from his hand and the wood burst with a bright blaze.

The samurai looked genuinely surprised for the first time since they had met him. He scratched his thin beard in wonder.

"I couldn't stand another night in the cold," the boy said with a shrug, "besides, it wasn't that easy before. We're now much closer to the…"

He glanced at the samurai nervously.

"…source of power."

"Yes, there is a strong vortex of mystic energies nearby," Master Dōraku agreed. "All magic in its vicinity will probably be similarly strengthened."

"And how do *you* know that?" Bran asked suspiciously, "are you a wizard as well? Is he telling the truth?" he turned to the wizardess.

Satō wasn't sure what to answer, but then she remembered her glove – she took it from her bag and studied the dial. It was fluctuating, trembling, as if great streams of magical energies flowed through it.

"He's right!"

Eager to test the discovery, she scrambled out of her bedding and cast a small freezing spell at a branch of a nearby tree. To her surprise, the whole tree became covered with solid ice from root to top. She jumped back, startled by her own power.

"*Eeh*! A fire wizard and an ice wizard!" the samurai exclaimed, "what fascinating company I find myself in! Are *you* a mage as well, priestess-*sama*?" he asked Nagomi. The priestess raised her eyes as if frightened that somebody would mention her.

"None of your business," barked Bran before Nagomi could answer.

"Bran!"

Satō clasped her mouth, shocked. The samurai glanced at the boy in amusement.

"What about that vortex of energies you've mentioned?" Bran asked quickly, avoiding her accusing stare.

"The Takachiho Mountain."

"Takachiho Mountain..." Nagomi repeated, whispering the words like a prayer.

"Ame no Uzume asked again – where shall you go and where shall the August Grandchild go? He answered and said – the child of the Heavenly Deity will proceed to the peak of Kushifuru at Takachiho, and I will go to the upper waters of Isuzu at Sanada in Ise," Master Dōraku recited.

"What is it?"

"An excerpt from an ancient chronicle," explained Nagomi. "The peak of Takachiho, where the August Grandchild Ninigi no Mikoto descended from Heavens, bearing the three Imperial Regalia. The Dwelling of the Gods. I never dreamed I would…"

"It's just over that summit," the samurai said nodding south, where in the last rays of the setting sun they could see a tall volcanic cone hiding in the clouds, one of several in the chain of Islands in the Mist. "We should reach it by tomorrow. If you get well rested tonight, that is."

He stood up and stepped out of the shelter, immediately disappearing from sight into the rainy darkness.

"Where are you going?" Bran asked nervously, but there was no answer. "I don't like to have him around, but when he's gone it makes me even more anxious," he mumbled.

"If he hasn't killed us yet, I don't think he will," replied Satō.

"He could be bringing his men now to capture us and carry us away to some dark prison."

"You worry too much."

"And you're too trusting."

"I have lived in this place for seventeen years. You only arrived a month ago," she said, feeling her anger rising. *How many times will we have to go through this?* "I will choose my allies as I please, thank you very much."

"But I never – "

"Good night, Bran-*sama*." She turned his back to him huffily, covering her head with a blanket.

THE ISLANDS IN THE MIST

CHAPTER VI

Chief Councillor finished reading the documents from the pile he had marked with a sign of a "Horse" and moved on to a pile marked with the sign of a "Ram". As the head of the government, the matters of the Empire lay solely on his thin, bony shoulders. Without some kind of sorting system he would soon be buried under the weight of documents, missives, reports and letters. At first he had them divided into three categories of urgency, but by now he had twelve separate stacks of papers, each stamped with a character from the Qin zodiac.

Even with this system, a lesser man would break down under the weight of single-handedly ruling the islands. Abe did not like to rely on secretaries and courtiers, like his predecessors. Their minds did not work fast enough for him. He had kept the ones he inherited with the job on court salaries, but never called on their services, leaving them largely to their own devices. That way, everybody was happy.

He had retained only one man at his side, the personal aide to the previous Chief Councillor himself, Hotta Naosuke. Master Hotta had appeared in the *Taikun*'s court in service of one of Ogasawara lords and had risen to the top almost as fast as Abe. Naosuke's unremarkable physiognomy, accented only by the cunning glint of his eyes,

113

hid one of the brightest minds Abe had ever worked with. It almost seemed as if the Councillor needed no sleep, food or drink. He worked constantly and without fail.

It was Naosuke who laboured on dividing the documents into zodiac-marked stacks as they arrived to the Chief Councillor's office. The "Ram" pile was for all matters of coastal defence, and it had grown so large lately, that it had to be divided into two, one of the stacks dedicated solely to the defence of Edo and surroundings. He fingered through the letters from the many *daimyo*s who had been ordered to provide Edo with men, supplies and arms.

"A thousand samurai from Aizu with armour and horse, a dozen war boats and five battle mages," he read to Naosuke, who scribbled down some notes. "Yes, the Aizu are reliable as always. The Matsuyama, the Takamatsu, the Kuwana... not as much as they could send. Note: admonish them for avarice." He continued going through the stack until he reached the bottom.

"Is there no answer from the southern provinces?"

"No, *tono*. Only Nabeshima-*dono* has responded. The Saga province is sending a token force of samurai now and preparing a larger detachment for later."

"What about Tosa? Chōshu? Higo?"

"They seem to have ignored your... the *Taikun*'s orders." Naosuke's face remained perfectly still, but his eyes glinted, betraying how satisfied he was with the news. Abe recognized a familiar ambition in the Councillor. He had no doubt that, sooner or later, Naosuke would replace him in the position. It did not matter in the long run; the court was like a boiling pot of *oden* – some would rise to the surface, others fall to the bottom. Such was the way of politics. If anyone were to take over the reins of government, Chief Councillor preferred it to be the wily, moderate Hotta rather than the hot-headed Kuze or one of the self-confident Matsudairas.

"The Southerners have mingled with the Westerners too much. They are no better than the Barbarians. I don't suppose Nariakira's response was any different?"

"He did not even bother with one."

Abe rubbed his eyes with a tired gesture.

"I know you two used to be close. Why don't you write him a personal letter? For old time's sake."

Naosuke shrugged lightly. "I may try, but we have not spoken to each other in years. Not since he stopped coming to Edo."

"Ah, yes. That's another thing. We will need to remind him about his duties. The Alternate Attendance system must be obeyed."

"He will not come," said Naosuke firmly. "You would have to drag him by force."

Abe smiled knowingly.

"That may not be necessary. Did you know he's sending his daughter to the Castle?"

Naosuke raised his eyes. "I didn't even know he had a daughter."

"Adopted, I believe. I'm not sure what he's planning exactly. Help with administrative duties, officially, but this is obviously just a ruse."

"Obviously."

For a moment they were both silent, pondering the mysterious plans of the Satsuma *daimyo*.

"What about Kiyō?" Abe said, picking up another piece of paper. "What do the *Rangaku* wizards say? Will they help?"

"Their answer is in the "Dog" pile, but I can tell they won't be terribly committed to the cause. Not after how the *Taikun* treated them."

"I will change these laws. I need the cooperation of the wizards. If a war with the West were to break out... I know what might convince them. That scholar under house arrest, what's his name – Takashima? I want him released."

"That might be difficult. He and his family have been outlawed."

"By whose orders?"

"Bugyō of Kiyō."

Fool.

"I will override it. Send the dispatch with the first post."

Naosuke nodded, but still looked doubtful. The wizards were notorious for their anti-government sentiments.

"What will you do if that isn't enough?"

"Then whoever takes my place will have to find a way to deal with those rebellious half-barbarians, one way or another. Whatever the cost, we need national unity in these difficult times. We cannot share the fate of Qin just because of some petty squabbles."

The other man nodded again in silence. At least on this, they were both in agreement.

Chief Councillor put away the bunch of papers and wiped the sweat off his brow.

"Tell you what, Hotta-*sama*. Why don't we leave this for now and go to get some saké?"

Naosuke looked up in surprise.

"Are you thirsty, Chief Councillor? Should I call for the servant?"

"No, no. I meant going to an inn. Have some leisure time."

Abe realised how unusual his request must have sounded. Normally he was the last person to be seen drinking and merry-making when he should be working. But these were not normal circumstances.

A smile slowly appeared on Naosuke's face. "Very well, Abe-*dono*. I know just the place."

The girl finished her dance, picked up the fan from the floor, bowed and left, followed by the *shamisen* player. The two men remained alone with their flasks of saké in an octagonal, Qin-style pavilion in the middle of a small garden at the back

117

of an opulent guesthouse. A nightingale sang inside a large hydrangea bush; blue-tinted buds swayed in the wind.

Chief Councillor picked up a strip of grilled chicken meat on a stick and chewed it for a while, deep in thought.

"If we fail this test, history will know us as the last Councillors," he said.

"And who would write this history?" asked Naosuke.

"The Barbarians, no doubt."

"That's very pessimistic. Bordering on treason."

"We both know there are none more faithful servants to the *Taikun* than the two of us. But we must acknowledge the facts. The Qin fell to the Barbarians in two months. Do you remember when the news first broke out about the war?"

Councillor Hotta nodded. "Of course. I will never forget it."

It had been ten years earlier almost to the day. Like many young idealists of the age, Hotta Naosuke had at the time been studying law and history at the famous Mito school, under Aizawa-*sensei*. He was just becoming aware of Yamato's dreadful situation under the facade of the *Taikun*'s "peaceful reforms".

He had been late that day. He noticed from a distance that the students had gathered on the main courtyard in a great crowd, instead of attending lectures or working on the Great History as they should have been doing at that time of day.

118

"Is this true? Is it really true? So fast... total rout!" He heard the voices as he approached the crowd. He grabbed one of his friends by the shoulder – it was Shimazu Nariakira, then son of the *daimyo* of Satsuma. They disagreed on matters of politics, but enjoyed each other's company whenever copious amounts of saké – or better yet, shōchū, of which Nariakira had always plenty – were involved.

"What's going on?"

"News from Qin. The Barbarians have destroyed their fleet and broken through the Barrier. They've captured Huating and Fan Yu."

"What? But the war's only just started..."

"And now it's finished. The Barbarians are at the gates of Jiankang. The Empire is pleading for peace."

"Is this news confirmed?"

"As much as any news from abroad can be."

The crowd hushed momentarily, as Aizawa-*sensei* walked into the courtyard. He was already an ancient man, wrinkle-faced, dry-skinned, his lips always pursed and twisted as if he had eaten something sour. He was a renowned scholar and tutor to the *daimyo*s of Mito, but his greatest claim to fame had been an incident twenty years earlier, when he was delegated to translate for the Western barbarian sailors who got captured while shipwrecked on the coast of the province. This meeting shook him to the core and he had devoted the rest of his life to developing a way for the Yamato to deal with future foreign threats.

119

The old headmaster approached the message board and squinted to read the black squiggly letters. He then harrumphed, shook his head and turned to the gathered students.

"There will be no lectures today. You are free to ponder this momentous event however you see fit. If anyone wants to discuss anything with me, I'll be in the garden, meditating."

"Say, Nariakira, do you still have that barrel of black yeast stuff you got for the harvest holiday?" Naosuke prodded his friend and, with a couple of other drinking and debating companions, Tenkō and Nobumitsu, moved in the direction of Shimazu's lodgings, ostentatiously to discuss the latest news, but in reality to have a taste of the famous liquor.

"Old Sourface must be overjoyed," Naosuke said. "Isn't this what he's always predicted? That the Barbarians will come and gobble us all one by one, like a pack of wolves eating up a herd of deer?"

"I don't think being right makes him happy today," replied Nariakira.

"The *Taikun*ate must react to this," Tenkō said, banging his fist on the table. He had one cup too many and his face was flushed. "If they ignore even this news, then, then…"

"Then what?" goaded Nariakira.

"Well then they're no longer fit to rule! And by the will of Heavens, they should be removed!"

"Don't you start with your Confucian fairy-tales," Naosuke said, waving his hand, "will of Heavens indeed! That's a traitor's talk."

"A traitor to what? The nation? The *Mikado*? The Tokugawas gained their power by force, not by legacy or divine intervention. They can be removed by force."

"And what would you have instead? Civil war all over again? There is no *daimyo* strong enough to take the *Taikun*'s place."

"You know very well whom I would have instead. We all think alike here, except you, don't we, lads?"

Tenkō looked around himself, trying to find support for his rebellious words. Nobumitsu said nothing. He was an expert in deciphering ancient texts, but modern politics was not his strongest point. But Nariakira nodded and grunted in agreement.

"There is a family that ruled Yamato for hundreds if not thousands of years," said future lord of Satsuma, "their line is unbroken, and they still are nominally monarchs of this country. Their legitimacy to rule is much greater than that of any *daimyo*."

"I can't believe you're being serious," Naosuke scoffed, "Bring the *Mikado* back to power? That puppet? You might as well put *Butsu-sama* on the throne, or Amaterasu herself! What good would that do?"

"It would be a symbol behind which everyone could rally. You know this might work. There will be no war if we all unite behind the Chrysanthemum Throne."

"That's just a dream. Tokugawas have half the *daimyo*s supporting them, if not more. There would be a war. More bloody than the last one. And while we fight amongst each other, the Barbarians will swallow us up, just like they did in Bharata."

"Well then, what is your solution, o wise Hotta-*dono*?" Tenko mocked him, pouring himself yet another cup, not noticing the warning look he was given by Nariakira.

"I don't know yet. But I don't believe the problem lies with the institution. It's the people who are the problem. As long as they rule, Tokugawas guarantee peace. Peace and time is what we need right now, not hot-headed intellectuals pursuing dreams of divine legacy. But there is stagnation creeping in, and with it, indolence and corruption."

"That's why we need a revolution!" Tenkō banged the table again.

"A revolution is chaos, and chaos would be used by our enemies. We need better reforms, smarter reformers."

"How many reforms have there been in the past century? And after each one, things get worse."

"That's why we need smarter people in the government. People like us. Isn't that what we study here for? To learn how to rule the country better?"

"We'll never get anywhere near the government," said Nariakira softly, his inner calm cooling the heads of the quarrelling friends, as always. "You're the only one of us who is from a *fudai* family, and you're what, thirteenth in line to succeed? The rest of us are *tozama*, outsiders. All our skill and knowledge will amount to nothing as long as the current system is in place."

"There must be another way than revolution," Naosuke put down his cup, deep in thought. "And I would give anything to find it."

"And have you found it? The way, I mean," asked the Chief Councillor having listened to the entire tale.

"I like to think so," Naosuke replied, but said nothing more, keeping the secret to himself.

"So that's what the conversations were like at Mito," said Abe, looking into his saké cup. "I've often wondered."

"We were young and hot-headed, all of us. Some have changed little – like Nariakira-*dono*."

"Do you think he still considers replacing the *Taikun* with the Divine *Mikado*?"

"His mind is too fast to dwell on one idea for too long. No doubt he has come up with a dozen different plans since then."

"I used to dread waking up one day to see Satsuma's banners at the gates of Edo. Now I would welcome them."

"They would certainly be of great help against the Black Wings," agreed Naosuke. "Unless, that is, Nariakira-*dono* deemed it more useful for his cause to *join* the invaders..."

"He'd never... do you think...?"

"He's always been a patriot at heart, but his sense of what's best for the nation can sometimes be... misguided."

Councillor Hotta's crooked smile and raised eyebrows expressed his distrust much more strongly than his words. He reached for the saké flask, put it to his ear and shook it.

"Alas! No more."

"Under the budding hydrangeas,

I reach for the white clay bottle:

Like my head, it is empty," chanted Abe and both men erupted in drunken laughter.

A hundred Qinese men stood in a loose column in the middle of the plain, holding on to their self-repeating rifles, their heads sweating under the green turbans in the sweltering sun. The navy blue of their uniforms stood out against the brick-brown of the muddy earth.

On the other side of the plain waited a thousand or so soldiers, wearing mostly grey studded kaftans and red trousers. The men brandished an assortment of weapons of all sorts, broad swords, spears, halberds, pitch forks and a few matchlocks. The arrangement was supposed to imitate a rebel rabble, but Dylan had strong suspicions that this was how the Imperial Army really looked.

"How ever did you convince old Pointy Beard to give us this demonstration?" asked Admiral Reynolds, observing the field.

"It was his proposition. I tried to convince him for three days and then suddenly he came back in the morning with this." Dylan waved his hand.

He had been training the hundred men for a week, with the help of other dragoons. The blue uniforms they wore were spares from the Admiral's stores, as were the rifles and ammunition. He knew the safety of the Concession depended on the success of this demonstration of the Western art of war – already the scouts were reporting that the rebels had been regrouping a large number of troops to the south of the Cheng River in preparation for a renewed assault.

As if we hadn't shown them enough how superior our tactics are, he thought bitterly. But he knew this wasn't the case. The Qin officials had to be convinced that the Western tactics could be applied to the mentality of the Eastern soldiers. And of that even Dylan himself wasn't certain.

"I must admit, you've done a great job, Ardian. They look almost human."

Dylan winced and scratched his scar nervously. He was trying to stamp out this sort of attitude in his own men, but he could do nothing about the Admiral's old fashioned prejudice.

"I had plenty of valuable help from that Lee fellow."

"The interpreter?"

"He turned out to be more than an interpreter. He's a sort of lieutenant to the Bohan, or a protégé. I have a feeling it was his whispers that led to us having this exercise."

He stood up in the stirrups and raised his hand. A hush spread throughout the battlefield. Both sides watched him, a small human figure on top of a great silver dragon. The respective assigned commanders – Edern led the blue-clad hundred – raised their own banners in anticipation. The Banneret's men screwed on their bayonets.

At the signal, the thousand men charged ahead with a variety of battle cries. A perfectly executed rifle salvo thundered and a flood of bullets whistled over the heads of the running rabble.

The first line of the attackers was to drop to the ground after the first salvo. This was, after all, supposed to be just an exercise. But nothing of the sort happened.

What are they doing?

"Cheating bastards!" the Admiral cried, waving his fist.

Edern cried a new order, but Dylan couldn't hear what it was. The blue-clad men aimed the rifles again, slightly lower this time. Another thunder of shots echoed throughout the mud plain and this time, a row of running soldiers stumbled and fell. Nine hundred men ran past their comrades rolling on the ground, wailing and groaning in pain.

The Admiral laughed a wheezing laugh, but Dylan frowned. He didn't want to start *another* war when the first one wasn't yet finished… but he trusted Edern knew what he was doing.

The Banneret's men shot twice more – two more lines tumbled under the feet of those running behind them – and then split into three groups, in a classic flanking formation.

Dylan's heart rose as he watched the perfectly performed manoeuvre. And they only had a week of training! The Qinese were proving to be just as good soldiers as his own men. He glanced at the Admiral. The old soldier was engrossed in the spectacle, his eyes wide open. His hand clapped against his thigh when the flanking troops pierced the now seven-hundred-strong battalion from both sides. The bayonets flashed against the swords and halberds. Most of the attackers wore heavy studded armour and their weapons were hefty while Edern's men bore themselves lightly and moved swiftly, and their bayoneted rifles held a nasty surprise that no spear or halberd could counter: once in a while a shot was heard, followed by a cry of anguish.

The Qin battalion fell into confusion and disarray when the middle group of the blue-clad soldiers charged head on, led by Edern whose hair and Lance shone like silver stars in the melee.

"Observe now, Admiral," said Dylan, "this is a modification to our usual tactics that Lee had advised us would suit best the Qin style."

Edern led a wedge of soldiers straight for the heart of the "enemy" formation. Disregarding their "losses", they charged onwards. For a moment, the silver haired head disappeared in the sea of blades and banners, but then a loud cry of triumph was heard and the remaining Qin dropped their weapons and surrendered. The battle was over.

"Aim for the head and the body will fail," Dylan said. "It's old fashioned, but seems to work here still."

The Bohan and his entourage marched quickly across the battlefield, stopping only for a moment to assess the injuries of his men. None of them were life-threatening. Edern's riflemen had been aiming for the feet and shins of the attackers, and their aim was accurate.

"How many of the rifles and uniforms can you procure?" the Bohan asked as soon as he climbed to the top of the small mound upon which Dylan and Reynolds stood.

His face was an impenetrable mask. No discussion of the result, no explanation for his men's behaviour during the exercise. The Bohan acknowledged his utter defeat without so much as a twitch. Dylan couldn't help but smile in admiration.

"I can send for a transport of three thousand from the Fragrant Harbour. It would be here in two weeks."

"Slow."

"It would be faster if we could sail past Ederra. And the messages take longer since the ley line's disruption."

The Bohan snorted and then grinned. His mood changed surprisingly fast.

"Come, Ardian. The Qin have secrets of their own – it's time I showed you one of them."

"What's going on? Where is he taking you?" the Admiral demanded. The entire conversation had been in Qin and he caught no word of it.

"I have no idea, Admiral, but I bet it will be an interesting trip."

CHAPTER VII

The three travellers lay around the fireplace in silence, the beating of the rain on the tent cloth the only sound of the night. The wizardess wrapped her cloak and blanket around her like a mummy. Nagomi lay on her back, hands on her stomach, in her usual pose. Bran turned away from the fire, facing the rain and darkness beyond the makeshift tent, contemplating what Satō had said.

She had the right to say it. It was her land, her people. Whoever he was, Dōraku, a *real* samurai who had lived in Yamato for his entire life, was closer to the wizardess than a Westerner. The boy felt a sudden, surprising pang of jealousy. He shook his head. He could not lose focus now. He had a mission to perform; a dragon to rescue. Emrys was now almost within his reach, no more than a couple of days walk away. He could feel the beast almost as strongly as if it was right beside him.

He reached a hand into the night and conjured a dancing sparkle of dragon flame. It came effortlessly, like a child's illusion. Dōraku was right – it was very easy to perform magic in this place. He could sense the currents of energies surging through him from all directions. With a wave of hand, he formed it into the shape of a rampant dragon, its wings spread widely. Then, just to see if he could, he sculpted the flame to show his own figure, dressed in the Yamato clothes, sword at his side. It seemed odd when viewed like this, it did not feel like him at all. The samurai uniform and haircut did not suit him. Another flick of the fingers and the dancing figure of fire changed to resemble the wizardess, with her tomboy posture and the *katana* in her hand. In his fiery vision, Satō wore the samurai gear much more comfortably and with more confidence. Just like Dōraku... Bran weaved his hand again and the flame split into two figures, one of him, one of Satō. The figures got closer. With another flicker, they were naked...

A twig cracked in the darkness. Dōraku returned from whatever his nightly errand was. Bran closed his hand, extinguishing the flickering flame sculptures, and pretended to sleep. The rain poured around the camp without respite.

The sweet smell of sizzling meat tickled her nostrils. She opened one eye and saw Dōraku, sitting by the campfire, holding a makeshift roost of long, sharpened sticks.

"Fish!"

She sat up immediately. Oil dripped from two fat trouts into the fire, sending out aromatic sparks.

"Where did you get it?"

"There are streams full of fish in these mountains, if you know where to look."

"So you're a fisherman now, too," said Bran, picking himself up on the other side of the campfire. "You are a man of many talents."

The samurai only smiled and turned the fish to the other side. He reached for his baggage and rummaged for a while. He took out a small bamboo box from which he poured some dark sauce on the fish, but something else caught Satō's attention; she glimpsed a corner of something round and white.

"Is that a... a theatre mask?"

Dōraku looked at her curiously and took out the mask. It was old, yellowed, fractured in places, trimmed with patches of white fur and painted in fierce red and black patterns.

"You like theatre?" he asked.

"I love it!"

The samurai gazed at the mask for a long time, then up to the sky with a faint smile, as if remembering something. He then turned to Bran.

"Will you hold the fish for me, Karasu-*sama*?"

Bran sighed grumpily, reaching for the roost. *What is it now?*

The samurai stood up, stretched himself and waited until Satō woke up the priestess. When he had the full audience at last, he put on the mask, bent his back and stretched his arms.

THE ISLANDS IN THE MIST

He began a strange wail, one in which Bran, at first, could barely discern the words. It was unlike any song he had ever heard, with no rhythm and scarcely any melody, yet strangely harmonious and haunting. It wasn't until he began to understand the lyrics that he realised Dōraku was telling a story.

Sore koso sashimo Atsumori ga saigo

Made michishi fuetake no...

Indeed until the last moment

Dia Atsumori keep the bamboo flute...

The samurai began to pace around the campfire on tiptoe, shaking his head and waving his arms, miming to the words. It was a tale of some duel in the middle of the battle, between a youth called Atsumori and an older warrior, Kumagai of Musashi province. The story was reaching its climax, and the song and Dōraku's movements were picking up the pace.

Uma no ue nite hikkunde

Namiuchigiwa ni

Ochikasanatte...

Ana on their horses they wrestled,

Then, falling into the waves,

Droppea one against another

At last…

"The fish!" cried Dōraku, tearing off the mask and leaping towards the campfire. He grabbed the roost from Bran's hands at the last moment – the sticks had almost burnt through; any second later, the trouts would have fallen into the fire.

"What happened?" asked Satō. "Who won the duel?"

"Kumagai," said the samurai, "but he did not rejoice in victory. Atsumori was the same age as Kumagai's son. The old warrior became a monk, dedicating his life to the atonement for his sins."

"But it was death on the battlefield. There is no wrong in that."

Dōraku looked at her with sad and strangely solemn eyes. "I pray that you never have to ponder this dilemma yourself, young warrior. But look, the fish is ready. Eat well, we have a long way to go."

As he sank his teeth in the tender white flesh of the trout, Bran heard a soft humming. He glanced at Dōraku. The samurai was looking into the fire, singing the rest of the song so quietly that Bran was certain only he could hear the words.

THE ISLANDS IN THE MIST

Kataki nite wa, nakarikeri

Ato tomuraite, tabitamae

Ato tomuraite, tabitamae.

If thou art not my enemy

Pray for me often,

Pray for me often.

By midday, the terrain got even tougher, as the travellers had to climb ever higher upwards, towards the summit of the mountain, along the needle-sharp, rocky ridges and jagged, weathered bluffs.

The black and grey mountaintops, naked, save for a few tufts of the shrimp grass or lichen-covered boulders, seemed to Bran indeed a good home for Gods and Demons to roam. This was how the world must have looked like when it was still young, in the age of Unbridled Fire. The red earth here was warm to touch. Plumes of steam spewed from fissures and rifts in the rock. Small, round craters were filled with clear blue-green water, boiling hot. There certainly was beauty in all this rough, rugged landscape, but overall Bran was thankful that they only needed to spend two more days climbing these volcanic slopes.

Based on the phases of the moon he was noting in his diary, less than a month had passed since they had left the Suwa Shrine. It seemed like a year. This journey had been by far the longest he had ever had to undertake. Any distance longer than a few miles back in Gwynedd, he would have just mounted Emrys and flown. The thin straw sandals the Yamato used for long-distance travel were barely any better than walking barefoot. His legs burned, his arms ached, his whole body cried "Enough! Get rest!"

He dared not complain. The journey was hard, but if the girls were managing to walk all this distance without so much as a whimper, so could he.

They never complain, he thought. *Not even Nagomi.* The priestess seemed excited to leave the city at first, but he could see clearly the recent events had taken their toll on her. She was more focused, more serious than when he had first met her.

She was the only one in Yamato who did not hide her feelings. She cried openly, and she laughed without restraint. All the other people he had met so far had worn masks of politeness, cheerfulness and indifference as impenetrable as Dōraku's theatre mask.

Satō is really good at this game, he thought. She played her role perfectly throughout the day. Seeing her, one could almost believe she was just on some country holiday with her friends. It was only at night that Bran could sometimes hear her sob, quietly. He never mentioned it. *I don't need to give her another reason to be angry.*

Before evening they had climbed almost to the top of Mount Takachiho, into the clouds covering the jagged summit, a gruelling trek through the empty and dusty lava fields. Weather up here changed abruptly. The day before they'd had to suffer a torrential shower, now Bran would have been grateful for a drop of water or a gust of wind to disperse the stale, humid, hot air. Below, spread the valleys

135

of Kirishima; seas of tall, bushy grass. But he could not see far beyond the hellish steams and sulphurous mists emerging from the cracked slopes of the mountain.

There was, at last, a patch of greenery, a clump of low azaleas blooming bright pink, huddled on the southern incline, which provided them with some welcome shade and shelter. They ate a brief meal there and, at Dōraku's advice, drank the last of their boiled water.

"Below that ridge the mountains end and, from there," the samurai said, pointing with his bamboo pipe, "tomorrow we start our descent straight to Kirishima. It's a cedar forest all the way down, pleasantly cool and dark at this time of year."

Satō moaned, discarding the ruined straw sandals and picking new ones from the bag. She was down to her last pair. "I can understand not going by the main roads... but this is not even a road!"

"It would be too easy to follow us through the woods. I needed us to stay out in the open, to see any incoming danger. From here, we can see far down but remain unseen from below."

Even Bran had to admit this sounded reasonable. How many enemies were now after them? The Magistrate, the Crimson Robe, the lord of the Kumamoto Castle... and whoever kept Emrys imprisoned. It seemed as if all of Yamato had turned against them.

This was the most desolate, miserable place he had ever had the misfortune to see. He had once flown to the top of a volcano on Brendan's Island, but it was surrounded with greenery, vineyards and orange orchards. There was nothing so abundant growing here, nothing to make a fire with. Only the lonely clump of wild azaleas, exposed to the elements.

He reached over and fluttered his fingers over the pink bloom. He knew a real samurai would at this moment think about the flowers in some poetic terms. Here was life, clinging desperately to a hellish wasteland, flourishing, ever hopeful in its fragile beauty. He tried to think like a cultured Yamato warrior, come up with a way to capture the beauty in words, but couldn't. His Western mind tried instead to assign a taxonomic rank to the plant, analyse the way the soil composition was reflected in the colour and size of blossom. At the Academy he had been taught botany, not poetry.

I will never be like them.

He picked a large, five-fold flower and, without thinking, crushed it between his fingers. A mocking chuckle resonated in his head.

Bran stirred, moaned and threw his head from side to side in his sleep before finally opening his eyes. They were black as the night around the camp.

General Shigemasa sat up and stretched the muscles of the boy's body. He looked around. The campfire was sizzling away into ashes, giving just enough light to illuminate the girls lying close together underneath their blankets and the dark silhouette of Dōraku who sat outside the tent cloth, cross-legged, in the pouring rain.

The General rose and crept quietly up to the samurai.

"I may be deep in meditation, but I can still hear you coming, *Taishō-dono*."

Shigemasa chuckled. "And thou canst even tell 'tis me?"

"The boy does not know how to sneak like that. Why do you disturb my exercise?"

"I see… things. This close to Mount Takachiho my senses are as sharp as in the Caves."

"Oh? And what do you see in the darkness and mist?"

"I see a head of the eight-headed serpent reaching out towards us. I see monsters coming from beyond the sea. I see one of the three perish, but I know not which one. And I'd rather it not be the boy."

"Two of these I am aware of," nodded Dōraku, "but what is this about the monsters from beyond the sea?"

"I do not see it clearly yet. I am worried, Swordsman. I require this body. I need it safe."

"I will do what I can to protect the boy."

Shigemasa scoffed.

"It is *thee* that I am worried about."

Dōraku uncrossed his legs and turned around. His eyes glistened in the campfire light.

"I am not like the…others."

"So thou sayest, but how can I believe thee?"

"Have I ever betrayed your trust, *Taishō-dono*? When we fought at Shimabara… have I ever done anything improper?"

"That was more than ten score years ago. A lot has changed since then, even the way people speak."

"I have not. Not like that."

Shigemasa looked into the night for a long while in silence.

"I will have to tell the boy about thee," he spoke at last. "Let him decide what to do."

Dōraku stood up.

"I would advise against it, *Taishō-dono*. He would likely do something unwise."

He stepped forward. Shigemasa shuffled backwards.

"Thou threatens *me*? By what power?" he said and laughed, but the laughter died in his throat when Dōraku stepped even closer and his eyes glinted gold.

"I was hoping I could trust you to keep a secret," the samurai said, "but if there be no trust between us…"

Like a striking serpent, Dōraku's hand flashed forward towards Bran-Shigemasa's face. And then there was darkness.

He was back on the plain of the red dust. The light from the tower on the horizon was dimmed, hazed by the distance.

Shigemasa sighed and started walking back towards it when he heard heavy footsteps thumping in the dust behind him.

He turned around and saw a giant. More than twice the size of a man, he wore a cloak of darkness and wielded twin blades of silver light, each as big as a glaive. Eyes like two pieces of gold shone brightly from under the hood.

"Thy tricks do not scare me, S-swordsman," Shigemasa started defiantly, but ended on a stutter. He drew his own sword – here he had his old armour and weapons – but it seemed a mere toothpick in comparison.

"These are no tricks, *Taishō*. Here, everyone shows their true form."

"If thou wishest to strive with me, then do it honourably, like the nobleman thou art."

"As you wish." The air shimmered and in place of the giant appeared the Dōraku as he was outside, with his ridiculous yellow and purple kimono and old-fashioned whiskers.

"Now – " he started, but Shigemasa did not let him finish. He charged with a short yell, so suddenly, he almost succeeded in surprising the samurai.

The blades clanged – once – twice. Shigemasa's sword raised a plume of red dust. A tip of one of Dōraku's swords hovered an inch from the general's neck, the other – at his heart.

"I don't even know what killing you here would do to you," the samurai whispered hoarsely, "but I am itching to find out." His eyes glowed like lanterns, his breath smelled of death.

Shigemasa blinked then threw back his head and laughed, genuinely this time.

"Dost thou expect me to beg for mercy? I am a samurai!"

Dōraku lowered his weapons and his figure seemed to shrink and darken even further.

"No, you're right. It is not proper."

He closed his eyes and whispered something unintelligible, then sheathed his swords and turned on his heels. Shigemasa tried to follow, but he couldn't budge. His feet sank into the red dirt like quicksand and the more he struggled the deeper he fell.

"What hast thou done to me?"

"I will release you when it's safe," said Dōraku without turning, "I cannot have you interfere with my plans."

The general snickered. "Plans? I could have told thee about thy plans. It is not *I* that shall be the cause of thy failure."

Dōraku stopped.

"Thy ears are pricked now, eh? But it's too late. I shall tell thee nothing."

The samurai's shoulders dropped. "Good," he said, "your prophecies were growing tiresome."

With that, he walked away into the darkness. A nameless wind blew across the featureless plain, picking up the dirt and shrouding the horizon in a blood red haze.

They huddled together in the darkness, in a large cave on the shore of the Kuma River, not daring to light a fire, not daring to make a sound.

Bats were their only companions, flying in their hundreds to roost as the evening fell. Further in, the cave expanded to a magnificent palace of limestone formations, but they stayed near the entrance, watchful, observant.

"He will find us," Azumi said, shivering. Rain and fog drenched her clothes and hair as they fled through the forest, but she had nothing to change into. "He will find us and destroy us."

Ozun kissed her on the forehead. A thunder struck in the distance and she shuddered. The rain started anew.

"You're a brave *kunoichi*. Surely you're not afraid of a storm now?"

"Don't mock me. You know what He's capable of."

"We will be all right," said Ozun, caressing her wet, cold back. "Tomorrow we will reach the sea, and from there we can sail to wherever we want."

"But where to? He'll find us anywhere in Yamato."

"Then we will leave Yamato. We will go to Nansei. His power doesn't reach there."

"I have a villa in Nansei," a darkly sweet voice said behind them, "although it's a bit too warm this time of the year."

They jumped up and turned around. In a flash of the thunderclap they saw a tall figure in a long robe of crimson, with eyes glowing gold. Stench of death and blood filled the cave.

Ozun stepped in front of Azumi, rising his jingling staff in defence.

"How brave," the Crimson Robe said, smiling. "And romantic."

"You can kill me, but leave her. She did nothing wrong."

"Kill? Who said anything about killing?" the Crimson Robe feigned surprise.

"But I thought…" Ozun lowered his weapon.

The Crimson Robe waved his hand and a powerful force cast the hermit against the cavern wall, knocking him out. Azumi cried and tried to run but she couldn't move; one word whispered by the Master was enough to hold her in a bind.

"Kill you, after what you've done for me?"

"I don't understand," she whispered. "What good have I done?"

"You've forced my old friend to come out of hiding! That must count for *something*. Thanks to you he had to show off his fencing skills and my other spies – you didn't think you were alone? – could have confirmed it was really him?"

"You… know this …swordsman?"

"Know him!" He laughed again. "Yes, I *knew* him."

Ozun stirred and moaned, trying to rise up, but the Crimson Robe snapped his fingers and the hermit's head was smashed against the wall again.

"Please stop it!" she cried. "You said you would not kill him!"

"I've decided to change my tactics," her master continued unperturbed. "Sending you out one by one will not do, not when that… man is around. I am summoning everyone from the old team – and once we're done here, I will need you both back."

"Done with what?" she asked and the way his golden eyes looked at her made her immediately regret the question.

"The tracks from the road lead here," Azumi said in a hoarse voice. Her ashen skin was almost the same colour as her tight-fitting uniform of the Koga province assassins. Her cheek twitched nervously whenever she had to address her master. His punishments left no trace on her body but drove deep scars into her spirit.

The Crimson Robe was standing atop a fallen tree, careful not to stain his robe with mud. His men were searching the forest floor around the earthen mound as he watched from beyond the stone circle. Azumi observed his unease with satisfaction. The power of the Ancients was still strong enough to keep the likes of him at a distance. The remnants of their presence permeated this primeval forest.

144

"Somebody made a very good effort at concealing them," she added.

"This is what I have spared you for," he said, smiling. She gulped and continued.

"There was a battle here as well, but much more … lethal."

"We found them!" cried one of the members of the searching party, shovelling away a pack of fresh dirt. The men all wore the grey uniforms. They were very reliable – and very disposable.

The Crimson Robe knelt by the bodies, already starting to swell and turn blue in the hot and humid spring air. A cloud of hungry flies buzzed irritatingly above until he snarled and made an impatient gesture; the insects dropped dead. He traced the pattern of the wounds with his hand and examined the way the head had been cut off the mage's body. His golden eyes glimmered with recognition. He chuckled.

"Only one man uses that technique with such precision."

He turned to the *kunoichi*.

"Have you found anything else of interest?"

"There was a dead wolf buried along with the bodies. It looks… familiar."

"Show it to me."

The men brought out the carcass of the slain animal. The Crimson Robe examined the wounds and let out a surprised laugh.

"How quaint. With all these dead bodies around… chivalrous as ever."

"I also found this on the floor of the mound," Azumi said, showing him several long hairs of deep red colour.

"The young priestess who was a friend of Shūhan's daughter… what was her name again?"

"Nagomi, I believe."

"So she's no longer dying her hair. That should make things easier."

He stood up and looked at the headless body of an *onmyōji*, thinking something over. He then looked at the people gathered around him.

"One of them is a wizard, right? I believe that gives them an unfair advantage…"

He leaned over and examined the corpse once more.

"Take this body with you. Burn the rest." He spat. "No, wait. One more idea. Ozun!"

The hermit appeared before him and Azumi winced. His left arm hung limply along his body and he slouched slightly, but in his eyes still glimmered the rebellious streak she loved him for.

Ozun's eyes narrowed when he saw the wolf's mangled body.

"I need your powers to hunt down the owner of this beautiful red hair," the Crimson Robe said and let the thin

copper-coloured thread float down with the wind onto the
yamabushi's outstretched palm.

"The spirits of the forest yearn for revenge," Ozun
said, looking at the dead animal.

"Do they, now?" The Master looked at the hermit
with interest. "Fine. Let them have it, then. But! The dragon
rider must be unharmed."

Ozun nodded.

"I need fresh blood. This is useless."

The Master whistled at one of the grey-clads. The
man came up and knelt down. Azumi turned her eyes away,
knowing what was about to happen. The great *nodachi* blade
fell and the *rōnin's* head rolled on the grass. Blood splattered
the dead wolf's body.

Ozun crouched by the animal and patted it gently on
the side, sighing. His fingers caressed the grey fur, now
turned red. He stood up, put the conch to his lips and blew a
solemn melody. At first nothing happened, but then white-
and-blue will-o'-the-wisps appeared in the crowns of cedar
trees. Spiralling, they descended to the ground all around the
glade, in their dozens. The forest reverberated with the
sound of the shell, and the wind and leaves joined in with
their own morbid song. The entire wood mourned the death
of the noble animal.

Wherever the wisps touched the ground, they turned
into ghostly wolf shapes. Soon there was a great pack of
them before the shrine, howling for vengeance. The largest
one approached Ozun, who let the beast sniff the
glimmering copper strand of hair. The hermit leant down

and whispered something to the leader of the pack, then stamped the jingling staff twice. The wolf snarled and launched into a chase. The other spirits followed in deadly silence.

"And you are certain they will find their prey?" the Crimson Robe asked.

Ozun nodded, pale and frail after casting the spell. "Nothing escapes my *yōkai*."

The Crimson Robe turned to the rest of his men who awaited further orders.

"Destroy this eyesore," he said, pointing at the earthen mound, his eyes glinting with grisly satisfaction, "I don't want a trace of the Ancients to remain."

CHAPTER VIII

Captain Kiyomasa came up to the campfire and poked it with a stick.

"This fire will go out in an hour," he said, "bring more wood."

Two guardsmen rushed to carry out the order. He clasped his eyes with his palm in exasperation.

"No, no, no, no! Never leave your post together, how many times have I told you?"

"Apologies, Captain Kiyomasa," the two soldiers bowed.

Kiyomasa sighed.

"You stay here – you get the firewood," he ordered. When the younger of the watchmen disappeared into the dark cedar forest, the Captain sat down on a log and gestured to the older of the soldiers to join him.

"I know what you think. I'm too rigid. A martinet. No, don't protest. Every night I make sure the watch is set up properly, the fires are lit, the weapons are at the ready. But you must understand, I don't do it for my own benefit."

He waited for a prompt, but the soldier was too overwhelmed by the presence of his superior to speak out.

"It's because of those highborn, the samurai," he continued, "they are not used to being in an army. You've seen them, a band of arrogant snobs. Each thinks himself equal to another – and they all think they're better than me. They would never follow my orders. I can't command them, but I can give them an example. Perhaps observing how disciplined you common footmen are will inspire them to act as warriors should."

The soldier nodded, then opened his mouth and licked his lips.

"You may speak."

"Forgive me, Captain… I don't understand. What are we even doing here?"

"You know the reason. We are to escort Nariakira-*dono*'s daughter across these wild mountains."

"But… thirty of Kumamoto's finest samurai and a troop of footmen? Who would dare to even think of attacking such a force?"

"I don't know. These matters are as over my head as yours. All I know is that I've got my orders and you have yours, and we must do our best not to neglect our duties."

Kiyomasa was lying. He had received his own secret orders directly from the *daimyo* on the day of their departure. He was one of the two people in the entire entourage who knew about the real treasure hidden at the Kirishima Shrine.

Twice already had a messenger arrived on horseback from the castle, carrying a coded message from lord Hosokawa, and rode back with the answer. The missives exchanged did not bring him peace of mind. The *daimyo* was just as unsure of what to do as the Captain. Were they to charge the shrine and capture the dragon by force from Satsuma guards? But that would mean an open conflict between the two *daimyo*, who had until now been staunch allies and, ostentatiously, friends. Wait and observe, hoping for a solution to arrive? They did not have that much time; the princess was expected at Edo in a month and that meant she had to depart Kirishima at most within a week from now.

"He's taking his time," he said, nodding towards the trees.

"There's something wrong with this forest, don't you think, Captain? It gives me goose bumps whenever I stray too far from the camp."

Kiyomasa nodded. The wood sprawling the steep slopes of Mount Takachiho was unlike any he had ever seen. The cedar trees grew into twisted and bent shapes instead of straight majestic pillars. Outcrops of sharp volcanic rock scattered among the wild ferns were bathed in the yellow vapours descending from the summits. No animals lived here apart from snakes and crows.

He stared into the evening mist and spat in disgust. He had never wished so badly to be back in Kumamoto.

Bran woke at dawn and looked around. The girls were still asleep, but Dōraku was sitting a few feet away, observing an azalea bush, a paper scroll on his lap and a painting brush in hand.

He yawned and walked behind the samurai to look at the paper over his shoulder. He expected to see a simple sketch, one that a pretentious warrior would draw to while away a sleepless night. The flower on paper, though marked with a few quick strokes of black ink, seemed more real, more alive than the one hanging from a twig. Again, Bran felt a twang of envy, recalling his own clumsy attempts at drawing.

Is there no limit to this man's talents?

Dōraku finished his sketch, stretched out the scroll, looked at it and nodded with satisfaction. He left the paper to dry, pinning it to the warm ground with four pebbles.

"Ah, you're awake," he said, noticing Bran behind him. His face was even more pale than usual, and his movements seemed slower, less energetic.

So even he can get tired.

"What do you think?" the samurai asked, nodding at the scroll.

"It's… astonishing." Bran couldn't lie.

"Yes, I'm rather glad of it myself," the samurai smiled and for the first time Bran saw him genuinely pleased about something. "You know, I once spent five years trying to capture the beauty of a peony flower."

A peony flower…?

The samurai put the writing utensils into one of the containers hanging from his sash.

"What do you keep in all those pouches?" Bran asked.

"Ink pillow, thread and needle, *tabako*, *yuzu* sauce, *shichimi* spice…" the samurai recited out. "Everything a man needs on the road."

"And the big one?"

"That's salt."

"*Salt?*"

"I guess I'm a little superstitious," Dōraku said, chuckling quietly. "They say some kinds of demons are afraid of salt."

"That's a lot to carry around just because of some superstition."

The samurai smirked.

"Some demons are bigger than others."

Bran started rolling up the bedding. The clouds had cleared a little, and from their position near the summit of Takachiho he could see far down towards the cedar forests covering the slope, and beyond, into the valleys.

"Is that the town of Kirishima?" he asked, looking at the chequered board of fields and orchards below the forest. There was a blue ribbon of a river flowing down from the mountains to the north and, where it turned west to circumnavigate another mountain, spread a small town of grey- and blue-roofed houses.

Dōraku nodded.

Several large structures of red brick stood on a hill on the outskirts of the town, across the river. They looked out of place in this otherwise idyllic landscape; the sprawling buildings reminded Bran of sleeping monsters, spewing white smoke from their nostrils high into the sky. It had taken him a while to realise what he was looking at. The last time he had seen buildings like those was in Brigstow.

"Are these… " Bran struggled to speak. His knowledge of Yamato failed him: there seemed to be no word for a *factory* in this language. "What *are* these?" he asked at last, pointing to the red brick buildings.

"The great workshops of Satsuma, boy; the first of many. That's a brewery, if I'm not mistaken, and that's a steel plant. The third one wasn't there the last time I was here."

"Where's the Shrine?"

"Higher up the slope, on the edge of the forest. You can't see it from here."

"I'm not sure we'll make it there this afternoon."

"There's a good road halfway down that lumberjacks use. It's not going to be like the last two days."

For an instant he tensed, his eyes narrowed.

"What is it?"

"Wake the others. There is something… odd in the air."

154

The girls woke and, after quickly eating a small, dry breakfast of pickles and rice cakes, they moved out hurriedly, urged on by Dōraku.

Bran kept thinking about the peony drawings. The memory lingered at the back of his mind, irritatingly. It was the same with Nagomi and her father. Another stirred recollection. If only he could stop, clear his head…

They walked for about a mile at a hurried pace. Dōraku's serious mood spread, and Bran was now also sensing some kind of hard to pinpoint dread. He looked to the girls – they were also silent, grim. None of them was saying anything.

He heard a faint howl in the distance, then another. Dōraku slowed down; he looked back toward the volcanic road as if searching something along the northern horizon, his whole body rigid and alert, like a hound that had caught the scent of its prey.

"What's going on?" asked Satō, but the samurai gestured to them to keep quiet and continue their march towards the trees. He sniffed the air. His neck stiffened, his gaze focused at a point along the ridge. His hands wrapped around the hilts of the two swords stuck in the sash.

"Keep walking at a normal pace," he said sternly, "but when I say run, run into the forest. Try to get to the road, there should be people there."

"What is it?" Bran repeated Satō's question. "More bandits?"

"I don't know yet – it's… something else. Look, there it is."

A grey dot appeared over the ridge, then another, and more. Soon there were dozens of them, running down the mountain in a tight pack.

Bran reached into the satchel for his spyglass.

"Are these... wolves?" The pack easily numbered twenty, thirty, maybe more animals. And still more were coming.

Dōraku drew his swords in a smooth, perfect, noiseless move. The blades glittered in the sun. The swords thirsted for blood.

"Go, now," he said.

"We can fight them," opposed Satō, "it's just some wolves. We are stronger here, near the vortex."

"These are not normal wolves. And they are after me, not you."

"How do you know? *What's going on?*"

"Does it matter? He's right, we need to get to that forest, it's too dangerous here in the open," Bran said, thrusting his spyglass into the satchel. He pulled Nagomi with him towards the trees.

"Satō! Come, I'm sure he'll manage."

"But..."

"Run, now!" the samurai barked at the wizardess. His cold, fierce eyes demanded obedience. For a moment, Satō hesitated. But the pack now grew to a horde, a sea of grey poured over the ridge down the slope, an immeasurable, unnatural multitude of blood-thirsty animals. There couldn't possibly have been so many of them in the entire forest. At last the wizardess started running alongside Bran and Nagomi.

They were a few hundred yards nearer the trees when the first two of the pack reached Dōraku. His swords moved faster than a human eye could register and, with a yowl, both animals were slain. Instead of falling to the ground, however, they perished into thin air with a quiet flash. Three more wolves jumped on the samurai. He cut them down in one smooth strike. Still more came, and still more appeared over the ridge, an unending army of vengeful ghosts. Dōraku's arms turned into a whirlwind of steel as he fought against the onslaught, but his body remained calm and still.

"They're coming towards us," Bran said. A few of the ghostly attackers ran past the samurai. He tried to pick up the pace, but Nagomi could not run any faster.

"I'm... sorry..." she started, panting, but Bran silenced her.

"Save your energy. We're almost there."

Far in the distance, on the barren mountainside, Dōraku's outline was barely visible under the attack of countless wolves, now swarming from every direction, swamping him under the sea of grey fur.

They ran into the shadows of the tall cedar trees, but the wolves kept on running. One of them caught the hem of Satō's *hakama* in its teeth. The girl stumbled, drew her sword and cut through the animal's body. It disappeared in the

157

same white flash as those slain by Dōraku. The other two wolves turned away and started running alongside the runaways, safely out of range of Satō's sword.

"The blade works against them!"

"If we stop now there will be too many for us to fight," said Bran, "if we get to the road, maybe we can find help."

As he glanced at the wolves running beside them – two more appeared on their left, seeking to encircle their prey – he thought he noticed something else in the forest, deeper among the trees. A glimpse of… crimson? His blood froze. *Are the wolves just a ruse?*

He ran out onto a wide dirt road. The wolves jumped behind them, but hesitated to attack, growling uncertainly. Bran turned around to see what made the animals stop. On the road before him stood a company of about thirty samurai, accompanied by foot soldiers, servants and porters.

"What's the hold-up?" a voice asked in a commanding tone. An important-looking samurai came forth to the front. He was short, stocky and round-faced.

"Why are we not moving? I want to be in the Shrine by evening! Oh…"

He stopped, seeing the three travellers and the wolves behind them. He frowned.

Bran noticed the symbol embroidered on the samurai's kimono. The same symbol had been stitched onto the soldiers' cloaks and banners on the horses. The eight circles; the crest of lord Hosokawa of Kumamoto.

He clenched the hilt of his sword tightly and made a step forward.

Two young samurai and a girl wearing the travelling clothes of a priestess stood on the road; a straw hood fell from her head, revealing her hair – red like a fox's fur…

The wolf growled, then another came out onto the road, head low, teeth bared. More howled, hidden among the trees. Kiyomasa counted at least a dozen of the beasts. What got into them? He had never heard of the wolves behaving in such manner, not even in the harshest of winters.

One of the boys, wearing a dark blue kimono, stepped forward, holding a long sword. There was fear and determination in his eyes.

"I am Captain Kiyomasa Katō, son of Kiyotada, of Kumamoto castle guards," the Captain introduced himself formally, "who are you?"

The boy eased a little and looked back to his companions.

"Please help us," said the other of the youths in a high-pitched voice. "We are pilgrims on our way to Kirishima". His vest was black and his kimono vermillion, like the pillars of a *torii* gate. Kiyomasa had never seen one of this colour.

The wolves, apprehensive at first, now started moving towards the group, growling quietly. The eyes of their brethren blazed among the trees. The horses in the train started neighing in fright, as they felt the pack close in from both sides.

His men whispered among themselves.

"Goblins! Demons! This damned forest…"

"Come," he said, gesturing at the three youths to join the convoy. "I don't think those wolves will attack thirty samurai, but even if they do, we're sure to make short work of them," he boasted, trying to encourage himself as well as the strangers.

"Thank you, Captain," the boy in the blue kimono said, bowing – though not deeply enough, Kiyomasa noted. He bore himself with the arrogance of a high-born samurai.

Kiyomasa gave the signal to march onwards, but nothing happened.

"What now?"

"It's the wolves, Captain," reported the sergeant, "they're not moving." The animals stood a few paces from the front of the group, growling fiercely. The soldiers lowered their halberds and the wolves' eyes lit up with an unnatural glow. The air in the forest turned cold, the mist smelled of blood.

The Captain, his hair standing on end, murmured a short prayer to the Goddess of War. *Benzaiten-sama, give me strength in combat ana valour in death.* He drew his sword and marched towards the closest of the wolves. He stomped the ground in an attempt to frighten the animal, but the wolf only growled back, showing its sharp teeth.

"Kuso!"

Kiyomasa slashed his sword, aiming for the head. The wolf disappeared in a flash. The Captain fell on his bottom in surprise, and everyone else gasped in terror.

"*Inugami!* The *yōkai* are back!"

The wolves sprang from all sides in silence. Lord Hosokawa's samurai started slashing around at random, some hid behind the horses and the wagons. The servants dropped their loads and ran away. But Kiyomasa's soldiers stood their ground, forming a triangle of spears around him and the three travellers.

"They may be ghosts, but they can be cut by steel," Kiyomasa cried to his men. He noticed the two boys joining him in the fray. The girl stood in the middle of the convoy, praying. A pale aura of sanctity surrounded her, repelling the *yōkai*. The beasts attacked in waves, without fear or remorse. One of Kumamoto's retainers fell down with a ghostly animal at his throat, then another. There seemed to be no end to the demonic pack; the samurai got pushed away from the footmen; the defenders were stretched dangerously thin, their line breaking. Another soldier fell down with a gurgling cry.

Like a herd of deer, thought Kiyomasa. *They will pick us off one by one. But the deer don't fight back!*

"Form an arrowhead!" he cried an order. The soldiers obeyed instantly, setting themselves up in a tight wedge of glistening spears.

"Charge!"

His fear disappeared completely, replaced by the rush of exhilaration. This was no exercise! This was a real battle,

161

the likes of which he had only dreamt of. His entire soldier's training led up to this moment.

He led the charge against the wolves, chasing the demons back into the forest from which they were emerging. His men cried and died, their throats, thighs and stomachs torn by the ghostly fangs, but they pushed on. Out of the corner of his eye he saw the two boys fighting alongside the soldiers. They fought well.

And then, as suddenly as they had appeared, all the wolves vanished. The forest was silent.

The losses were grave. Five of Kumamoto's retainers were dead, either slain by their own companions' indiscriminate hacking, or torn apart by the wolves. Six more were too wounded to walk on their own and had to be carried on stretchers. Of the footmen, a third were either dead or incapacitated. Blood turned the sand of the road into mud.

"I lost many good men here!" the Captain burst out, feeling his face turn hot. "I demand to know what just happened! It's no coincidence –"

"Captain Kiyomasa!"

He scowled hearing the shrill voice.

"Gensai-*dono*," he said calmly, bowing before the young, fierce-faced samurai. Kawakami Gensai was one of lord Hosokawa's most trusted men. He emerged from the battle unscathed, but Kiyomasa knew it was not because he had strayed from a fight.

"There are wounded men awaiting your attention, Captain. I will take care of our noble guests."

The military convoy turned into a funeral procession as the bodies of the slain samurai were put on the wagons. The servants and soldiers were buried on the spot in the hard volcanic soil. At Master Kawakami's request Nagomi had agreed to oversee the funeral rites.

The samurai poured saké from his own flask into two small white cups and offered it to Bran and Satō.

"I've heard stories about the *yōkai* of Satsuma forests, but I never imagined I'd see them with my own eyes," he said. The corners of his mouth twitched slightly under the thin moustache and Bran realised this was Master Kawakami's way of smiling.

Thick, dark eyebrows accentuated a plain, strong face. His hair was tied in a tight ball-like bun, stretching the skin on his forehead in what must have caused constant irritation. A thin, badly stitched scar ran from the corner of his right eye towards the ear.

"We were just as surprised," said Satō.

"Oh, I'm sure, I'm sure. But what were you doing off the main road? These mountains are not hospitable to lonely strangers, even without demons roaming about."

"We... got lost in the mist," Bran said. This excuse had worked once before. The samurai narrowed his eyes and his lips twitched again.

"I hear you're both good with the sword," he changed the subject. "We must spar later. You're on your way to the Kirishima Shrine, aren't you?"

"Yes."

"This little affair set us back a few hours, but we should reach it before night. Ah, I believe the young priestess returns. That hair of hers is quite remarkable. We best be on our way, lest Captain Kiyomasa gets all irritable again."

The samurai's lip twitched one last time.

"He suspects something," Bran said to Satō quietly.

"Obviously. You should've let me speak to him."

"And what would you have told him?"

"I'd certainly come up with a better explanation than being *lost in the mist*."

Nagomi joined them, wiping water off her hands.

"Do you think Dōraku-*sama...?*"

"Who knows," said Bran, "but we must assume the worst."

"That's twice he's saved our lives," said Satō, "we need to honour his memory."

Bran let his mind wander, observing the soldiers marching around him with curiosity. The only other time he had seen Yamato footmen was at the picket in Kumamoto, but Captain Kiyomasa's men seemed much more like a real army than those shivering guardsmen. They bore a range of weapons, spears, swords, long-barrelled rifles of antiquated design, but he was most interested in their *naginata* glaives. They consisted of long curved, widening blades attached to wobbly bamboo poles. They looked remarkably similar to his father's golden Soul Lance. He asked one of the soldiers to let him hold it for a while; it was well balanced and hefty. It felt good in his hands.

Once out of the cedar forest, the road descended steeply towards the market town spread below the Kirishima Shrine, amongst a thick carpet of pink-blooming azaleas and, further down, vast tea plantations. The sky was hazy grey.

It was the time of the harvest. The white headscarves and pointy straw hats of peasants bobbed up and down between the bushes as they filled baskets with freshly picked leaves. Bran had never seen a tea plantation up close. He wondered how the thick, moist green leaves were transformed into the hard, black brick with which he was more familiar. The Yamato *cha* was served either as a bright green, foamy, soup-like liquid or a yellowish-green drink, bitter and refreshing. Neither of those resembled the 'tea' he knew from home.

"Milk and sugar," he said, tracing his fingers over the young tea leaves.

"What?"

"We drink *cha* with milk and sugar," he repeated.

"Ugh!" Satō said. "Why would anyone do that?"

Bran shrugged. "It's just a custom... we like sweet things. I've heard that in Shambhala, in the mountains west of Qin, they eat the leaves with butter and salt. Everyone has their own way."

"Did you hear about the Way of Tea?" Satō asked. "I studied it, but only got as far as folding the cloth. It's very difficult."

"The Way of Tea?"

"The *Cha* Ceremony, a proper way to drink powdered *cha*." She then started to describe a complex and highly ritualised procedure. He tried his best to feign interest, but quickly got lost in the many small rules.

"You'll have to teach me later, when this is all over," he said when she finished and thought, *Liar. There will be no "later".*

A group of nearby labourers in red sashes and dark blue tunics erupted into song. The first harvest must have been a joyous occasion to the entire community.

Without the Cursed Weed money, you would have no tea for breakfast, Bran remembered his father's words from Fan Yu. He imagined the Yamato peasants lying on the side of the road, their minds addled with laudanum, as clipper ships filled with cheap tea sailed from Kiyō harbour to Lundenburgh.

Satō shook him by the shoulder – the road turned abruptly and he was almost about to walk straight through the tea bushes.

"What is it?" she asked with concern. "Suddenly you've grown all dour."

"You told me once your father desired a change for Yamato… but what if the change brought only more suffering?"

"You mean like in Qin?"

"You know what happened in Qin?"

"Of course! Everyone was shocked to hear of the humiliation brought upon the Emperor…"

"It's not the Emperor you need to worry about, but the people."

"How do you mean?"

He told her briefly of his experiences in Fan Yu. She stared at him with her eyes growing wide, but when he finished, she shook her head.

"This would never have happened here. The days of Qin's glory are long past, but Yamato is still strong and virile. It just needs some reforms…"

"I may know little of the situation here, but I've seen enough of the world outside. If the Westerners – if *we* come in force, do you think we will be impressed by your reforms? By your swordsmanship, by your calligraphy, by your *cha* ceremonies?"

"If your people do come in force, we will fight them and remove them from our lands – or die trying," she said with defiance, her hand inadvertently reaching for the sword.

"Then you will die trying," he replied unhappily.

THE ISLANDS IN THE MIST

CHAPTER IX

Ardian ab Ifor was sitting at his desk in the cabin on the first deck, buried in some papers. Samuel tried to discuss with him Bran's upcoming birthday, but the Ardian paid him no attention, mumbling something in response.

"I'm sorry?" said Samuel.

The Ardian raised his head and repeated the murmuring. It had a strange, droning quality, like the monotone hum of a mistfire engine. It filled the entire cabin, drowning out all other sounds.

The Doctor woke up. He was on a canvas bunk bed. The droning sound continued in the darkness. He reached out and his hand touched a cold metal surface, vibrating in tune with the hum.

A curtain opened, letting in some light from a table lamp. A bearded man in a green cloak looked at him intensely.

"*Gut.* You waked," he said with the harsh Varyagan accent.

"I… yes, I am awake," Samuel replied weakly. "Are you a doctor?"

He was still dizzy and nauseated. The bearded man nodded and handed him a bowl to retch into; Samuel gestured it wasn't necessary.

"I'm a doctor too. Samuel Ben Hagin," he said.

"I am Magnus Ingvarsson," the other man said, shaking Samuel's hand. "You rest now. I bring Admiral."

Admiral?

"Please, just tell me – where am I? What is this place?"

Ingvarsson smiled but said nothing. He turned around and disappeared down a long, narrow corridor.

The Admiral was a short man, like all sailors on this mysterious vessel but, unlike the others, was clean shaven except for abundant sideburns, flaxen yellow like the rest of his hair. A large, straight nose dominated a determined face.

The cabin they were in had rounded walls, made of thick metal sheets joined with thick iron rivets, and was very sparsely equipped except for a console filled with gauges, switches and dials beside the Admiral's table. There was a small, thick-framed round window in one of the walls, but Samuel could see nothing but darkness behind it. The constant, irritating humming filled this place as well. The air was stuffy, smelling of dozens of men cramped in tight quarters.

"Fridrik Otterson," he said simply instead of a greeting.

"Admiral, I hear."

"Well, *ja*, but let's not dwell on *formalitaet* too much. What were you doing in the middle of the ocean? We saw no other castaways and heard of no Western shipwrecks in these seas."

"I drifted off far from where my ship sank. We were at anchor before Huating."

"That is far indeed! You were very lucky we found you at all. We're *tva* hundred and fifty miles north-by-northeast from Huating."

Samuel recalled the navigation charts with some difficulty – his head was still spinning.

"You're headed for Chosun?"

The Admiral laughed.

"*Nej, herr Doktor.*"

"But… there is no other land between here and Tyr Gorllewin. Unless you're trying to reach…"

"The fabled islands of Yamato? *Ja,* that is exactly where we're going."

Samuel leaned back in his chair and tried to gather his thoughts.

"The storms… the maze of waves… the navigation problems," he said, trying to remember all the many reasons he knew for nobody but the Bataavians being able to reach Yamato.

"All of this, we have discovered, working only on the surface of the sea," said the admiral, smiling.

"This ship…" Samuel understood at last. "We're sailing under water!"

A buzzer sounded on the steel wall. The admiral pressed a button on his console. The heavy round door swung open and into the cabin came another man, silver-haired, wearing a dinner jacket and round metal glasses. In his hand he held a pocket watch on a chain that he kept checking nervously.

"*Doktor* Nobelius," the admiral introduced him. "The finest naval inventor in the *Khaganatet*."

"Honoured," said Samuel.

"Likewise," said Nobelius swiftly. "*Amiral*, in ten minutes we need to make another *tryckkontroll*… A pressure check," he added for Samuel's benefit.

"*Ach, ja, Doktor*. We'll be right with you."

The inventor left hastily.

"I'm guessing the existence of this ship is supposed to be a secret," said Samuel.

"Oh, it is – for now. But you won't be telling anyone in the West about it for a while. We've set our course and will not surface until we are in *Dejeema*."

Dejeema. The name invoked an even greater sense of mystery.

"The *Khaganatet* has been trying to chart these seas for years," the Admiral continued, "ever since we've reached the coast of the *Stora Havet* – the Great Ocean – and built the harbour at Alexisborg. We have learned many *sekret* – the Bataavians are not as good at keeping them as they think.

But, we wanted to make sure we knew what we were doing. There is only one such *boot* in the world and we didn't want to lose her."

"Just like *Ladon*," said Samuel quietly, remembering the vastness of his own ship.

Each nation is trying to outdo everyone else in making the machines of war... where will this race end?

"Pardon? Anyway, we found out we were late to the party. Another power is heading for Yamato as we speak. Hence our hurry – and the poor *Doktor*'s *angslan*... uneasiness. This *boot* was never properly tested."

"Another power? Not the Dracaland – I would know..."

"You wouldn't," said the Admiral with a laugh, "but *nej*, it's not the Dracaland. Nor Breizh, nor Midgard, nor any of the old ones. There's a new child in the nursery, as they say, and it's eyeing Yamato as its new *leksak*... new toy. And if we don't hurry there will be nothing left of it to share."

A sailor appeared in the cabin's round door and cleared his throat.

"*Ach, ja, naturligtvis*. Nobelius is waiting. Excuse me, *Doktor* – you may return to the infirmary. And it's probably best if you hold on to something for the next ten minutes."

Three loud whistles echoed throughout the vessel. He heard many heavy boots running to and fro around the deck amid barked orders. The tongue of the Varyagas, like those of their Western kin in Midgard and Niflheimr, was most suited to pronouncing orders, he had always thought.

Their vast empire stretched across two continents, from the cold Venedian Sea in the West all the way to the borders of Qin in the East. Most of this enormous landmass was poor and inhospitable – dark northern forests or arid open steppe, with little value other than some furs and fish; but the Varyagas possessed an insatiable hunger for land and discovery, a legacy of their Norse ancestry. It did not surprise Samuel that once the Varyaga explorers had reached the Great Ocean, the Khaganate decided to push still further eastwards, beyond the known charts.

He felt the change in the air pressure in his ears and then the bulkheads started creaking and groaning worryingly. Within five minutes everything was over; another three whistles announced the end of the pressure test.

He lost count of the many exercises and training routines the crew of the *Diana*, the underwater ship, had performed over the past two weeks. He would have lost the count of days if it hadn't been for the calendars hanging on the wall of almost every cabin. The vessel surfaced only by night, to replenish the air stored in Doctor Nobelius's ingenious tanks, and nobody but the maintenance crew was allowed outside.

Samuel had been allowed to see the outside world through the round window in the Admiral's cabin, but he saw only the gloomy, dusty murkiness, barely illuminated by a faint evertorch. On one occasion the Admiral showed him the surface through *Diana's* periscope. He realised immediately they were in the middle of the famous sea maze.

The storm waves rolled back and forth in random directions, heedless of the prevailing winds; the clouds and mists covered the sky and the horizon with an impenetrable curtain of grey. All the navigation devices behaved as if broken. Only after submerging the ship to below a hundred feet the compass started showing north again.

"How do the Bataavians get through this?" he asked the Admiral later.

"There is one route always open clear for them. Every year they send only one ship. A sailing ship, mind – the Yamato do not allow *maskines*… engines. And when it returns with cargo it also brings the details of what the route will be the next year – for it always changes. It is a much more elaborate system than the crude *barriaer* of the Qin."

"Is Yamato really worth all this effort?"

"I have spoken to a *Midgaerd* spy who sailed on their ship once – he told me of the riches the land keeps; there is *koppar*, *kamfor*, silks, cotton, *porselin*… but most of all, there are people who were, he said, among the most ingenious he had ever met. The years he had spent on *Dejeema* had been the best of his life – and he had travelled far and wide. And they are fiendishly clever. It is a waste to keep a nation like that under lock and key."

"But they obviously wish to keep their doors closed from us."

"The rulers, maybe. But Philip – the *spion* – told me there were many people in Yamato who demanded a change. All they need is a little… *assistans* from outside. The Bataavians are too weak and too set in their ways for this."

"So this is not just about taking the Bataavians' place," Samuel guessed. "You want to start a revolution. That's a bold ambition for a commander of a single ship."

"A ship that can sail under water, mind. But my mission is just a beginning. If I succeed, we will build more ships like *Diana,* merchant ships and war ships and eventually the rulers of Yamato will realise the *futilitet* of their boundaries."

"And what about that other… *Power* you've mentioned?"

"One thing at a time, *Doktor.* For now my greatest worry is reaching *Dejeema* in one piece. The closer we seem to be to Yamato, the deeper we have to go to avoid the effects of this sea *labyrint.* Hence all the tests and exercises."

"How deep can this ship go, if need be?"

"We don't know," Otterson smiled. "We have never sailed as deep as we are at the moment."

Samuel wriggled uneasily in his chair. The creaking of the bulkheads overhead suddenly seemed a lot more ominous.

The Bohan had set up his headquarters in the same stone-and-water gardens that the Heavenly Army had used during their brief hold on Huating. Dylan landed his dragon on a square in the middle of the walled city, surrounded on all sides with tall buildings of white walls and black tile roofs. The town was loud and crowded with refugees, soldiers and merchants. The guards led him through a sculpted gate past a tall wall and immediately the din quietened, replaced by the babbling of water and the chirping of sparrows.

The paths in the garden were as angular as the wrinkles on Bohan's face, a convoluted labyrinth of bridges and gates designed, not out of convenience, but following some greater, Heavenly scheme. At select places stood intricately eroded stones or statues, pavilions overlooking flower ponds or grand old trees, with boughs sprawling like wooden snakes, supported by bamboo poles. Dylan knew there was nothing random about the placement of these features; the Qin left nothing to chance.

Following the guards, he was trying instinctively to map the garden paths in his head, but soon gave up. He had seen the Gardens from dragonback; it was just a tiny space in the middle of the bustling city. But they had been walking now for far longer than it would take to traverse this space from one side to another in a straight line, and they seemed no closer to their destination.

I am literally a-mazed, he thought, with a chuckle which made one of the guards look back at him and frown.

Another gate and another wall appeared before him on top of which coiled a dragon sculpted out of blue clay tiles. Past this wall the garden was even quieter, only an early cicada buzzed in the top of a great pine tree.

This tree must have been planted when this place was just a village, Dylan thought, admiring the gnarled, twisted, blackened trunk.

The guards stopped.

"Please," the Bohan gestured him to follow further, into an expansive bungalow, the walls of which were open and airy, carved with intricate latticework of wood and lacquer. This was the largest and most opulent building Dylan had seen so far in the Gardens.

The Bohan led him along a corridor of wooden planks, polished to such perfection that they seemed to be covered with glass. Water trickled in a covered gutter alongside, cooling the entire house down. His navy boots squeaked on the slippery surface and he was finding it hard to keep up with the pointy-bearded man without stumbling. At last they reached their destination – a small square room. Red lanterns stood on black iron stands in the corner; a golden screen showing a coiling dragon adorned the opposite wall. The Bohan closed the door behind them carefully.

A table of polished wood stood in the middle of the room on four tall legs of eroded stone. On the table lay several thick brushes, an ink stone, several pieces of paper, a lacquer tray filled with what looked like sand and a copper brazier in which blue fire burned. Dylan immediately sensed magic.

"Sit, please," the Bohan pointed to two chairs on both sides of the table. "We shall write a formal request to the *taipan* at Fan Yu."

He reached for the brush and paper and Dylan dictated what should be written. When they finished, the Bohan blew on the ink, rolled the paper carefully and dropped it into the flaming brazier.

He turned to Dylan with a smile.

"It will take a moment to decipher the message and deliver a reply. Let's have some tea."

The Ardian knew better not to question what had just happened. At his host's signal the golden screen slid apart, revealing a hidden entrance. Two men entered the room. One was a servant carrying a pot of fragrant, straw-coloured tea and two white china cups. The other wore the robes and the hat of a priest. He held a sharpened bamboo rod in his hands.

The Bohan poured the tea from on high, splashing it all over the tray – a sign of luxury. By the time Dylan had finished his second cup, the priest staggered, touching his forehead with his fingers.

"Ah, good," said the Bohan, "it was faster than I expected."

The priest rolled his eyes up and started to shiver in spiritual ecstasy. The servant who had brought the tea now guided his hand holding the bamboo rod over the sand tray.

The rod trembled and started moving, as if on its own, writing Qin letters in the sand. The Bohan copied them onto paper. The message was brief, but the priest seemed exhausted by the ordeal and the servant had to escort him out of the room.

"The ship will be dispatched in two days, with the right of passage through Ederra Strait," the Bohan read out the characters.

"That means they will be here in a week," said Dylan, still reeling from what he had just seen. At last, here was the explanation of the astonishing speed with which information seemed to travel throughout the Qin Empire. He pointed to the sand tray.

"What – what was that?"

"Magic," the Bohan replied with a self-satisfied grin.

The vast watery expanse of the Qian River spread like a narrow sea between the tall pagoda underneath which Dylan had set up camp and the opposite shore, almost two miles away.

"You were right, Ardian," the Admiral said, studying the brown, stormy waters through the long, heavy telescope attached to his iron hand. "Hard to believe that's not the Sea. I could wage an entire battle between these shores."

"Perhaps you will have it, if we fail to establish a bridgehead."

"Are you certain this is necessary? I could defend this crossing with a few gunboats for years."

"It's not just the crossing. There's a trade port on the other side that the rebels might use as an alternative to Huating. We have orders to assist the Imperial Army in its capture, if we can."

The Admiral ran his fingers through the balding hair and sighed.

"Ah, politics. How I loathe it. Interfering with a good war."

"Sir?"

"I also got new orders yesterday. Once this here battle is over, I'm taking my ships up north, to Ta Du. Don't worry – there are a few gunboats coming to take my place, and the Qin fleet is supposedly on its way. You shouldn't be lacking in ships."

Dylan frowned. "I haven't heard of any new developments over there."

"I don't know what's going on either – but we can both guess it's going to be something big."

They both nodded in silence. The storm clouds and crow flocks had not yet been fully dispersed here in the south and already they had started gathering elsewhere.

There is always war in Qin, he remembered his son's words. Bran – for the first time in weeks he recalled the boy's face, his voice. He looked eastwards, where the great river entered a broad, funnel-shaped bay of the Qin Sea. A line of Reynolds's warships obscured the horizon, reminding him instantly of the upcoming battle.

"Let's make the best of what time we have, then," Dylan said with a dry smile.

He gazed down on the camp. Three thousand men in blue uniforms busied themselves among the white tents – an army with no name. It seemed an impossible task to train so many soldiers in such a short time, and yet he had succeeded – with great help from his lieutenants and officers of the Twelfth Light Dragoons. The dragons of both regiments rested in the hastily built stables a bit further to the west. There had been little need for them so far – the rebel scouting parties had fled as soon as they saw their glinting scales in the sky. Both the men and the beasts itched for a fight.

"You know, Ardian," the Admiral spoke just as they were about to return to the camp, "I've been thinking lately about what happened to your son."

Over the few weeks, the two men had exchanged many tales. Reynolds knew now with details the story of *Ladon*'s final journey, and they had both agreed that the Ifor serving under the Admiral in the days of the Kyrnosian Emperor must have been Dylan's father.

"Sir?"

"I had a certain idea of my own... but it will have to wait until after the battle. Look, here she comes," the Admiral said, pointing downstream, "our signal."

A ripple formed on the horizon, which grew fast to a white foaming wave, stretching from shore to shore. A giant tidal bore, many times greater than the famous wave at Môr Hafren in Gwynedd, rushed towards them with the speed – and sound – of a steaming omnibus, taking everything with it. Only the most tightly anchored vessels could withstand its terrible force.

Dylan knew that the Heavenly Army on the other shore also waited for the wave to pass towards the floodplains upstream. There would be a full day to attempt the crossing before another bore came rumbling down from the sea.

"Now there's a sight," the Admiral said, his eyes gleaming with youthful joy, "I'm glad I came all this way to see it. Ardian – " he continued, turning to Dylan as the crest of the wave roared deeply beneath them, "I believe it is time. To battle!"

"To battle!"

There was a soft knock on the workshop door, barely a scratch, so quiet that Master Tanaka had not heard it at first, too busy with adjusting the pressure points of his new mistfire engine.

The knocking repeated, louder this time.

"I'm busy," the mechanician murmured.

"Hisashige-*sama*!" A commanding voice spoke.

Master Tanaka dropped the octagometer and hurried to open the door. He lay prostrate on the floor.

"*Kakka!* I am most sorry, I was not informed of your visit – "

"I am glad to hear that. This is not an official visit, and I'm not here in my capacity of the *daimyo*. Please, stand up, Tanaka-*sensei.*"

The lord of the Saga province, Nabeshima Naomasa, entered the room. Even wearing the plain indigo clothes of a low-ranking samurai, the well-groomed, weary-eyed man exerted an unmistakable presence. Here was a man born and bred to rule. His ancestors were friends to the *Taikun*s, his domain's forces guarded the entry to the Kiyō harbour – arguably one of the most important positions in the Empire.

"Is this the engine you were telling me about?" the *daimyo* asked, stepping up to the desktop.

"Oh no, *kakka*. This is just a toy, a testing piece. The other one I had already brought down to the harbour."

"Do you think the boat is going to be faster than the Satsuma one?"

"Difficult to tell. They had the Bataavian plans, I had to figure out everything from scratch… I will be trying it out next week."

"I may need you to do it sooner."

"*Kakka?*"

The *daimyo* reached into his sleeve and took out a curious item: a small ball of cork with a dozen long black feathers glued to it.

"A Bataavian shuttlecock," said Hisashige. "I have received one too. But I do not yet know what it means."

"It's a message from the Overwizard of Dejima. It means one of *our own* is in danger, and we are called on to help in any way we can. And there is more. There have been many messages coming from Kiyō – strange and dire news."

"I was too busy with my experiments…"

"I know. That's why I decided to visit you and explain the situation personally."

The *daimyo* sat down on the straw matting and gestured the mechanician to do the same. Master Tanaka listened to the tale with increasing disquiet.

"So that's why I never heard from Shūhan-*sama* again… and here I thought he was just busy, like me. And Sakuma-*dono* returned to his Chūbu home… none of this bodes well."

"No," the *daimyo* agreed, "and this is why I have come to you for help. I need your divination machine."

Hisashige's face turned dark. "Why not ask the priests of Yutoku?"

"I have asked them for a general prophecy, but nothing detailed. I do not trust them as much as I trust you, *sensei*. Is something the matter?"

"My divinations are... not as accurate as they once have been. The future is strangely clouded. But I will endeavour my best."

The Inari Shrine of Yutoku, where Master Tanaka had his home and workshop set up, rose in many-pillared, vermillion terraces on a wooded slope overlooking a rapid, broad river. A tunnel of bright red *torii* gates lined the path descending towards the pier. The dawning sun cast a crimson shadow on the water.

He stood on the pier with two other men and a boy, his adopted son Daikichi. A long and narrow boat, of the kind used for cormorant fishing, was moored to a thick bollard, bobbing in the fast current. A great ironbound chest rested in the middle.

"I should be sending a detachment of my samurai," said Lord Naomasa. "They would be ready to go in one day."

"And they would reach Shimabara in four," replied Hisashige. "The eighth hexagram speaks plainly: *Whoever comes too late, meets with misfortune.* But if I'm not back in a week, please send your samurai, *kakka.*"

"At least allow me to accompany you, *sensei*. Or failing that, go in your place. It is a dangerous quest and you are not young."

The mechanician bowed his grey head. "The boat takes two, and only I know how to control the engine. Do not fear, *kakka*, for the eighth hexagram also says *there is a movement towards the union of the greats, and good fortune.* And the fifteenth hexagram adds *he who is humble employs the strength of his allies. Modesty brings good fortune.*"

Lord Naomasa laughed quietly. "How can a lowly *daimyo* discuss with the mighty oracle! Very well. Etō-*sama* will have to suffice for the entire force of the Saga province."

The third man bowed swiftly at the mention of his name. He was short and tense, his eyes darting left to right as if in constant expectation of a foe, his hand held on to the hilt of his sword.

Master Tanaka bowed back and then turned to the boy standing aside.

"Daikichi, take good care of my machines while I'm gone."

"Yes, Father."

"Remember to oil the gears and clean the pipes, as I have instructed you."

"Of course, Father."

The old mechanician opened his mouth once more, but then found nothing more to say and closed it again.

"Well, I'd better be off," he said, turning back to the *daimyo*.

"And you are certain of the direction of your journey?" asked Naomasa.

"The blood signal is still fresh in my head. I'm surprised you can't sense it."

"One more proof, if proof were needed, of my lack of any magical talent," said Naomasa with a sigh.

The intense pulsing of the blood magic beacon had reached Hisashige in his workshop the night before, when he was still busy calibrating the divination circuit on his clock. He had recognised the spell signature right away; it was similar to the blood pattern he had been given by Shūhan to weave into the glove. Now he understood what the beacon meant. Takashima Shūhan was alive and desperate enough to call for help using the most forbidden type of Western magic.

"I will bring him back, *kakka,*" Master Tanaka said firmly.

He climbed into the narrow, wobbly boat carefully and held on to the mooring ropes waiting for Etō to join him. Daikichi untied the ropes and pushed the boat into the current. Etō stood up, grasping an oar and guided them downstream. The pier, the *daimyo* and the little boy soon disappeared into the dawn haze.

The river carried them swiftly past the small town and a bridge into the narrow inlet of the Ariake Sea. Hisashige waited until they were out in the open waters, out of sight of the shore. Morning sun was already high upon them when he reached for the iron-bound chest in the middle of the boat and opened it with a creak.

Inside was the small mistfire engine, a tangled mass of copper pipes, coils, valves, shafts and gears. He grasped a brass lever and pushed it forward, then turned two valves on the side of a large glass cylinder. He spoke the words of command. The elementals awoke slowly, released from their copper prisons into the cylinder. Steam rose inside an iron funnel when the seawater mixed with the emanations of the fire sprites. The entire boat trembled as the crankshaft turned.

"Careful, Etō-*sama*," the mechanician said, pointing to the glistening iron rod rotating furiously under their feet without any protection. "I'm sorry, I did not have time to build a cover."

The samurai mumbled something and focused on the oar in his hand, now serving as the tiller. Hisashige pulled another switch inside the chest; a large gear clicked into place and suddenly the boat leapt forwards. Etō almost fell into the water, but held on to the edge of the boat valiantly. The water rippled behind them in a broad v-shaped wake.

"It worked, at first try!" Hisashige rejoiced. "And she *is* fast. Let's take it as a good omen for the rest of our journey!"

Etō only grunted as he struggled to keep the boat on course against the rolling waves.

CHAPTER X

A small square building of unpainted cypress wood stood not far from the shrine's main gate, overlooking the wide platform of the dance stage.

"It will be a noisy and smelly place in the evening," said Satō, wrinkling her nose.

The landlord bowed, his narrow eyes squinting apologetically.

"I beg your forgiveness, noble guests, but all other rooms have been reserved for Atsu-*hime* and her entourage. Perhaps you may find something more suitable in the town below?"

"Perhaps we should," she said, eyeing the building with contempt. *This is almost like going back to the stables.*

Bran pulled her aside.

"Remember what that monk at Unganzenji said? The demons can't stand anything holy. It may be just a legend, but I wouldn't take my chances. We're safer here, on the Shrine grounds."

"Very well, we'll take what you have left," Satō told the landlord.

"Settling yourselves in?"

Master Kawakami approached them from the direction of a larger, far richer building nearer the main hall, where he and other Hosokawa retainers had their accommodation.

"Almost, Gensai-*sama*," Satō said with a bow.

"Let me know if you need anything. I still want to clash swords with you later."

"It's a wonder he hasn't recognized us yet," Satō whispered as the samurai passed under the main gate and descended towards the town, "with Nagomi's hair and my *Rangakusha* outfit…"

"These men were ahead of us in Hitoyoshi, and were moving slow," said Bran, "they must have marched out of Kumamoto a long time ago. Let's just hope they take that princess they came for and leave before they realise who we are."

"I don't think they're here just for the princess. That's not an escort, that's a war party."

"You don't think…"

They looked at each other in mutual understanding.

"Can you… sense the *dorako?*

Bran closed his eyes and breathed in.

"Over there," he said, pointing towards a tall fence separating the shrine's public space from the inner sanctum. "They keep it in a cage. It's still asleep, but not for long… I can feel Emrys struggling to waken."

"*Emu- emris?*" she repeated.

He blinked at her.

"Emrys – my dragon. I never told you its name?"

"I didn't even know dragons had names."

"Of course they do. How do you think I call him? *Come here, dragon?*"

He chuckled.

"Naming a dragon is important," he added, "much more than a horse or a dog. It's a creature of magic, so there must be some magic in the name as well."

"And what does *Emris* mean?"

The dragon rider opened his mouth to speak, but then shook his head.

"That is a long tale to tell. Let's wait for supper, when Nagomi joins us."

"Ah! Supper! That's right."

She hadn't eaten a proper meal since leaving the shores of the Sendai River. The shrine fare was not much to expect, but at least it would have been warm – and made by somebody else.

The priestess was luckier than the two of them. She was allowed to live with the other priests and, in this way, she had gained access beyond the shrine's fence.

"They're making some repairs to the inner compound," she told them at supper. "Preparations for the festival – or so they said."

"A festival?" Satō asked.

"In three days there will be a *kagura* dance on that stage over there."

"There will be crowds."

"Hundreds, the priests tell me."

"This will be a good time to strike."

"*Strike?*"

Bran stared at her over the bowl of buckwheat noodles, frowning. He took a bite of a pickled herring and chewed it in silence for a moment.

"We haven't really thought this through, have we," he said, chuckling.

"No, we haven't."

Satō started to laugh as well. She had no idea what was so funny, but she couldn't stop until her sides started hurting. Nagomi looked at them both and then joined the laughter.

"We... we do have to come up with a plan now," the wizardess said at last, wiping tears from her eyes.

"First we need to find out exactly where and how Emrys is being held captive."

"*Emris?*" It was Nagomi's time to ask.

"You were supposed to tell us the story of the *dorako*'s name," said Satō.

Bran slurped the remaining noodles and gulped the broth from the bowl before speaking again.

192

"This is how my mother told me the tale, when I was a child," he began.

Satō leaned closer. Bran had never told her any legends from his country before.

"A long time ago – in the Age of Heroes – our land, the Island of Prydain, was invaded from across the Sea. The enemy flew on dragons white as snow, and was unstoppable for there were no dragons on the island at the time. We lost battle after battle and, in the end, the Kingdom of Prydain was reduced to a small country in the westernmost corner of the island, defended by a king from the Faer race, called Arthur."

Bran sipped some *cha*, his eyes wandering about as he tried to remember the story.

"King Arthur was trying to build a great fortress to make a last stand against the invaders, but the walls of the fortress kept crumbling. At last, there came a boy with the powers of prophecy." He nodded towards Nagomi and she smiled. "The boy guided the warriors to a cave. There was a pool inside the cave, of water dazzling bright like liquid silver. The boy ordered King Arthur's warriors to search the bottom of the pool. When they did so, they found a giant round stone."

"What was it?" Satō asked eagerly.

"A dragon egg, of course. Its magic was so powerful that it prevented the construction of the fortress. Once King Arthur ordered the egg taken out of the cave, it hatched into an enormous red dragon, larger than any ever seen by mortal eyes. With a dragon like this by their side, the Prydain warriors finally had a chance to fight against the invaders."

"Have the invaders been defeated?"

"That's another tale, I'm afraid," Bran smiled.

"So, I take it that the red dragon's name was Emrys," Satō guessed.

Bran shook his head.

"It had no name other than Y Ddraig Goch, which simply means 'The Red Dragon' in our language. But the boy was called Emrys Wledig. He later grew into a great warrior and a poet."

"Your warriors are poets too? Like the samurai?"

"Not anymore," Bran replied sadly.

She pondered the tale in silence. A shy servant girl came out of the kitchen to take away the empty bowls. Satō glanced at her and reached out her hand.

"You, girl, wait! Show me your face."

The servant lifted her head, frightened. Her eyes were blank, covered with the mist of blindness, but there was no mistaking her face.

"Don't you have a sister in Suwa?"

"Y-yes, *tono*," she stuttered.

"I knew it! What's your name?"

"Yōko."

Satō smiled.

"Your sister is in good health and well taken care of," she said.

"Thank you, *tono*!" the girl fell on her knees. "That is great news."

"Are you happy enough here? Do you need anything?"

"I am, *tono*. No, *tono*. T' priests provide me wit' all I need."

"You have your sister's smile. I will let her know I've met you."

Yōko lay prostrate on the floor in gratitude, but Satō bade her get up, slightly embarrassed.

"What is it?" Satō asked Bran and Nagomi when girl left the room. Both looked at her bemused.

"Nothing," Bran said, shrugging and pretending to focus on his food.

"You've never seemed more like a samurai than now," said Nagomi, "it's as if you'd suddenly grown up."

We both have, the wizardess thought. Sudden heaviness pressed on her heart. Her friend's face somehow seemed no longer as innocently childish as it used to be. She didn't smile so much, and blue crescents under her eyes showed plainly how much trouble they had been having lately.

Do I look the same? She wondered. *I feel worse. All the running, all the fighting – it's drained me so much…*

Bran yawned and stretched his arms

"I know we should be thinking up strategies, but all *I* can think of is a well-stuffed *futon*."

She could not agree more.

When he had first arrived in Yamato, Bran had trouble telling its people apart. All the men and women on the streets of Kiyō seemed too similar, with their uniformly black hair, brown eyes and flat, pale-cream faces.

Looking at the crowds filling the main courtyard of the shrine, a square of polished stone floor surrounded by a colonnade of vermillion pillars, he understood his early mistake. Every person in the multitude of pilgrims looked different. A commoner with a nose like a squashed *taro*; a noble lady, her face covered with white paint, one eye slightly larger than the other; a samurai with thick eyebrows joined above the nose and an innocent expression, oddly unsuitable for one who wore two sharp swords at his side.

There must have been hundreds of people here, coming and going, stopping for a moment before the talisman shops, then proceeding to the Offertory Hall where they had only enough time to clap, bow and throw a small coin before another of the pilgrims pushed their way in. How many thousands of copper coins jingled daily against the sides of the offertory boxes? And this was an ordinary day – how this place would look like on the day of the festival!

He was confident they had made a good decision to stay within the Shrine grounds. With crowds like these even the Crimson Robe would think twice before attacking. *Was it his shadow I saw in the forest?* The wolves must have been the demon's doing – and Bran suspected a lurking presence beyond the Shrine walls. *Will he come just for me, or for the dragon, too?*

He stood among the pillars, observing the crowds, sketching the details of the shrine precinct in his notepad, noting what he had learned throughout the day. The inner compound spread to the north and east, up the slope of the Takachiho Mountain in what looked like three terraces. The majestic undulating gables of the Inner Sanctuary rose above the ochre-coloured roof of the Offertory Hall. The shrine, he had learned, had been dedicated to some ancient *Mikado* and his family, all now deemed Gods by the priests and their following.

A path branching east of the courtyard led past the dance stage to the cemetery, laid out among the pine trees. Earlier in the day the funeral procession of the slain Hosokawa's retainers had passed through the shrine. Bran managed to stay out of sight of Master Kawakami, who no doubt would have insisted on him and the girls joining the ritual. They had no time for this.

Bran noted the dimensions of the fence surrounding the inner precinct and wondered if it was so high and strong on all sides, when a sudden commotion caught his eye. A group of burly bodyguards were making their way through the crowds, pushing people to the sides with their hands and bamboo poles.

"Make way for Shimazu Atsu-*hime*!"

Shimazu! The crest of a cross in the circle flashed in Bran's mind. The Shimazu were the ones holding Emrys captive. Overwhelmed with curiosity, Bran squeezed through the crowds, hoping to catch a glimpse of the mysterious "princess".

THE ISLANDS IN THE MIST

First came the servants and retinue, carrying banners with the circle-cross, then six strong men hauled a massive palanquin, decorated with black and gold, with a brass spout sticking out of the roof. But the palanquin was empty, its grid open. A woman walked slowly in silence beside it, accompanied by a servant girl. Her long kimono of black silk embroidered in brightly red and purple flowers, bound with a wide, pink *obi* sash, reached the ground, hiding her feet so that the woman seemed to slide over the grey stones. She was wearing a straw hat with a wide rim folded to the sides, concealing her face from the crowd. Bran could not make out any of her features, or tell whether she was old or young, beautiful or ugly, even though she passed him so close he could smell the faint scent of sandalwood perfume from her hair and clothes.

A light punch with an end of the bamboo pole reminded Bran he had got too close. He pulled back and made his way back to the house by the dance stage.

The cedar trees cast short, flickering shadows in the light of a flamespark hovering faintly over Bran's shoulder. Confused moths and night flies flapped distractingly about his head. A bat fluttered from tree to tree. He adjusted the black scarf covering his entire head except his eyes and mouth – a technique Satō had taught him before he had set out on the nightly escapade – and moved on.

He walked carefully along the outer fence of the shrine. Seven feet tall wooden planks surrounded the compound on all sides. There was a small gate in the north-western corner of the perimeter, but no other openings. Bran knew the rough layout of the inner precinct from Nagomi's description. There was a storage area immediately beyond the corner gate, living quarters for the priests beyond that and, to the west, a garden and a small villa where the Shimazu princess had her dwelling. The storage area was his best bet when looking for a place where Emrys could have been kept, but the two armed guards posted outside the gate were discouragement enough from trying to get through that way.

Whoever had prepared the shrine's defences had made a thorough job of it. The fence boards were all well-maintained, freshly lacquered, any loose or rotten planks recently replaced with new ones. The trees in the immediate vicinity of the fence had their branches cut so that no spy or assassin could use them to climb over the wall.

But Bran had certain advantages over any regular spy. He found his way to the darkest, most remote part of the compound, halfway down the mountainside. He used the sword's scabbard to calculate the distance and angle. There could be no mistake. He calmed his breath, closed his eyes, focused on the centre of gravity of his body, just above the sternum. He weaved his hands in a spiral move, tracing a ballistic curve, a line of sparkling light in the darkness.

When he was happy with the projected trajectory, Bran made one step back and bounced himself off the ground with a light tap. He let his body be carried over the fence in a somersault along the spiral line of kinetic energy, hoping at least this time his enhanced acrobatics skill would not fail.

It was a smooth jump all the way to the top. He caught a glimpse of the inside of the precinct, a small pond surrounded by flowering reeds, when his foot tripped over one of the planks in the fence. He waved his arms futilely and the damp grass hit him in the face.

He heard a soft outburst of laughter.

A pair of brown eyes stared straight into his. A woman in a rich, cream-coloured kimono was sitting no more than ten feet away from him. A paper lantern in her hand illuminated the whole scene with a faint, pale light. In the other hand she was holding a white folding fan.

Her skin was smooth, unpainted; the lantern's light gave it an almost angelic glow. Her face was flawless, symmetrical, exquisitely proportioned, with cheekbones and chin prominent but not offensive and a small, pointed nose over full, slightly pouted lips. Eyes of a roe deer, almond-shape, deep, reddish brown, glistening like a polished carnelian, stared at him with piercing intelligence from under the thin, gently curved, raised eyebrows and elaborate hair-do. She was a girl, really, no more than a few years older than him, but there was maturity and wisdom in those eyes belying her age.

She showed no fear and made no sound or movement. Bran sniffed, and smelled the familiar scent of sandalwood. The garden was silent, a single frog croaked in the lily pond. His face stung where he fell.

"You are the clumsiest *shinobi* I've ever seen," she said. "Are you here to kill me?"

Who is she?

"N... no."

"Did my father send you, then?"

"My business is with the shrine, not you," he replied.

"I see," she said and pouted her lips. "Come closer."

He hesitated. The girl stood up and approached him instead, lifting the lantern to his face. She was surprisingly tall for a Yamato woman, only a few inches shorter than Bran. The sweet smell of sandalwood overwhelmed his nostrils.

"What strange eyes," she said upon closer examination. "Green like jade."

"So I've been told."

She touched the black scarf.

"Are you hurt?"

"I'm fine."

"You're not an assassin."

"No."

"I know who you are," she said.

"Oh?"

"You're one of those three pilgrims Gensai-*sama* met in the forest. He told me all about you. I've seen the red-haired priestess in the afternoon, helping with the altar."

He didn't know what to say to that.

"You must tell me why you are here," she decided suddenly, "or I will cry for help."

Bran glanced behind – he could try and jump back, but he wasn't sure he was able to focus clearly enough in this situation. And even if he did, she would then no doubt alert the temple guards. The advantage of surprise would be lost, and he would probably never get another chance to steal his way into the inner premises. Worse still, the security of the shrine would have been compromised and the dragon would no doubt be moved to another secret location.

"You can trust me," she said, still looking boldly into his eyes. "All I want is a good story. I'm so bored here. Everyone is so old, polite and tedious. Please?"

She looked at him pleadingly with the carnelian eyes. He felt his heart melting.

"Are we safe here? Will nobody eavesdrop on us?"

"This is my private part of the garden," she assured him, "and everyone's asleep by now."

She motioned him to sit beside her on a long stone bench on the bank of a lily pond.

"It's about the treasure, isn't it?" she asked before he could say anything.

"The treasure?" Bran's heart started beating even faster than it already was.

"Nobody ever tells me anything, but I am smarter than they think. There are two dozen samurai armed to the teeth guarding this shrine. My father had a great iron oxcart accompany my entourage. He told me it contained a gift from the Gods. You're here to steal it, aren't you?"

She grinned.

Her father...?

"Not steal. It belongs to me," he said.

"How exciting! But what is it, tell me?"

He opened his mouth but a female voice cried in the distance.

"Princess Atsu! Please come back, it's late."

"Oh, how I hate that woman," the girl said, standing up. "A living chaperone is such a nuisance compared to an automaton!"

An automaton?

"Atsu... you are the Shimazu princess!"

"Of course! Who did you think? I have to go. You must visit me again tomorrow!"

"I will," he blurted, "I mean... I'll try."

"I shall wait," she smiled at him with a smile warm like summer sun and ran off into the garden.

He shook his head, trying to maintain focus. He measured his distance again and leapt over the fence. He almost made it this time.

There was a rope hanging across the fence, tied to a black pine growing on the other side. He tugged it to check if it held fast and climbed across, as quietly as he could. She was already waiting for him by the lily pond.

"I thought a rope might be of use to you," she explained, "I found some in the gardener's shed."

"That was very thoughtful... but what if somebody noticed?"

"I told you, nobody ever comes here. Now sit down and tell me your story. My chaperone thinks I'm meditating – we have all night."

He gulped.

"You must first tell me yours, princess," he said.

He had spent all day thinking about the girl, wondering what she was doing in the shrine.

"Oh, but my story is nowhere near as interesting as yours!"

"Such is my condition, *hime*."

"Very well, but don't blame me if you're disappointed. And don't call me *hime*, all my friends call me simply Atsuko."

"But we've only just met…" he started, but seeing her pout again, he added, "Atsuko."

She smiled, looking not at him but at the floating lilies, their buds closed for the night.

"My current life started when the *daimyo* of Satsuma, Shimazu Nariakira-*dono* adopted me as his only daughter. My real parents came from a poor, distant branch of the clan, so they were glad to be rid of me. Later my father had to commit suicide for some minor offense and my mother died soon after."

No shadow marred her beautiful face as she was saying these words, only the light of the lantern flickered in her big brown eyes.

"I have lived alone in the Kagoshima Castle for years, trying to learn as much as I could about the world from the books in my new father's library."

"Satsuma is so far south – it's almost outside Yamato," she explained, "so we're more connected to the seas than to the land beyond the mountains. My father was always very keen to expand his knowledge of the Western magic and technology and there were always some foreign envoys or scholars in the castle, sneaked in secretly from Dejima or the Nansei islands in the south. Sometimes I've managed to talk to them."

"You speak Bataavian?"

"Just a little. Not as well as my father."

"Have you ever been to Kiyō yourself?"

She shook her head with sadness.

"This is the first time I travel out of Kagoshima. It is not acceptable for a woman of my standing to journey without good reason."

"And where are you going?"

"Edo."

From the map he had seen in Lady Kazuko's room Bran knew the *Taikun*'s capital city was weeks away from Satsuma.

"That's a long journey! Aren't you excited?"

"Maybe," she said with a shrug, "but I fear I will not see much. They carry me around in a shuttered palanquin everywhere. They will put me in a windowless cabin on the boat, and then lock me somewhere in the *Taikun*'s palace, where I am to do secretarial work for my father and his officials."

"So what are you doing in this place?"

"Oh, I was just waiting for those samurai from Kumamoto to escort me across the mountains. Now that they're here, in a few days, I will have to leave."

Bran felt a sudden pang of sadness. He turned his eyes away from Atsuko's face, pretending to admire the reflection of the moon in the pond.

"Now, your turn," she insisted, "what is the treasure you seek?"

"A *dorako*," he said without a moment's hesitation.

"*Ah!*"

The excitement and admiration in her almond brown eyes was worth betraying his greatest secret.

"I am a dragon rider. I come from a land far away, and I lost my dragon in battle off the shores of Qin…"

She pouted, irritated.

"Now you're making fun of me. I can tell you're just a Yamato boy underneath that mask."

"I'm telling the truth! Wait here."

He knelt at the edge of the pond, cooling his face with the water to lessen the pain of the transformation.

206

"Are you all right?" she asked.

He turned to her, removing the black scarf. She gasped and hid her face behind the paper fan.

"I am Bran ap Dylan o Cantre'r Gwaelod," he said proudly.

"Fantastic!" She clapped her hands. "How did you do that?"

At first he spoke cautiously, in short, broken sentences, but she was so eager to hear more and looked at him with such expecting admiration that, before he noticed, he was telling her of all his adventures in Yamato, from waking up at the infirmary, through the visit to the Cave of Scrying, to the clash with the *onmyōji*. By the time he had finished, it was well past midnight.

Her next question threw him off balance.

"That samurai girl and the priestess… are they pretty?"

"I... I think Nagomi is regarded as a pretty girl…"

She giggled.

"But not the other one?"

"It's difficult for me to judge people of your race. I – "

He looked into her almond eyes, staring at him expectantly.

"I never thought I would find an Eastern woman as beautiful as you," he blurted.

What am I saying?

Atsuko was as unlike all the other girls he had fancied as a rose was different from a field daisy: mature, bright, polite… and her smile, sincere and wise… there was no fault in her smooth, shapely face and carnelian eyes.

She startled at his confession and turned her eyes away. For a while they enjoyed the sounds of the night and each other's company in silence.

"I will help you," she said, "I know the man who will tell me everything. His name is Torii Heishichi-*sama*, and he's my father's *Daisen* – Arch Wizard. I wondered why he was chosen to accompany me on this journey! And I can demand access to every room and every building in this shrine. I will find your *dorako*."

"You really shouldn't… it's dangerous."

"I know!" she said, beaming. "That's what makes it exciting. Oh, it's like I'm in a *kabuki* play. A secret prince who comes at dusk and disappears at dawn, a dragon, mystery, magic and action!"

Bran felt his cheeks redden at the words "secret prince".

"Tell me something in your native tongue!" she asked.

He thought for a moment and then started singing, softly at first, ending on a louder, though shaky note as the song's melody brought with it the memory of the rolling hills of Gwynedd and the slate walls of his home in Caer Wyddno.

Ar lan y môr mae rhosys cochion
Ar lan y môr mae lilis gwynion
Ar lan y môr mae 'nghariad inne
Yn cysgu'r nos a chodi'r bore.

"What does it mean?" she whispered a question after a long pause.

"Beside the sea red roses grow,
Beside the sea white lilies show,
Beside the sea my love resides,
By day she walks, by night she hides."

He choked on the last verse of the translation.

"So you're also a poet."

"No!" He laughed. "That is an old song, a fireplace song."

"Your tongue is strange. At once harsh and sweet. And so unlike Bataavian."

"It is much older than Bataavian. When the oaks at Mona were yet acorns, my people already spoke Prydain. Some say its roots are in the speech of the Faeries."

"The Faeries?"

He told her of how the golden-haired Tylwyth Teg danced under the stars in the old elm woods along the Taf

Fechan, in the Great Forest of Brycheiniog. He hadn't spoken these names in such a long time they sounded strange to his ears, still they rolled smoothly off his tongue.

"There is nothing in my father's books about all this!" She clasped her hands together in awe. "I have learned so many new things tonight."

He tried to smile but it came out as a yawn. His eyelids felt heavy and sticky.

"Oh, how thoughtless of me. I've been keeping you awake all night."

"It's all right," he said, stifling another yawn.

"No, no, your days must be busy while I spend mine lazing about and strolling in the gardens."

"I... I haven't really slept since yesterday," he admitted.

"Then go and rest. But you *must* return tomorrow."

"I will," he said, this time with certainty.

CHAPTER XI

The dream was a story.

Out in the middle of a vast plain, covered with tall grass that waved like the sea in the wind, stood a great castle, once magnificent and white, now fallen in disrepair and ruin after long years of neglect.

Three men desired to enter the castle; one had a long beard, the other wore a grey hood, and the third had eyes as green as jade. But try as they might, they could not breach the mighty wall of grey stone that encircled it.

The fourth man, a red-haired merchant, had the key to the single gate in the wall. He would come to the castle once a year with a cartload of goods from the valleys and mountains beyond the grassy plain. The lord of the castle shunned him, but coveted the exotic wares from the cart.

After many long years, each of the three men devised a different way of breaking through the castle walls. The bearded one dug a tunnel underneath it. The grey hooded one rode a flying beast over it. And the jade-eyed one ambushed the merchant and stole from him the key to the single gate.

THE ISLANDS IN THE MIST

All three met at the courtyard and the lord of the castle came out to greet them and he was old, frail and trembling. They drew their swords.

Lady Kazuko was right. The priests at Kirishima had recognised her status and guided her to the more luxurious accommodation higher up the slope of Mount Takachiho.

She had not seen such opulence in Suwa, rich though the Kiyō shrine was. There was gold leaf and jade everywhere, precious silks and exotic woods. Her mattress was soft as snow, the clothes chest was encrusted with red lacquer and ivory. A servant maiden, who brought tea in an expensive Qin pot, wore richer robes than Nagomi herself.

Wandering around the compound she noticed the priests had put her in a room far away and separated from everyone else. She quickly guessed the reason. They may have been too polite to make any mention of her hair, but their nervous glances gave them away.

Their nervousness increased after the funeral of the fallen samurai, when the rumours of the wolf attack spread around the shrine. She caught a whispered "goblin" or "*yōkai*" whenever she passed by a group of younger acolytes or maidens. The elders still smiled and bowed at her welcomingly, though their smile disappeared as soon as she pretended to turn away.

There was plenty she could help with around the precinct. Of late a small earthquake had caused a landslide near the Offertory Hall and once Nagomi had rested she was more than happy to put her hands to some physical work to take care of the injured workers.

After a day of such work one of the chief priests took her aside.

"We appreciate your assistance, priestess," he said, "but it does not speak well of our hospitality that we let a guest do such hard work."

"Really, I don't mind."

The priest lowered his head.

"I must insist…"

"Oh."

"The workers are simple people, they would not understand all the… circumstances. Any other time, perhaps, but not with all the rumours of the *yōkai* coming down from the mountains…"

"I see."

"I'm sure there is enough to keep one as industrious as yourself busy. Is there anything I can help you with?"

"Can you tell me what's over there?"

She pointed to a fenced-off area to the north-west of the main compound.

"Oh, that's… that's just a storage area. Nothing of interest."

"That's a lot of guards for just storage. And a big fence."

"*Eeh*! Very perceptive." He laughed and lowered his voice. "It is actually our main treasury, priestess. We don't need the thieves to know where we keep our most precious offerings, do we?" he said and winked.

"Of course not," she said, winking back, feeling slightly sickened.

She was picking up the withered flowers at the altar of *Mikado* Jimmu to replace them with fresh ones, when she noticed Bran, browsing the souvenir stalls. She came up to greet him.

"You're working?" he asked. "Aren't you supposed to be a guest of the shrine?"

"I can't stay restless for long. At Suwa I was always busy with something."

"Did you find out anything interesting yet?"

"There's a closed-off area in the north-western corner – I could see the roof of a large building over it. The priests say they store most precious treasures in there."

"I'll try to check it out tonight."

"Be careful, there are many guards."

"Oh, now, that definitely sounds interesting," he said with an absent smile. He was twirling an *obidame* buckle in his fingers, a simple souvenir piece carved out of a deer's horn in the shape of an orchid.

"What *are* these things, actually?" he asked.

"Noble ladies wear them around their waist sashes, tied on a cord – like that one," she lowered her voice and pointed to an elderly, heavily built woman passing by, wearing too much make-up. Her kimono was as noisy and gaudy as herself, and her *obidame* was golden, encrusted with jewels.

"How is your arm?" she asked, as she had been asking every day. With Bran's increased resistance and lack of attunement to the spirits, she worried his wounds might never fully heal.

"It's barely a bruise now."

"You seemed so surprised, back then. Don't you have priests in the West?"

"We do, but they are not healers..."

"Miracle workers then? How do you call them... thauma...?"

"No, they're not thaumaturgists, either, unless they decide to learn some magic on their own."

"Then what is their power? I have never spoken to the Bataavians about their religion."

"I... Nothing like this, certainly." Bran hesitated. "I have rarely paid much attention to the Sun Priests," he said at last. "Matters of religion are left to the Church and, in exchange, the Church tries not to interfere in the matters of wizards. These days, I don't think they have any *real* power."

Nagomi looked at Bran curiously, not sure if she understood him properly.

"No power? Then what good are they?"

Bran shrugged, "What priests are usually good for? They preach, they teach, they offer advice to the confused and help to the poor. The Church used to fight the wizards in the old days, blaming them for all sorts of calamities... Now, priests and mages mostly ignore each other."

The priestess nodded.

"I see. I've heard about something like that. Sometimes a priest would be abandoned by the *kami*, lose the power of healing, and start some new cult claiming he's found new, better Gods."

Bran chuckled. "Sounds about right to me."

He studied her for a moment.

"You look healthy," he said. "This place serves you well."

"It's a busy shrine," she said, shrugging, "and that reminds me of Suwa... but I wouldn't like to stay in this place too long. The priests here are... different."

"We won't be long here, anyway. In a few days it will be all over, one way or another."

There was gloom in his words and she didn't like it. It reminded her of her own dark visions that kept haunting her in the night.

"You can see the future, right?" he asked, as if reading her mind.

"Sort of... sometimes..."

"Can't you tell how this story ends? Can't you see if we are succesful?"

"Well…" she stumbled on words, "scrying's not as simple as that."

"But surely you have seen *something* about our future?"

"I have seen nothing that would show that we are going to fail," she lied with a smile.

Satō wandered aimlessly about the shrine's courtyard in the sizzling noonday sun. She came up to the talisman stall, picked up a few cloth pouches embroidered with lucky spells and then put them back without looking. She bought a few joss sticks, but forgot to light them. She drank some cold tea and ate some sweet bean *mochi* at the pilgrims' teahouse.

She was feeling increasingly useless. She had neither Bran's sixth sense nor Nagomi's authority to investigate the shrine and its surroundings. In the end, she climbed up the hill towards the *Butsu* chapel beyond the cemetery, to pay for a prayer in Master Dōraku's memory.

She could not understand why the other two did not seem to mourn their guide in the slightest. He had sacrificed himself to save their lives! But Nagomi and Bran never mentioned his name again.

What is wrong with them?

As she stood before the chapel's statue of the bodhisattva Jizō, her head bowed in prayer, she noticed somebody standing beside her.

"Who do you pray for, young man?" Kawakami Gensai asked. He was wearing a fine kimono of soft grey silk and only the short sword at his side.

"A friend."

"Do you mind if I join you? I also have fallen friends to mourn."

"Not at all," she said, stepping aside. "I'm sorry for the deaths of your comrades."

"Such is the samurai's lot."

They prayed for a while in silence, then bowed before the statue and to each other.

"Is that a Matsubara?" Master Kawakami asked, glancing at the handle of her sword.

"Yes."

"*Eeh!*" I have never fought anyone wielding a Matsubara before."

It was the first time she had seen his face take on a genuine expression of joy. She gave it not a moment's thought.

"I have little else to do today," she said eagerly, "so whenever you have the time…"

"Most excellent. I will send a messenger in a short while – you're staying in the annex, aren't you?"

"Unfortunately, yes," she said, embarrassed.

She stepped under the vermillion gate with some apprehension, hoping Bran would not notice. He was very vocal about them not leaving the precincts of the Kirishima Shrine, fearing the Crimson Robe's attack. But she could not refuse Master Kawakami's invitation and they obviously could not fight on the sacred ground.

The samurai's servant led her off the main road, onto a glade of freshly mowed grass. Master Kawakami was there already, dressed in his grey and blue fighting clothes. A flask of saké and two cups rested on a lacquer tray on a tree stump.

"Welcome," the samurai said, bowing.

"What is this place?"

"A duelling glade – for those who felt insulted on the grounds of the shrine. It is still maintained, though not used as much as it used to be."

He gestured to them to sit down by the tree stump. Satō poured saké into his cup and then hers. She gulped the liquor.

"It's sweet," she said, surprised. It tasted quite unlike her father's sakés.

"Northern style, from Aizu," Master Kawakami replied. "You like it?"

She nodded. "It's exquisite."

"A refined taste for one so young. Now then, let's see if your swordsmanship is just as good," he said, standing up and drawing his sword. It was wider and longer than most *katanas* she had seen, a thick, heavy blade that seemed almost crude to an untrained eye; but she recognised it at once.

"*Dōtanuki?*" she raised her eyebrows.

"I know, I know. My teacher mastered one and I got used to the heft. It's not as bad as you might think – of course, if you have the original, not a copy."

He had the right part of his kimono pulled down for more freedom of movement. Veiny muscles rippled on his arm and torso, developed by years of carrying a blade a good pound heavier than usual. A grim, fierce tiger stared at Satō from an elaborate tattoo spread across the samurai's chest.

She assumed a stance and noticed a glint of interest in Master Kawakami's eyes. The stance of the Takashima school was significantly different from the more well-known styles; the blade closer to the chest, the hands on the hilt closer together. His stance also surprised her. She was expecting one of the slow, precise styles, suited to the heavy blade, but Master Kawakami stood softly and lightly on his feet, more like a martial artist than a swordsman.

He's going to be fa –

She barely managed to reflect the coming blade. Her shoulder shook with the power of the blow. Her opponent gave her no time for respite; another cut came from above, then another from below, a quick one-two. She felt her wrist twisting dangerously, almost spraining. She jumped back, the samurai's blade swishing where her head had just been.

That would have gouged my eyes!

She blocked another blow and stepped back again. She had to be careful: the grass under her feet was moist and slippery. *If I could use my magic… but that would be against the –*

Master Kawakami pushed on with the attack, thrusting and slicing without pause, not letting Sato strike even once.

220

Blood flowed away from his face, giving it a morbid pale hue, like a *kabuki* mask. His expression was solid, focused, only his eyes moved swiftly, following and anticipating her every move.

Is he mad?

Her back touched a tree trunk. There was nowhere else to retreat. The *dōtanuki* blade flashed again before her eyes. She cast her head back and hit herself on the tree behind. In a daze, she slashed wildly, without looking. The two weapons clashed, and she let out a cry of pain as her left wrist finally gave way. Her sword whirled in the air before falling into the grass. The tip of her opponent's weapon hovered an inch from her eyes. The samurai's face as fierce and focused as that of the tiger on his chest.

"I yield!"

He smiled, took a step back and bowed, before sheathing his sword. He hardly even broke a sweat, but Satō felt so tired she feared she'd throw up.

"Well done," the samurai said, handing her the dropped weapon, "but why were you holding back?"

"I did not!" she protested, panting. She needed to sit down.

"You hesitated. You have skill, but lack confidence." He studied her for a moment. "You have fought recently, and lost."

"I have," she said.

"Why does it trouble you so? You are still young. There will be many fights you will lose."

"I chose a coward's way."

"You ran from a fight – so what? Don't believe all that *bushido* nonsense. These are just some rules in an old book. The real war has no rules."

She stared at him in confusion.

"I did not get to where I am now by dying whenever somebody bested me in combat," he said. "If you survive now, you get a chance to win later. Take time to train, study your opponent, grow stronger, and come back to fight again. Shinmen-*sama* often had to run away from a fight before he became the master."

"Shinmen-*sama*…?"

"Have you not heard of Shinmen Takezō, the greatest swordsman in Higo?" He seemed taken aback by her ignorance, and she was herself surprised that there was a famous samurai she had not yet heard of. "I have to send you one of his books later. My master learned everything he knew about fighting from his works, and so did I."

"I will be most grateful," she bowed deeply.

"And if I may offer more practical advice, you will be slightly faster on the upper block if you hold the sword like this," he said, taking her hand in his and guiding her in slow motion. "Oh, I'm sorry," he added, seeing her wince, "you need that wrist looked after by a priest."

"It's… nothing, really," she said, stepping quickly away. Her ears were burning. The samurai looked at her curiously.

Did he see through my disguise?

She sheathed the sword and tightened her kimono. "I was not aware Kumamoto Castle had not one but two such great swordsmen."

"Two? My teacher is long dead, and though I loathe boasting, I'm not sure who might be the other man you speak of."

"What about Dōraku-*sama?*"

Master Kawakami frowned.

"I am not familiar with this name."

"He came from Kumamoto .He said he was a retainer of Yōkoi-*dono.*"

"A retainer? What did he look like?"

She described the fallen samurai in great detail, including the two swords he had wielded with so much prowess. Master Kawakami was silent for a long time after she had finished speaking.

"I have never heard of such a man, either in Kumamoto or anywhere else on Chinzei – and believe me, I would. I know the school of sword you describe – it was one of the styles invented by Shinmen Takezō – so he must have been trained locally. How did you meet him?"

"He… on the road from Hitoyoshi."

"And where is this elusive swordsman now?"

"He fell defending us from the same wolves that killed your comrades. It was him that I prayed for at the chapel."

"Ah. Well. Nothing to worry about then." The samurai's lips twitched in a smile. "An odd story, no doubt, but finished now."

He tilted the flask, but it was empty. He let out a short "Hah!" and gestured at the servant to take it away.

"I need to go down to the market," he told Satō, "I cannot trust my servants to pick the right flask by themselves."

She raised her eyes. "Oh – can I go with you?" she asked without hesitation. It was her best chance to go down to the town safely. Surely, not even the Crimson Robe would dare attack a samurai of Kawakami Gensai's stature.

"I'll be honoured," he said with a smile.

The small town below, huddled between the mountain and the river, was filled with visitors from all over the province, here to see the famous *kagura* dance of the Kirishima Shrine. All the guesthouses were full, all the tea and saké shops were brimming with patrons, loud and rowdy, their faces flushed from too much of Kirishima's famous black yeast spirit, shōchū. The main street was lined with stalls on both sides, and the crowd moved slowly from one vendor to another like a giant, easily distracted caterpillar.

Master Kawakami disappeared inside a large liquor warehouse, leaving the two girls to themselves. Satō had taken Nagomi along. The priestess had been at first reluctant to leave the shrine but once they reached the lively market she forgot all her fears.

"Look here!" she led Satō to a stall marked with a dial of a Batavian clock.

Here were sold items which were rarely seen out in the open anywhere other than Satsuma. These were Batavian goods – from toys and sugar candies to simple magic items, like perpetual whirligigs, bouncing balls or tiny glass baubles with electric sparks trapped within for eternity.

"How much for this?" asked Satō, pointing at a glass lens hidden among mostly worthless colourful trinkets.

"Ah, excellent eye, *tono*," the vendor bowed, "I had it delivered only last week. That's ten silver *monme*."

"*Eeh*! That's less than half of what it's worth in Kiyō," Satō shook her head in astonishment. "And so easily available!"

She moved to another stall. This one was full of books and scrolls, mostly samurai adventures.

"I loved these when I was little," she said, flipping through the pages. "Look, this one's about the warrior monks of Mii-dera."

"One of my favourites as well, young swordsman," Master Kawakami spoke behind them, giving the girls a fright.

"*Ah*! Gensai-sama! Have you found what you've been looking for?"

"Somewhat," he grimaced, "all they care about here is shōchū. I have pressed the landlord long enough and it turns out he had a whole batch of the Fukushima's finest."

A few drops of rain fell on the books and the vendor began to hastily cover them up.

"We should go back," Nagomi said.

"Oh, can't we stay a while yet?" said Satō, "I wanted to go and see the workshops across the river. I've heard so much about them..."

"Karasu-*sama* will be worried," the priestess gave her a telling look. "Maybe some other time."

Master Kawakami looked to the dark clouds. "It will pass soon. But as you wish."

The crowds split into two currents. One flow headed for the inns clustered on the southern edge of the town, the other – for the shrine, where some of the pilgrims were yet hoping to find some accommodation. Satō, Nagomi and Master Kawakami joined the former, moving slowly forwards as the rain changed from a spitting drizzle to a drenching torrent. His servant strove to keep them all under one bamboo umbrella, pummelled by the sudden onset of wind.

Just before the bridge to the shrine the samurai stopped abruptly, causing the entire crowd behind them to also stop and wait in the downpour.

"What is it?" Satō asked.

"For a moment there I thought I felt – a presence…" his hand released the hilt of his long sword. "Nothing. Never mind me. Let's press on!"

Satō looked at the colourful multitude around them but saw nothing. She felt Nagomi grasp her by the hand and pull her closer.

"We must not get separated in this crowd," the priestess whispered. "And let's stick close to Gensai-*sama*, just in case."

"In case of what? What did you see?"

"Nothing, but… somehow I don't feel safe here."

Only when they were safely back beyond the shrine's great red *torii* and behind the closed door of her room, did the priestess sigh with relief.

"What happened there?" asked Satō.

"Didn't you feel it?"

The wizardess shook her head.

"I think something is out there, waiting for us."

"The Crimson Robe?"

Nagomi shrugged. "It could be anything. That evil presence from Honmyōji, whatever it was… or something we stirred in the forest... We must tell Bran."

"He will be angry at us for leaving the shrine. But I guess we have no choice. Where is he, anyway?"

"He must have gone on his nightly scouting mission already."

There was a knock on the door. Satō reached for her sword.

"I bring a gift from Kawakami Gensai-*dono*," a servant's voice announced.

She was wearing a different kimono this night, of plain black, glistening silk with crescent moon and stars embroidered in silver. The dark robe enhanced the lightness and smoothness of her skin and neck and made her seem even more mature and regal. She smelled of rosewood.

"Come with me, my secret prince," she said with a slight giggle and led him by the hand, beyond the lily pond and her lodgings, into the outer precinct. By the faint light of the paper lantern they passed along an ancient clay wall, covered with thick moss and mould. The grass was wet with fresh rain.

"This is where the priests live – and your red-haired friend," Atsuko explained.

Manoeuvring between some sheds, pavilions and huts of unknown purpose, they reached a massive storehouse in the middle of the storage area, a rectangular building supported on tall pillars of cedar. The thick stone walls had no windows.

"I think it's here. It's the only place in the shrine I'm not allowed in," she whispered, "and I've seen Heishichi-*sama* coming in and out of it every few hours."

They were huddled in azaleas behind a low wall. There were two guards stationed outside the storehouse, whom he recognised as Hosokawa's retainers. Bran could feel his heart beat faster than ever. Atsuko was so close he could now smell not only the rosewood on her clothes, but also the faint, chalky aroma of her make-up. He felt the warmth of her skin, heard her quiet breath.

"Well, what do you think?" she asked.

I think you're wonderful. I think I want to stay here forever.

Reluctantly, he turned his attention to the storehouse. He cast True Sight and the sheer amount of energy surrounding the structure almost blinded him. Magic currents surged through and around the building, powerful fields and multiple knotted spell threads interconnected with each other. In the middle of it all the silhouette of Emrys shone with a familiar bright green light. Bran's head began to hurt.

"Yes, this is the place. Why are Kumamoto soldiers guarding it instead of your Father's men?"

He didn't like them being here. The eight-circle crest of the Hosokawas on their clothes brought back memories of the fight in the forest.

"They are my escort. Kumamoto is famous for its warriors, and has more of them to spare. Lord Nariakira agreed to this to strengthen the alliance between the two domains."

"And you're not afraid of betrayal? What if something happened to… to you?"

She shook her head.

"They wouldn't dare. It would bring shame upon the entire clan. But if they did… My Father would proudly accept my sacrifice."

"You're a *bait?*"

"I am just one stone of many on the *igo* board," she said. He did not know what game she was referring to, but he understood the metaphor well.

"Let us return to the garden. Will you know how to get here on your own?"

"I think so." He looked around to get his bearings. "There's the Jimmu shrine, and beyond it – the main offertory and worship hall, right?"

She nodded and turned to leave.

"Wait, I want to try something."

He closed his eyes and focused on the Farlink connection. There was a resistance at first, and not only because of the magic barriers around the cage. Emrys was fighting him back. Bran pressed on, forcefully at first, then, when this only made the dragon resist more, gently, soothingly, caressing the beast with his mind. At last the dragon yielded, recognising its master. It stirred in its cage uneasily, snorted and grunted. Even the guards outside heard the noise and stepped away from the warehouse with a start.

A slim man wearing *Rangakusha* clothes appeared on the garden path, pacing quickly towards the building. Bran recognised the lanky face and horn-rimmed glasses from the visions he had shared with Emrys. The wizard entered the warehouse and shortly Bran could feel the dragon fall asleep again, the mind link between the beast and its rider weakened. Whatever the wizard did, it had worked – for now. Bran was satisfied with the results of his little experiment, though more than a little perturbed by the initial resistance.

"Who was that?"

"That was the *Daisen,* Heishichi-*sama.* You need to watch out for him. Now come, before we're found out," she said and pulled him back towards the lily pond.

They sat down on the stone bench in silence. Stars frolicked on the surface of the pond, rippled by the wind. Bran noticed she did not let go of his hand.

"I… I brought something for you," he said and presented her with the *obidame* buckle.

It had taken him all day to come up with a gift fit for a princess before remembering his grandfather's black box.

"Oh – it's beautiful!"

The intertwined golden dragons glistened in the light of the lantern as if alive.

"I'm afraid it's missing a stone…" he said.

She shook her head.

"It doesn't matter. I haven't seen such craftsmanship outside my father's treasure chest. Thank you."

"It belonged to the woman my grandfather met in Kiyō."

"But it's such an important thing! Are you sure you want me to have it?"

"Yes. Please."

Moon danced for a moment in her eyes, but then her gaze dimmed back again and she turned her face to the lily pond; still she did not let go of his hand.

"I wish I could wear it to the shrine dance," she said.

It took him a while to realise what she was telling him.

"I see."

"I asked them if I could yet stay a day more, but they won't let me. Gensai-*sama* insists I must leave tomorrow."

"Can they take you away just like that? Aren't you a noble woman?"

"Oh, my prince!" she said, laughing bitterly, "I may be a noble woman, but I'm still a woman, and my words mean nothing in this world of men."

"The wizardess, Satō... she once told me that in Yamato, only men can be truly happy."

"I should very much like to meet that girl in samurai clothes one day. But tell me, oh stranger from far away land." There was no mockery in how she addressed him, only wistfulness. "Surely the women of your people are also slaves to the men? They are also bound to a life of misery and imprisonment in their golden cages?"

"I... don't think it happens that often anymore," he said, "not among mages, at least."

"Then they must become lonely spinsters, mocked by their families, free to be taken by any man strong and willing enough?"

"No!" Bran cried out with genuine surprise. "They just – live their own lives, I suppose, have lovers, husbands… I'm sure my mother always loved my father, and that's why they're married. Maybe the royals or high nobles arrange families to keep blood purity... but those are rare occurrences these days."

He fell silent. All this talk of mother and father made him remember his little home, with walls of slate, by the beach, on a green hill, far beyond the three oceans. He suppressed tears swelling in his throat.

"Oh, my secret prince! What wondrous tales you tell me, how heavenly is your land!" Atsuko cried and suddenly started sobbing discreetly. Awkwardly, unsure, he pulled her to his chest and embraced tightly, letting her tears wet his kimono.

She raised her head. Tears destroyed her make-up, tracing lines of dark mascara on her cheeks, but her beauty was undiminished.

"Thank you, prince. I will always remember you and your tales. They will give me hope in the dark, dull life that awaits me, even if they sound like fairy stories."

She brought her face close to his until their lips met for one fleeting moment, a heartbeat. She pressed something in his hand and then stood up and disappeared into the darkness of the garden; only the paper lantern yet flickered for a moment, like a trapped firefly.

He opened his hand. It was a small carved wooden container, of the sort the samurai attached to their sashes when they needed to store small items, with a bead of carnelian stone as a fastener. With trembling hands he opened it and unrolled a piece of paper hidden inside. It smelled of rosewood.

Edo is a great and faraway place

But the world is even greater

If East and West met once

They may yet meet again.

My secret prince,

Tomorrow I leave for Edo; maybe I will see you in the crowd, but not recognize you. It is as it should be; our meeting was just a bright spark, a candle in the darkness that envelops my life. If it lasted any longer, it would burn a hole in my heart too big to heal. As chance had it, it only burned out a memory.

I hope all goes well with your plans. I will pray for you and your friends. If you ever find yourself in Kagoshima and are in need of help, remember this: my father's name is Shimazu Nariakira, and our family code word is "Shōhei" — "Tranquillity".

And now, the spark dies down, the black curtain falls. The lily pond grows over with weed.

Atsuko

Bran gazed at the surface of the pool, rippled by the soft night breeze. A sad, lonely owl hooted in the distance.

Since dawn there had been preparations all around the wooden stage. Guests at the nearby lodging house had been woken by hammering, sawing and polishing of decorations, cries of carpenters and builders, mixed with the stomping and shouting of dancers rehearsing before the big day.

In the morning, on the hour of the Snake, a double cordon of samurai formed a corridor from the northern compound to the gate at the end of the main courtyard, separating the crowds of pilgrims from the stone path.

With heavy feet and heavy heart Bran moved through the crowds to a raised platform near the talisman shops from where he could observe Atsuko's entourage leaving the shrine. She was carried slowly in the black and golden palanquin. Hosokawa's retainers surrounded the vehicle, with Captain Kiyomasa leading the convoy at the head of his soldiers.

The princess did not wear her straw hat this time, and had the blinds of her vehicle open so that everyone around could witness her mysterious beauty. The commoners prostrated themselves in the presence of a great lady and only Bran and a few nobles remained upright, bending over in a polite bow as she passed them.

She was looking around, as if trying to find somebody. Bran's heart sunk when he realized she had no way of recognizing him. She had not seen his Yamato face under the mask. To her, he was now just another samurai in a crowd of onlookers. He tried to catch her eye, hoping to somehow convey all his feelings in a single look, but her gaze just slid over him without noticing, and she passed by, leaving only the scent of rosewood behind.

Behind the palanquin, marched Master Kawakami. He did notice Bran and bowed slightly, his lips twitching up and down in his imitation of a smile.

"She's so pretty," said Satō with a sigh. Bran spotted her only now, standing beside him on the platform. She had a pained look in her eyes.

"Oh, to have her looks and her position... If any woman could find happiness in life it would have to be her."

"Sometimes beauty and wealth are not enough," he replied, his eyes still fixed on the procession now leaving the shrine through the main gate.

"Aren't you philosophic today," she said but then turned serious. "Is something wrong? You look as if you're sick."

There I go, showing my feelings to everyone, like the Barbarian that I am.

He tried to force his face into a cheerful mask, as he had seen the wizardess do so often.

"I'm fine, just… a little tired, that's all."

Satō stepped off the platform and winced.

"You don't seem so good yourself. Does your wrist still hurt?"

"No, it's healed. It's just a headache. I've had it since morning," she said and laughed. "Look at us. You'd think we've already been through a battle, not just preparing for one."

236

He nodded with a smile. The shrine gong rang out the hour.

"The dances start soon," said Satō and took him by the arm. "We should find Nagomi before the crowd grows."

THE ISLANDS IN THE MIST

CHAPTER XII

The instructor put another painted board onto the stand. All riders craned their necks trying to see the drawing. The shape of the creature drawn in ink and water colours on the board was roughly humanoid, but its face was bright red and its body was covered in thick blue hair.

"This one is a Sheng-Sheng," the instructor said. "Don't be fooled by their appearance – these are more than just some mountain apes. They are cunning, fast and stronger than five of you together. Avoid getting in the melee range – let your dragon deal with them. Luckily, they are most likely to fight in tight groups, separate from the humans."

"Will lightning to the head stop them?" one of the soldiers asked, waving a thunder pistol. He was of the fresh draft, same age as Wulfhere, and kept asking the same question about every magical creature the instructor described.

"Once again, Eadweard, the answer is yes. If you manage to hit it from dragonback. Their heads don't make the best targets, as you can see."

"Is it smaller than an apple, sir?"

239

The instructor sighed "No, it is not smaller than an apple. And if you try to bore us again with your tale of shooting apples off your cousin's head, I'll have to assign you to first aid duty."

Laughter rippled through the regiment and Eadweard sat down, his cheeks red.

Wulfhere ignored the exchange, focusing on his notes. "Big, red, strong. Dragon flame and pistols, no melee," he noted. This time, he was going to be extra careful with his choice of enemy. He had lost Eolhsand, his old mount, on patrol north of Fan Yu. Recklessly, he had charged a camp of the rebel scouts without waiting for backup. The rebel war machines proved more than a match to the dragon. He managed to fly away from the battle, but the beast was too heavily wounded and had to be put down.

His father's name had prevented him from being stripped of rank but, not being an officer, he had not been given a spare mount. Instead, he had been assigned as co-rider to the Flight Leader.

Hywel ap Cadell. It had taken him weeks to swallow the insult. He, a Warwick, serving under a peasant from some backwater beyond the Dyke! He still shuddered with anger thinking about it. How long would he have to suffer this humiliation?

There was a rumour of a transport of spares coming from the south. A battle was at hand, and there were always casualties in battle – dragons more likely to fall than the riders. A regiment of light dragoons could afford one mountless rider, especially one as unpopular as Wulfhere was among his comrades, but further losses had to be replaced if the troop was to remain operative.

All he had to do was survive.

It started with a single white flare, shooting up into the grey clouds. Then the line of ships standing at anchor at the river mouth erupted in bright flashes. A second later a prolonged thunder rolled through the river, the smoke trails of rockets covered the sky and suddenly, the opposite shore turned into one great explosion, spanning half a mile. The ground shook first, before the sound of the barrage reached the soldiers gathered in the barges on the northern side.

"That's our prompt," murmured Hywel as the bombardment moved further south. The commander raised his Soul Lance and, one by one, the dragons of the Twelfth Light sprang into the skies. Their task was to cover the western flank of the landing party – the Second Marines doing the same thing on the opposite side. The first wave of the barges launched from the moorings.

"Where's the enemy?" Wulfhere asked, straining to see anything among the smoke and dust raised by the shelling. The barges were almost halfway across the river and there was still no response from the rebels. He felt nervous. The dragons flew slowly, to let the barges keep up. *We're sitting ducks here*, he thought.

"Maybe they ran away," replied Hywel hopefully.

"Look, they dug trenches along the river bank."

Several rows of dugouts ran parallel to the shoreline, now mangled and partially buried by the barrage. Nothing seemed to move inside.

"We're flying too low," said Wulfhere. "Why are we flying so low?"

"Don't be a coward, Wulf," said Hywel, but his voice trembled.

An easterly wind picked up, dispersing the smoke clouds, and they saw a line of the rebel war machines, standing on the top of a tall cliff like patient spiders, their cannons aimed at the middle of the river.

"There they are," said Hywel.

"For the Dragon Throne!" the commander yelled. The dragons roared in response, and fifty winged beasts swooped down as one.

They were sitting in the canteen tent, by the long table, finishing their meal. Fighting still raged on the other side of the river, but half of the regiment was allowed to fly back to the camp for a brief respite. The battle was obviously going in their favour.

"Our naval guns are making mincemeat out of the enemy," said Berthun, a black-haired, thick-browed rider from Rheged. His voice was not boastful and his face was grim, a face of a man who had seen too much for one day. "This battle will be over before nightfall."

"Mincemeat... now there's something I'd like to eat instead of all this rice and fish!" replied another boy and many laughed, though not all.

"You're not drinking your rum?" Hywel asked. Wulfhere sat quietly over his bowl, a tin mug filled with muddled brown liquid untouched.

You call this swill "rum", he thought bitterly. *In my father's house we would drink the finest of Burdigala wines.*

He wasn't sure where the sudden memory came from. He shook his head.

"I have a feeling we may yet need our clear heads."

"You worry too much. Berthun is right, with the ironclads on our side nothing can stand in our way."

"I've heard a rumour the fleet is ordered to set sail on the morrow."

The Gwynedd boy looked at him sharply. Wulfhere may not have been a reliable soldier most of the time, but his good connections made him a valuable source of gossip.

"It will be all over by tomorrow," Hywel said at last.

He grabbed the Seaxe's mug and drank the rum in one gulp, snorting.

"Did you know Bran was supposed to be here with his father?" he asked.

Wulfhere shook his head. "I thought he stayed at the Academy."

"No, apparently he's gone missing in the *Ladon* disaster."

"Dead, you mean."

"Nobody here seems to think so. The Seal of Llambed saved him, but nobody knows where he is. Imagine if he was here, though – three boys from the same year on one battlefield!"

Hywel laughed, his cheeks already rosy from the drink. Wulfhere sat silent. The memory of Bran, and of his humiliation at the Red Dragon *tafarn* spoiled his mood completely. He pushed back the bowl and stood up.

"I'll go check on the dragon."

Hywel nodded. "We'll be flying again in ten minutes anyway."

Wulfhere stepped outside the flapping tent door and gazed across the muddy river. The waters flowed calmly now, unaware of the carnage on the southern shore, undisturbed by the smoke and flares.

There was a sudden quiet thunder strike in the distance, and a great flash in the sky. A ball of flame hurtled, rolling and tumbling from beyond the southern horizon, like a meteor. Long before it reached its destination, Wulfhere guessed what the strange missile was aiming for. The flaming rock hit one of the warships dead on, smashing through all the decks, straight for the ammunition storage. A blink of an eye later a tremendous explosion tore the hapless ship asunder.

For a moment everything was deadly quiet. Then the debris started falling down on the camp – half a mile from the blast – and the dragon riders poured from the tent to see what was happening.

"By the Red Dragon's Breath…" Hywel whispered, sobering up in an instant. "That was the Admiral's frigate!"

A swarm of Qin dragons headed towards them like a cloud of colourful ribbons in the wind.

"Look at that," whispered Hywel, "there must be dozens of them."

The regiment divided into two groups; one squadron, led by the commander, flew upwards and to the West, to strike at the enemy dragons with the sun at their backs. The other split further, into individual flights, to deal with the danger on the ground. Hywel was a Flight Leader – a rare promotion for one so young – and so he and Wulfhere found themselves leading a group of four riders, speeding low over the heads of both the enemy and friendly soldiers in the direction from which the flaming boulders were coming. The mysterious cannon – if cannon it was – took a long time to reload. It had shot only twice more since the Twelfth had scrambled. Neither of the shots was as precise and deadly as the first one, but the ships were forced to stop their bombardment and engage in evasive manoeuvres. It was imperative to locate it and destroy it fast, before the enemy regained their initiative.

"It came from beyond that low line of hills," said Wulfhere, one of the few who had seen the first shot fired. Hywel's flight turned along an irrigation canal running southwest across the rice fields towards a crest of sand dunes.

Something was running towards them down from the hills. At first it seemed like a cavalry of ponies, or a battalion of warhounds.

"Watch out!" Hywel cried to the other riders, "It's what's-their-faces, the leaping lions!"

"Bishiu," Wulfhere corrected him grimly.

In his notepad the name Bishiu was circled in red. Though the vestigial wings on the backs of the horned, lion-shaped creatures did not give them the power of flight, they could still pounce a hundred feet or more into the air to bring down any beast unfortunate enough to fly so low. Their strength and fierceness were legendary, and although one-on-one they were no match for even the smallest of dragons, they always travelled and fought in great packs.

"Up twenty!" Hywel commanded and the four dragons climbed to two hundred feet. The Bishiu were now following the flying beasts at speed, howling and barking, and leaping without much effect.

"Let them howl!" Hywel said, laughing, but at the same moment one of the lions leapt farther than any before it and its claws grasped a hind leg of one of the dragons. The mount snorted and dropped a few yards, flapping its wings desperately, trying to shake the beast off.

Two more of the Bishiu reached the dragon, pulling it further downwards. Hywel turned the flight back to save the hapless rider. Lightning and flame poured like rain on the heads of the leaping lions and the beasts scattered, squealing like pigs on fire. Soon, however, they began regrouping again at the foot of the hills, growling menacingly.

"Up ten," shouted Hywel with a tired voice, "and keep those shields on! Next time you're caught, you have to fend for yourselves. We've had enough delay as it is. That infernal cannon is about to make another try at our ships, I bet. Onwards, men of the Twelfth!"

It was difficult to assess the size of the enormous mortar until they got close enough to see the crew and soldiers bustling around it, and even then it was hard to comprehend. Each of the six wheels upon which the heavy wooden platform rested was at least twelve feet in diameter. The barrel of the gun, painted bright red and decorated with coiling hieroglyphs, rose menacingly into the sky like a giant chimney, leaning at a slight angle towards the battlefield.

"If *these* are the rebels," asked Wulfhere, "how come they have access to such weapons and not the Qin army?"

Hywel shrugged. "You want to switch sides?"

The Seaxe did not answer.

The cannon was manned and guarded by what seemed at first like very large men in bluish-green uniforms.

"*Sheng-sheng,*" whispered Wulfhere when they got closer.

A hail of musket balls and flaming arrows bounced uselessly off the *tarians*. A few rockets exploded between the dragons without harm.

Hywel reached out his right hand and summoned a bluish Soul Lance. He gestured to the rider at his left side – grey-eyed Eadgyth – ordering her to take out the rocket launchers and war machines on a ridge to the south. Hywel and one other dragon, led by a silent, tattooed man from Alba called Nechtan, swooped down towards the gun. There were only three of them left in the flight; the fourth rider flew back to the rest of the army to announce the discovery of the gun's position.

"Shouldn't we wait for the others?" Wulfhere asked.

"No time. At the least we can distract them from making another shot."

The *sheng-sheng* dispersed, cowering before their dragons and the gun halted its slow rotation. But the dragon flame could not penetrate the casing. The gun carriage was magic-proofed. Only the iron bindings of the wheels started melting in the fire, settling the entire machinery deep into the ground.

"Cover me, I'm going down," announced Hywel, standing in his stirrups.

"*What?*"

"You heard me. I'm going to dismantle that thing from the ground."

"That's insane! Didn't you hear the instructor? Those furry apes will rip you apart!"

Hywel's eyes glinted with battle rush and pride. "That's why I need you to cover me. You should be happy – if I die, you get to keep the dragon."

"But – "

"That's an *order*, ensign. Bring us close to that cupola at the back, that's where the steering mechanism must be."

Reluctantly, Wulfhere took over the reins and guided the dragon down. He could see Hywel's lips move wordlessly as the Gwyneddian calculated the trajectory of the enhanced jump. Nechtan circled above them, checking the crowd of the *sheng-shengs* with precisely aimed balls of dragon flame.

Hywel leapt down, somersaulting in the air before landing upon the platform. His Lance flashed, cutting an opening in the iron dome and he disappeared inside.

Wulfhere cursed, bringing the dragon to heel. There were more enemy soldiers swarming from all sides, and there was no sign of their own reinforcements coming, except Eadgyth returning from her mission. Several war machines smouldered on the ridge.

He's as good as dead, the fool.

Wulfhere and Nechtan were doing their best to keep the enemy from returning to the gun carriage, but both they and their mounts were growing tired with the prolonging battle. His mount struggled to keep airborne. Now that he was in charge of the dragon, he could feel the chaotic whirlwind of magic currents around the machine, disrupting the flow of the Ninth Wind. It was like flying through a tornado.

There was a small explosion inside the vehicle and one of the great wheels broke off, falling down with a thud, burying a few of the *sheng-sheng* combatants underneath.

Nechtan whooped, but the cry of joy died in his throat. Wulfhere felt it too. There was a dark *presence* on the battlefield beneath them. It did not take him long to find its source. A Qin man in simple red robes and long uncut hair was walking unhurriedly towards the gun, accompanied by several soldiers carrying long bronze tubes. The ranks of rebel soldiers parted before him like grass. The *sheng-shengs* dropped to their hairy knees.

The Alba rider, recognising an officer of some sort, let out a battle cry and dived down. The strange man looked up with eyes shining gold and Wulfhere was certain he smiled wickedly, though it was too far to see his features. The man raised a hand. His soldiers aimed their bronze tubes and launched flaming spears carrying what seemed to be fishing nets made of silver, glittering thread.

Wulfhere pulled up out of the range of the missiles, but Nechtan was too late. His dragon's wings got entangled in the nets and the beast tumbled down to the ground. The *sheng-shengs* swarmed to it, swamping both the dragon and its rider with their bodies.

"We need to retreat! Where's the Flight Leader?" shouted Eadgyth.

"Inside," Wulfhere pointed grimly at the gun carriage, from which the sounds of a fierce battle were still coming. The two riders tried to get close to the bombard but the nets launched again, keeping them at bay. The enemy footmen were now climbing onto the platform on all sides and the strange Qin man was reaching for a rope ladder.

"*Swyfen!*" the Seaxe cursed, "I'm coming after him. Cover me!"

He dived in and, swerving back and forth to avoid the nets, he landed the dragon on the carriage, in the middle of a troop of the *sheng-shengs*, who dispersed in an instant.

"Stay here," Wulfhere commanded the beast. The dragon had enough sense of its own to understand the order, despite their weak Farlink connection. "Guard the entrance."

The Seaxe looked up one last time towards Eadgyth circling above and then leapt through the opening in the iron dome.

He found Hywel on a narrow staircase reaching deep into the bowels of the war machine. The Gwyneddian was limping towards the exit, his side covered in blood and his cavalry sword broken, but a broad grin lightened his face.

"That gun won't move again. But what are you doing here? I told you to stay up."

"We have to get out of here. The others have still not arrived and there are enemy reinforcements outside. Can you fly?"

"I can try."

With Hywel hanging on his shoulder, Wulfhere climbed out onto the platform only to see a swarm of strong arms covered in blue fur reaching towards him. He pulled back inside, hacking at the *sheng-shengs* furiously. Hywel joined him, but with a broken sword and not enough power to sustain the Soul Lance any more, he could do little against the onslaught.

Several of the creatures grasped the jagged iron edges of the opening and, with tremendous strength, tore it apart. Others poured in through the breach, forcing the two riders further down the wooden stairs. Rocks and arrows flew, bouncing off Wulfhere's *tarian* with a shimmer. One of the beasts moved forward, wielding a heavy spear with a blunt bronze head. The blade penetrated the shield with a crackle, hitting Wulfhere's side and pinning him to the wall. He hit his head and his legs gave in. The *sheng-shengs* trampled and tumbled over him and a red darkness shrouded everything around.

The cold wind woke him up, but he dared not stir or open his eyes. The harsh, ineligible howls and barks around him told him he was still among the *sheng-sheng*. He wasn't bound – they must have thought he was dead. The wound in his side ached.

Very carefully, he opened one eye by a slit, just to get his bearings. He was laid on the gun platform, not far from the iron cupola. Hywel lay beside him, to the left, not showing any signs of life. Further along the Seaxe could make out the outlines of two more bodies: Eadgyth and Nechtan, he guessed. The *sheng-sheng* stood around them in a circle, agitated.

What are they doing to us? Some kind of sacrifice?

Another kind of cold passed through his body and he sensed the strange Qin man coming up to the riders. Wulfhere's skin got covered with goose bumps. The *sheng-sheng* fell silent and stepped aside. The man reached for the first of the bodies – Nechtan, judging by the hair colour, though the body was mangled almost beyond recognition – and raised it to his face. A sleeve of the robe slid down, revealing a tattoo of a black lotus flower on the forearm.

The Qin man's eyes turned from gold to black and he plunged his teeth into Nechtan's neck. The Alba soldier woke suddenly, gasped and twitched briefly, before falling limply to the floor.

Their tormentor moved to Eadgyth. Wulfhere closed his eyes and tried to calm his breath and heart to stay undetected. What was this *creature*? No briefing mentioned anything like it.

The man – the *demon* – now leaned over the body of Hywel. He turned his back to Wulfhere for a brief moment. This was all the boy needed. A Soul Lance appeared in his right hand and he leapt up, striking the enemy under the ribs. The Lance went straight through the lungs and heart. The Qinese let out a terrible shriek which made all the *sheng-shengs* fall down on their faces in fright.

Gathering all his strength, Wulfhere pulled the Lance downwards and to the side. There was no blood, no guts spilled from the gash, just rotting flesh. The creature reached back with a hand blackened with blood, but the dragon rider pushed on the Lance and the demon tripped over Hywel's body, falling.

It's still alive. How is it still alive?

The creature flailed its arms, trying to stand up. Wulfhere grabbed Hywel and, dragging him along the platform, hewed his way through the crowd of terrified *sheng-shengs*.

A ball of flame dropped from the skies, then another, then a lightning bolt. He looked up. Coming from over the sand dunes, the dragons of the Second Marines were coming to the rescue on the northerly wind, led by a man wielding a shining golden Soul Lance.

He sighed with relief and turned around. The platform was empty. There was no trace of the *sheng-sheng* soldiers, the two dead dragon riders – or the mysterious demon.

CHAPTER XIII

Dry wind blew volcanic dust across the arid highland. Particles of dark grey fell onto the torn and tattered remains of Dōraku's kimono and covered gaping, open wounds with a thin layer of ash. The samurai lay sprawled on the ground. His arms, thrown apart, still held on to both swords, but most of his upper body was ripped and slashed to pieces by ghostly fangs and claws, which pierced through the clothes and the mail shirt underneath like paper.

The wolf spirits disappeared, having fulfilled their purpose, leaving Dōraku's corpse exposed to the elements but also allowing it to slowly regenerate. The spell started working its way through the wounds as soon as the battle was over. Shredded veins and tendons linked up, nerve connections began slowly rebuilding themselves, muscles and skin grew back over the gashes and lacerations.

Dōraku needed neither blood nor oxygen to function. His heart, even fully regenerated, lay still in his chest without a single beat. His lungs did not move, no air pumped in or out of the trachea even as it grew fully back from the damage done by the wolf spirit's jaw. Even though they did not perform any vital functions anymore, the spell's power unhurriedly restored his inner organs to their former state.

His consciousness slowly returning, Dōraku moved fingers first of his right, then left hand, making sure he could feel the hilts of his swords. The muscles and tendons in his limbs were not yet fully regenerated and all he could do was lie and wait for full control of his motor functions to come back eventually. He felt the warm rays of the midday sun on his newly regrown skin and concluded it was a pleasant feeling, like lying half-asleep in a warm bed, long into the late morning hours.

He knew not how many hours or days had passed since the battle with the wolf ghosts. Since he could open his eyes, a night and half a day had gone by and that was his only frame of reference. At noon he could bend his wrists and wiggle his toes, move muscles of his face. In the afternoon, he could move his hand to where his waist had been and touch the soft leather of the salt pouch. The lungs and throat were not yet reinstated enough for him to speak comfortably, but it was only a matter of hours at worst.

A shadow fell across his face. A tall man towered over him, blocking the sun.

"It's your own fault, you know, old friend. Why drink a wolf's blood when there were so many humans to choose from?"

"Ganryū," Dōraku whispered hoarsely, straining his newly reborn voice box, "I have never been your friend."

The crimson clad Fanged stood leaning on the scabbard of his great two-handed *nodachi* sword, his long hair flowing in the dry hot wind, his silhouette black against the midday sun. He chuckled.

"Now, now. Don't you remember all the good times we had?"

"Have you come to reminisce, or to brag?"

"I have no time for either. I only wanted to make sure you won't be standing in my way tonight."

"Tonight? What day is it?"

"The seventh."

"Four days and you still haven't made your move?"

Ganryū shrugged, "There's been a troop of Hosokawa's retainers in the shrine. I don't wish to antagonize Kumamoto right now through impatience."

"Hosokawa will never join your cause."

"We'll see about that once I get my hands on the dragon."

"The dragon is in the shrine?" Dōraku tried to laugh but his throat failed him. "Then you can't get anywhere near it."

"Unlike you, I don't work alone. My people don't share our hindrances. All I have to do is to wait for them to come back with the *dorako*. Isn't it precious, Takezō? Or whatever name you are using for yourself these days."

The man in the crimson robe leaned closer towards Dōraku's tense face.

"I can't join my team, but neither can you help your companions. I wonder who will prevail in this contest; three city kids or a troop of trained warriors and assassins?"

"You underestimate them."

"Perhaps. I wouldn't mind a challenge for a change. Your performance against my wolves was sorely disappointing."

He examined Dōraku's body. "You regenerate faster than I expected."

"It's the Takachiho Mountain."

Ganryū pulled out the great sword from its sheath in a slow, deliberate move.

"I've always wondered how long it would take you to regrow your head."

He raised the *nodachi* to strike down, but at the same instant Dōraku swung his right arm at the Fanged's feet. Ganryū leapt at the last moment, somersaulting back a few steps. The *katana* cut through the air with a whistle. Dōraku brought his left hand up, throwing the pouch of salt at his opponent.

Ganryū cried out and spluttered, cursing and rubbing the white crystals out of his eyes.

"I don't have time for this," he snorted, "by the time you'll be able to stand up, I'll be long gone."

With that, the Crimson Robe turned away and walked down the slope towards Kirishima.

The Admiral seemed frail, weak and somehow older. The green cloth of the infirmary tent cast an unhealthy hue on his wrinkled face.

"That was a good battle," he said quietly and burst into a dry cough.

"We were reckless," said Dylan. He, Edern and the Admiral's *aide-de-camp* were sitting by the old man's bed. "That's the second ship I lost to the Rebels on my watch."

"Every ship's destiny is to sink," the Admiral said. "Victory is all that matters."

"And we've won splendidly," said Edern, "though our losses were great."

"The enemy's losses were much greater," said Dylan with a bitter smile. "The Ever Victorious Army is what our troops are called now. By the Emperor's edict!"

"And by my edict, they will now have a Commodore to lead them."

Reynolds gestured feebly at his *aide-de-camp*. The young man reached into his pocket and gave Dylan a sealed envelope.

"If I could make you an Admiral, I would," the old man said. "A better soldier I have not seen since my father's death. And the Pointy-Beard will respect you more if you have a proper rank. I could see how uneasy he was, having to deal with a mere Ardian."

"Thank you, Sir, that's a great honour."

"I only wish I could see all the victories you will win, Commodore."

"Perhaps after you return from your assignment at Ta Du – "

The Admiral laughed and then started coughing again. Blood spattered the bed sheet. He looked at the mangled, twisted remains of what was once his right arm. His iron leg was torn off at the knee.

"I am nothing but a broken machine… I should have died with my ship, but I won't fall far behind her. It doesn't matter. I had a long life. All my old crew mates are gone – from the Culloden, the Terpsichore, the Phaeton…"

His eyes opened wide.

"The Phaeton! That's what I wanted to tell you about!"

"Sir?"

The Admiral looked around him. "This is too confidential even for our lieutenants."

Edern and the other young man nodded and left.

"Tell me, Commodore, did your father ever tell you about the time we invaded Yamato?"

Yamato? Is he delirious?

"No, Sir."

"Good." The Admiral chuckled lightly. "So he had kept his oath. We were all sworn to secrecy as soon as we returned from that accursed place – and paid well to keep it."

"Paid?"

"How else do you think I could have afforded all this?" He pointed to the remains of his automated limbs and chuckled again. "Even after I was abandoned by my own men in shark-infested waters… But it doesn't matter. I've kept my part of the bargain. But it didn't mean I forgot – oh no, I never forgot it, and I bet neither did Ifor, for his own particular reasons."

With an increasingly weakening voice, in short sentences interspersed with bouts of coughing, the Admiral told the astonishing story of the Phaeton's raid on the city of *Keeyo* and the harbour of *Dejeema* and of the mysterious woman they had brought back to Dracaland.

"*Dejeema!*" Dylan whispered, remembering suddenly. "Bran asked me about that place the night before the disaster."

The Admiral nodded. "That would confirm my suspicions. I figured if your boy was somewhere in Qin, we'd have heard about it already. Even if the magic transported him all the way to Fan Yu or Temasek, we would have had some news by now. But there is nothing. And there is only one place secretive enough for this to happen."

He wheezed loudly, but managed to stop himself from coughing. What he had to say was too important.

"What if your son had found some information about his grandfather's journey? Maybe even some souvenir from it? Something Ifor had brought with him to Gwynedd? Could this have influenced the way the Seal worked?"

"The ring…"

"What's that?"

"My father gave Bran a ring and told him to always keep it with him. We never learned where it came from. A shard of a blue stone."

The Admiral closed his eyes, straining to remember.

"The memories are faint after so many years… That woman. She wore a brooch of gold with a blue stone around her waist. She and Ifor were very close. I don't remember what happened to her – I think she was taken away when we moored at Brigstow."

"But if all this is true…" Dylan said, thinking quickly, "and if Bran really is in Yamato right now, then that means – he's lost to me! Nobody knows the way to Yamato."

"Ah! But – no!" the Admiral cried, raising himself off the pillow, "there is a greater secret than the Phaeton's journey!"

He fell back and breathed hard for a while.

"My *aide* will give you access to all my papers," he continued at last, "what's left of them after the *Wintoncaestre* blew up. There you will find coded notes – the boy knows the code."

"The Bataavians changed the course of their ships after the *Phaeton* incident. I have tried to figure out where the new passage was, but then… my crew got restless again… and I was reassigned to the Cape Colony, not long after we got it from Bataavians.. It was there that I met a certain doctor, a spy in Bataavian employ. He told me everything."

The Admiral paused, gathering strength.

"There is only one ship in the year, and only its pilot knows the route. It sets sail from New Bataave in the late spring, past Temasek and Tagalogs. You will find all this in the notes."

"Late spring – that's… right now."

"Exactly."

The Admiral closed his eyes and focused on breathing. Dylan could see life trickling away from the frail body.

"You will do with this knowledge as you see fit," the Admiral whispered with increasing difficulty. "I trust you will... make the right decision."

He said nothing else. Dylan waited a moment and then touched the Admiral's wrist; there was no pulse. He stood up quietly and went outside.

He woke up feeling something was not right. The tent seemed somehow different in the pink light of dawn, the bedding was in the wrong position, and the table was folded.

A warm, soft hand touched his shoulder and then he remembered.

"Good morning, Commodore," said Gwenllian. He sighed.

"The night was too short."

"And now you're off again."

"There's a war on, you know," he said, smiling.

"Not right now. The battle is over."

"The Bohan's armies are still besieging Shanglin. They will need our help."

"Let them fight it out themselves. I'm still not sure we should be helping the Emperor rather than the Heavenly Army."

He chuckled. "Not you too! I find it hard enough to quell rebellious moods among the ensigns."

"And who can blame them? I despise the Ta Du court. Have you seen what they are doing with their women?"

"You mean the feet? It's been like that for centuries."

"The Rebels have disallowed that custom. And they are giving away the land to the poor peasants for free."

"But they refuse to trade with the West. They decline our envoys and kill our smugglers."

"And that is reason enough? That they don't want to peddle the Cursed Weed?"

"You sound like Bran." He shook his head and sat up, reaching for the uniform.

"Don't go yet," she pleaded. "I'm sorry."

She ran her fingers down his back, scratching the scars left on his body by all the dragons he had once ridden. A pleasant shiver ran down his spine. He thought about something for a moment, looking through the white canvas walls at the rising sun.

"Come with me," he said. "There is still some time before the siege recommences. I want to show you something."

They flew on the back of Afreolus over the vast, flat plain south of the river, a battlefield stretching from where the Ever Victorious Army had first made its landfall to the walls of Shanglin overlooking a long and narrow lake. The Bohan's army encircled the city on all sides.

"Is this what you wanted to show me?" asked Gwenllian. "How the Emperor's Army destroys the last Rebel stronghold between here and Jiangkang?"

"No."

The silver dragon dived towards the southern end of the lake. Dylan landed it on a spur of land between two outflows, beside a ruined villa of some Qin dignitary. He led her down an overgrown path to a green mound. Bits of white protruded from among the grass.

"Are these... bones?" she said with a shudder.

"Porcelain. But come over here."

She joined him at the top of the mound and, looking down, gasped. The ground beneath was strewn with shards of pottery as far as the eye could see, white, ivory and celadon green.

"These are the great celadon kilns of Yue – or what's left of them after the centuries of wars that rolled through these plains."

"Why are you showing me this?"

He did not answer. Something caught his eye, glinting in the sun. He came down and rustled through the pot shards. He found a piece of celadon pottery, a large round bead, an inch in diameter, polished so smoothly it seemed like a true gemstone – a piece of beryl or jade. Some hair-thin Qin characters were carved carefully into the clay, but they were eroded beyond recognition. There was some magic still left in the stone; Dylan could feel its slight buzz in his hand.

On an impulse, he pulled out the leather cord from the hood of his cape. He threaded the bead onto it and climbed back to the top of the mound, where he tied the cord around Gwenllian's white neck.

"It's… it's beautiful," she whispered, admiring the jewel's green shimmer. Her black eyes turned sad.

"Something troubles you."

He said nothing again, just gazed eastwards, beyond the besieged city, towards the sea.

A sudden roar of guns broke his meditation.

"I have to go," he said, "that's the Bohan's army, breaching the walls of Shanglin."

CHAPTER XIV

The messenger from Kumamoto galloped for a full night and day across the mountains, without respite, changing horses several times before reaching the procession. He was now resting in the Captain's palanquin while Kiyomasa walked beside it, carefully perusing his orders, written in the *daimyo*'s personal code.

"Silk is cheaper than jade. Make friends with the wizards for the time being. The winds blow strong from Higo, but the tide is higher in Sasshu."

The Captain frowned. The courier was almost too late – Lady Atsuko's entourage had already departed from the shrine, but they were still close enough to turn back. The first words of the missive meant that the protection of the *dorako* was more important to Lord Hosokawa than the safety of his ally's daughter. Kiyomasa was to take as many of his men as he deemed reasonable and go back to Kirishima. It was a risky gamble and a costly one.

The last sentence was an unnecessary reminder of his precarious situation. Lord Hosokawa had sent reinforcements from Kumamoto – Higo in the *daimyo*'s code – but so had Atsu-*hime*'s father – Sasshu indicated Satsuma – and these would arrive first. If Lord Nariakira decided to

267

move the *dorako* again somewhere else, the Captain would be unable to stop him.

"You're back," Heishichi said, not even looking up from the scroll he was studying. "Did something happen to the princess?"

There was no sign of worry in his voice, not even a feigned interest.

"Atsu-*hime* is safely on her way, with the rest of my men. I have returned to aid you with the protection of the Treasure."

"I don't remember Shimazu-*dono* agreeing to this arrangement."

"I take my orders from Kumamoto, not Kagoshima."

The wizard finally raised his eyes. He removed his horn-rimmed spectacles and his sad eyes seemed suddenly smaller, narrower. His hands trembled slightly.

"My men are more than capable of taking care of the safety of the shrine."

"You have not seen what our enemies are capable of."

"You mean the ghost wolves? Pah!" Heishichi scoffed. "Those *onmyōdo* tricks are no match for the power of my wizards."

Kiyomasa struggled not to scowl. Everyone had warned him that *Daisen* Torii Heishichi was as arrogant as he was bright. "*Too clever for his own good*" was an often repeated description of the wizard. Too radical, even for the Kiyō community, this merchant's son could only find a refuge and recognition for his skills at the Satsuma court.

"How many men do you have?"

"Six – and me. The best in Satsuma. I picked them myself."

"And I have twice that – also hand-picked. I'm sure the shrine can accommodate for all of us without a quarrel."

"Do as you wish," the wizard waved his hand, "just try not to disturb me too much. I have a lot of work to do."

"I would like to see what security you already have in place," the Captain remained standing. Heishichi crumbled the scroll in his hand and sighed deeply.

"Captain... Kiyomasa, was it? Do you know what we have in there?" he asked, pointing vaguely with his Western-style pencil in the direction of the storehouse. "Something that could change the fate of Yamato. And all the combined powers of Satsuma's best wizards can do is to keep it bound safely in the cage. I have already lost two men to this beast's uncontrollable wrath; one of them died. I'm at the end of my wits here, trying to make it do our bidding. And you want to check my *security detail?*"

Kiyomasa waited patiently for the rant to end.

"All your research and sacrifice will come to naught if somebody steals it from us."

"*Let them have it!* I want to see how *they* deal with the monster! But no, you're right." He calmed down as abruptly as he had exploded. "Very well. It is time for the changing of the guards anyway. Come, Captain."

Three mages in ill-fitting black and vermillion *Rangakusha* robes stood in the corners of an equilateral triangle, their hands outstretched towards the centre of the warehouse's floor, where an eight foot tall cage had been set up. Within the cage, bound with heavy steel chains, lay a celadon-scaled dragon, half-asleep, half-stunned by the efforts of the mages. A large thaumaturgic device – a tangled mass of pipes and gears – tick-tocked rhythmically in the corner, serving some unknown purpose.

This was the first time Kiyomasa had laid his eyes on the terrible beast and cold sweat trickled down his back. It took all his soldier's training not to run away screaming. He gained a new respect for Heishichi, who calmly paced around the dragon making notes. At the end of his round, the wizard leaned over to the machine in the corner and adjusted some dial.

Two more wizards entered the chamber, ready to replace their colleagues. All five men looked at their superior. The *Daisen* nodded and raised a hand with four fingers extended. At the count of four, the two of the standing mages quickly switched positions with the newcomers. The dragon snorted, but remained motionless.

Heishichi nodded with satisfaction. The replaced wizards stretched their hands and backs and quickly left the warehouse.

"Six times a day," the wizard replied to an unspoken question.

"And you're here every time this happens?"

"Of course. Somebody has to control the situation."

"Aren't you tired? All this and your research?"

"Exhausted. If it wasn't for the extract from the *maō* plant, I think I would be dead by now."

Kiyomasa looked into Heishichi's eyes. His pupils were large and the whites of his eyes blood-shot. A barely discernible twitch pinched his lower left eyelid.

"*Maō* plant?"

"A certain physician from Kiyō prepares this wondrous concoction. I have had no need for sleep in a week."

"Do your men also take this… extract?"

"Of course! Though not as much. I do let them sleep for a few hours a day, that's why the shifts rotate."

"And you said you only have these six men?"

Heishichi gave him a long look.

"I know what you're driving at, Captain, and I can assure you, the risk is – "

"Never mind. Hopefully this situation will not last too long. I just needed to know what our resources are."

"So I'm free to go back to my studies now?"

"I will let you know about my own arrangements later."

The wizard rolled his eyes and it was obvious he cared little for Captain Kiyomasa's "arrangements".

Satō mingled into the throng of pilgrims surrounding the stage. The performance was to start at noon and last well into night. People of all classes and professions had gathered to witness the dance, a colourful throng of craftsmen, merchants, local samurai and travellers from neighbouring towns and villages. The men were accompanied by their wives, mothers and daughters in pastel-dyed spring *yukatas*, or by mistresses in gaudy kimonos and overdone make-up. As the multitude of people grew in the courtyard, the usual hangers-on appeared: street hawkers, snack vendors and an occasional pick-pocket.

"So what's all this about, then?" Bran asked. He had been looking gloomy all day and Satō was growing increasingly exasperated with his moping. The headache she'd been suffering all day didn't help her irritation.

"They're going to perform a *kagura*," explained Nagomi, "a holy dance. It will tell the story of the shrine and its *kami*."

"And what is the story?"

"You'll see for yourself. Most will unveil long before dark."

They had planned to make their strike after nightfall, but not before the crowds dispersed, hoping that the performance provided just enough distraction.

"It's about Watatsumi, the King of the Dragons, and his daughter Otohime," she added.

"How apt," said Bran.

"Shh, it starts now!" Satō tugged him on the sleeve. "Let's come closer."

In a flash of smoke and fireworks, the announcer appeared: a priest in a fiery-red robe and a white dragon mask. He spoke loudly, in an archaic, theatrical manner, waving his hands and stomping his feet exaggeratedly. He greeted the audience and told a few bawdy jokes to put them in a good mood. When he decided they had had enough, he stepped back and a puff of white smoke appeared from behind the curtain.

"See now the first tale of the Dragon Dance - a tale of how the Great Creators, the Goddess Izanami and her husband the God Izanagi, created the world."

Two actors in long, flowing white robes, in male and female disguise, came onto the stage. To the haunting sounds of bamboo flute, drum and wooden beaters, they performed a slow, majestic piece known as the Birth of Gods. The crowd was obviously familiar with the traditional dance, for it cheered and reacted in all the right places, sometimes even slightly before the appropriate moment for applause arrived.

"In their wisdom the Gods spawn the three Dragon Kings to rule the Upper Sea, the Middle Sea and the Bottom Sea", said the announcer, "but as the last of the dragons passes through the divine mother Izanami, it burns her so badly she dies!"

The "Goddess" lay still on the wooden floor, the other actor weeping over her body. Suddenly his face burst with bright red light of the setting sun.

"From the tears of divine father Izanagi," the announcer cried from behind the curtain, "comes forth the Sun Goddess Amaterasu!"

At this prompt, the crowd murmured a brief chanting prayer. Satō noticed Nagomi bend piously in a deep bow. Even if she was only represented by a prop on the theatre stage, the Goddess's presence was almost tangible.

The next scene was the dance of Ninigi, grandson of Amaterasu, descending upon Mount Takachiho with the Imperial Jewels, to rule the world from its top. This was met with great applause from the locals in the crowd, as Takachiho, rising majestically beyond the shrine, formed a natural backdrop to the performance. The actor's dance was long and exhausting, martial in its nature. Ninigi danced with a wooden lance, a bow and a sword, conveying the many battles he and his father had to win in order to conquer and rule the land of Yamato.

Near the end of this part of the performance the actor in female guise reappeared on stage. The two performed a symbolic marriage dance. The announcer spoke once more:

"Many were the victories of Ninigi, and at last the land was subdued. He wedded an Earth Goddess and she bore him a child – a brave and strong son, prince Hikohohodemi, the Hunter prince."

Satō joined the enthusiastic applause, but when she turned to Bran she caught him yawning.

"You did not like it?"

"I'm sorry, I'm sure it is all very impressive and symbolic for you, but most of it just goes over my head. I don't even understand half of what is going on."

"Maybe that general in your head could narrate you an explanation." She was joking, but Bran frowned.

"Shigemasa is keeping silent lately. I think he's too overwhelmed by all the magical energies of this place."

It was a hot, humid day. Dark clouds hovered above the shrine, but not a drop of rain yet fell. A nearby vendor was selling cold *amazake*. Bran bought a whole flask of the drink and gulped half of it in one go before passing it over to Satō. It was sweet and refreshing. Just then, the announcer reappeared on stage.

"And now for the tale of love, love found in the strangest of places. See how prince Hikohohodemi descends into the depths of the sea and discovers his beloved Otohime!"

The prince's descent was another long and complex dance in which the journey to the bottom of the sea was created through minor illusions, conjured images of exotic fish, shellfish, corals and other "wonders of the deep". At long last, the prince arrived at the Dragon King's castle. The actor climbed an imaginary fence, and saw the princess sitting alone in the coral garden. Together they performed a complicated courtship dance. Their moves were exceptionally smooth and attractive, at times almost acrobatic.

The music got more dramatic as the princess's father, the Dragon King, appeared on stage. Smoke and sparks blew from its nostrils. The King was played by two actors in a dragon costume, its body and head fiery red, rolling its artificial eyes, lolling the cloth tongue and gnashing wooden teeth to the great amusement of the audience, especially the children. The prince and the princess managed to calm the Dragon King with another bout of dancing, and the prince was allowed to marry Otohime and remain in the undersea castle.

This time Bran joined the applause at the end.

"You've enjoyed this one?" Satō asked.

"Oh, yes! Very much. Have you noticed the magic?"

"You mean the illusions in the Sea Dance?"

"There's a wizard backstage, I can see his aura. Must be one of Hei – " he stopped.

"One of what?"

"One of the troop," he finished, though she was certain this was not what he meant.

The crowd around them started to thin out.

"Is it over?" asked Bran with a rather disappointing voice.

"No, it's just a break, the actors need to rest and eat," Satō replied, laughing. "Come on, we should eat something too."

The dining room was full of people and they had to wait an unusually long time for their meal of rice, cold soymilk skin and stewed vegetables.

"Have you noticed anyone suspicious?" Bran asked the girls.

"In this crowd? Impossible," Satō shook her head, "there could be a whole army hiding among the visitors. Listen, what if the Crimson Robe decides to strike today? He too must know this is the best moment."

The night before, Bran had at last shared his suspicions with them. Satō and Nagomi agreed that there was a dark presence prowling outside the shrine walls and together they concluded it could have been none other than the Crimson Robe – even though only the wizardess had seen the enemy up close, and long weeks had passed since then.

Perhaps we want it to be him, Bran thought. *Better the demon you know…*

He turned to the priestess. "What do you think, Nagomi?"

"Me?" the girl looked at him, startled.

"You're the only one who's not here to fight. You are with us because you want to be here, not because you have to. It ought to be your decision."

"I…" Nagomi took a deep breath. "We will fight, of course."

"Are you sure?"

"What other choice do we have? Your dragon, Sacchan's honoured father… it's not like we can run away."

"But what about you? This could be a battle to the death. It would be safer-"

"You're my friends!" she interrupted him. "Do you think I will just stand by and let you get hurt?"

Friends? We've only known each other for a month... He looked to Satō. Their eyes met and she smiled reassuringly.

Friends it is, then.

"It's decided then. Let us prepare ourselves and meet back in my room. Listen – " He paused for a moment. "I'm not sure how this will end, but we may find ourselves having to flee again. If you have anything you feel will come in useful on the run, take it with you."

"No, no, no, NO!"

Hurrying feet thumped on the corridor and Satō's alarmed face appeared in the door of Bran's room.

"What happe – "

She stopped, noticing the mess on the floor. Bran was kneeling among the items thrown mercilessly around, holding his leather satchel.

"They stole the ring," he said.

"*Eeh*! Who did?"

Bran shrugged. He was calming down now and started to put the items back into the bag.

"Did they take anything else?"

"No. These weren't common thieves."

A servant girl walked past the door with a tray.

"Yōko!" Satō called her over. "Have you noticed anything suspicious?"

"What happened, *tono*?"

The girl touched her way into the room and bowed.

"There were thieves here," explained Bran.

"Oh no! I must tell t'landlord!"

"First tell us if you've heard anything."

Yōko wrinkled her nose in thought.

"There were some… samurai. I could tell by t'way they walked. It seemed strange that they did not greet me – now I think they thought they could just sneak past me."

Satō dismissed the girl and turned back to Bran.

"Hosokawa's men," he said.

"*Eeh*? What would they want from your ring?"

Bran asked the wizardess to sit down and explained what he and Dōraku had discovered about the *onmyōji* and the involvement of Lord Hosokawa in the ambush.

"We are harassed constantly since Kumamoto. That *daimyo* is onto something. All those samurai we met on the way here, they're not just here to protect the princess – you said so yourself."

"You don't think he's in league with the Crimson Robe…?"

"No." Bran shook his head. "We would be in much worse trouble if that were the case. I think he's got his own agenda."

"You should've told me sooner. I wouldn't have spent so much time with Gensai-*sama*."

He looked at her sharply.

"What have you told him?"

"Not much," she shrugged, "he doesn't even know my name. But I – I told him about Dōraku-*sama,* thinking they knew each other."

"And did they?"

"He's never heard that name."

"*Strangers you meet on the road,*" said Bran pensively. "We should have been more careful. It must have been that Captain, Kiyomasa."

"Captain Kiyomasa hasn't left with the others. I've seen him outside, just now, discussing something with the priests."

Nagomi entered the room. The priestess wore a thick hooded cloak and carried a small bundle.

"I have some soap, a towel, a flask of water, bandages… couldn't think of anything – what's happened?"

Bran gathered his belongings back into the satchel and stood up. "Somebody stole my ring. But we'll deal with that later. Let's solve one problem at a time."

Just as they made their way back to the stage, the announcer jumped on it again. He was wearing a blue robe now, and his dragon mask was red.

"You have seen how love was found in the depths of the sea. But alas! Nothing lasts forever. Three years have passed and prince Hikohohodemi is feeling homesick. His land is on the surface after all, not in the depths of the blue ocean!"

The prince and the princess reappeared. Their costumes were now richer, indicating how their status and wealth had grown over time. But the prince's dance was melancholic, his moves and gestures wistful and nostalgic, his whole body pointing upwards where his kingdom lay.

The dancers moved in the same disjointed, purposeful manner as Dōraku had on the night of his performance. The haunting music, based on strange, jarring harmonies, resembled the samurai's song. The memory of their rugged camp in the desolate, wild mountains seemed like a dream to Bran, as he stood in the measureless crowd of onlookers.

Has it really been just a few days?

At last, the princess allowed the prince to return to the surface. The Dragon King then came on stage, bearing gifts for the prince's departure: a fish-hook and two magical jewels, orange-sized orbs, glowing white and blue. As the announcer explained, these were the *kanju* and *manju*, stones that controlled the ebb and flow of the tides. With these, the prince returned to his homeland and, as a mercifully brief dancing routine showed, won a war against his former fishing companion, recapturing the land.

The announcer returned on the stage.

"A few months have passed and princess Otohime sends a message – she is with child. She agrees to give birth to her son on land, not under the sea, but she bids the prince promise he would not spy on her at childbirth."

The princess came from under the sea with her fish-like entourage. She hid inside a wooden hut to give birth. But the prince, sneakily, crept up to the birthing shed, among bursts of laughter from the audience.

In the most impressive flash of special effects and fireworks so far – it was already getting dark – the princess disappeared and in her stead emerged a writhing, fiery, blue-headed dragon. It spotted the prince and, ashamed, flew away, leaving the new-born child on the sand.

"The princess closed her heart before the prince, and closed the sea before all men," explained the announcer. "Their love was but brief, like a candle in the darkness, but the memory of it remained forever."

Bran stood transfixed. It was no coincidence. *Their love was but brief, like a candle in the darkness...* Atsuko must have hoped he would watch the Dance and understand.

Satō pulled him back into the crowd.

"The sun is almost down. We have to go."

"I... yes, of course. But what about the dance? Will it really continue into the night? The story seems over."

"That's just the first part," Satō waved her hand. "Now they will show the tale of Jimmu, the first *Mikado*, who was born of Otohime's child. There're a lot of stories left to tell."

"I heard they're going to do 'Amaterasu in the Cave' at dawn, at the special request of the High Priest," added Nagomi.

"Oh, that would have been nice! Too bad we can't stay. Come on, Bran! I'm starting to think you don't really care about our quest anymore."

The sun set beyond the cedar trees. Bran led them into the forest, along the compound's western fence. They reached a place he assumed to be near enough to the big storehouse, but out of sight of the guards by the forest gate. He made ready to burn through the boards in the wooden fence. There was no need for ropes or acrobatics this time.

"Bran?" Nagomi asked quietly just as he was about to cast his spell.

"Yes?"

"What are you planning to do once you get your dragon back?"

He turned around and saw Nagomi look at him intently, waiting for an answer. Her face, in the flickering light of a flamespark, was serious and sad.

"We'll run away and hide somewhere in the forest. Emrys should manage all three of us for a brief flight."

"That's not what I mean. What will you do *after* that?"

What was she expecting him to say? He was a stranger in a foreign land, a fugitive with a price on his head. His home was Gwynedd, far beyond the western horizon, not the alien land of Yamato...

"I... I'm not sure," he lied. "I should probably fly to Dejima, and get some help there... find out what happened to my father, maybe, if he's still alive..."

"I see," replied Nagomi and said no more. Her lips were pursed tightly, and her eyes darted away from Bran, into darkness.

Satō sighed and stood between him and the priestess. "Let's leave that until we have made it through, shall we?"

Nagomi nodded.

Bran touched the fence with his open palm.

"*Llwch!*" he whispered, and with a flash, the boards turned to sawdust, leaving an opening big enough for them to squeeze through.

Suddenly he staggered back and almost fell. Satō supported him.

"What is it? Surely that little spell – "

"No, that's not it. It's Emrys, for a moment I thought it..." Bran frowned and shook his head. "Now it's gone. Let's hurry. I've got a bad feeling."

Captain Kiyomasa's battle instinct told him this was the perfect night for a surprise assault. Everyone in the shrine was busy preparing, watching or taking part in the *kagura* performance. There were crowds in the courtyards and among buildings of the outer enclosure; there was chaos, loud noise and bright lights. There had already been a disturbance the night before, when the dragon suddenly awoke in the middle of the night. It turned out to be a false

284

alarm, but it was enough for the Captain to order all of his men to stand guard throughout the night of the *kagura*.

Satsuma's wizards were also agitated, though none of them could quite tell why. Their magically enhanced intuitions warned them about some vague threat. Between them and Kiyomasa's men, whoever decided to attack the shrine would have to be desperate, mad, or have access to resources available only at the rank of a *daimyo*.

There had been no open conflict between the *daimyo*s since the last of the rebellions, over two hundred years ago. Any lord who dared to wage war on a neighbour faced the full wrath of the *Taikun*'s armies – and utter disgrace. Besides, which *daimyo* would be able to strike undetected, here, in the middle of Satsuma territory? Saga was too far away, Sagara too weak…

Logic, then, advised against there being any threat of a major strike against the shrine, either on this night or any other. But this was not the time or place to depend on logic and reason. There was a real, living and breathing dragon kept asleep in the inner compound. There were wolf spirits attacking armed men in the middle of the road. Some evil lurked in the dark woods around Kirishima. No, logic could not be trusted anymore. Something was bound to happen on this night, the Captain could feel it with every hair on his body.

Once again he made sure that the sentries were awake and watchful, that the weapon and armour racks were in place and that Heishichi's wizards were doing their job, whatever it was.

THE ISLANDS IN THE MIST

As night fell, evening fog began to rise from the wet grass. It thickened quickly in the stale, damp air.

"This is just what I needed," he scoffed, "mist so thick you can barely see the end of your sword. Where did it come from? I don't remember it being so bad last night."

He shrugged and wrapped his kimono sash tighter.

"Can't be helped, I suppose. It's been a muggy evening."

He ordered the lookouts to announce their position loudly once in a while and went towards the outer compound, hoping to catch at least a glimpse of the performance before the change of guards.

They hurried between two long houses with wide colonnades of cedar under broad eaves, towards the storehouse. Bran could still hear the noises coming from the dance stage, the fireworks and sound effects going off and the cries and applause of the enthusiastic crowd.

In contrast, the inner shrine was eerily quiet and empty. There were no birds singing, no frogs croaking, no insects buzzing, none of the background noises he remembered from the previous nights. It was as if all the living things had disappeared from the shrine. The compound was filled with an evening fog so thick and pale it seemed unnatural.

Nagomi whispered, confirming his fears.

"I know this mist."

"How?" asked Satō.

"It's the same mist as in Honmyōji."

As they ventured deeper into the shrine, the fog thickened even more around them. Bran could only see for less than thirty feet ahead.

"It's going to be hard to find our way around if it gets any worse," said Bran.

They found a low wall and azalea bushes to hide behind and tried to crawl as close to the storehouse as they could without arousing suspicion. Was it the same wall he had hidden behind with Atsuko; the same bushes where he had smelled her skin?

He soon spotted the great, dark blue shadow of the stilted building, carved out of the gloom by a few stone lanterns spread throughout the compound. The fog seemed to be at its densest here, as if emanating from the storehouse itself.

"Something's wrong," Bran whispered. "There should be guards."

As a waft of wind spread the curtain of fog apart for a brief moment, they saw the bodies of five samurai lying face-down on the grass before the storehouse. The building's gate had been shattered open. Bran closed his eyes, trying to contact Emrys. The link was still there, but it was much more subdued, as if the dragon had been hidden behind some new kind of barrier, even stronger than Heishichi's spell. In that instant, the noise from the outer courtyard quietened as there was a pause in the performance.

"I hear battle!" Satō stood up from behind the wall, trying to pierce through the fog. The clanging of weapons and the sound of battle cries came from the direction of the forest gate.

"It's over there!"

"I know," replied Bran, "that's where my dragon is."

"Then the Crimson Robe must be there too," said Satō with blazing eyes.

CHAPTER XV

He woke up with a headache more intense than any pain he had ever suffered. Every heartbeat released lightning strikes from the corners of his eyes. He could barely stand up. Moaning, he crawled to the basin in the bathroom and splashed his face with icy cold water. It helped a little, enough for him to gather his senses.

With his head bandaged with wet cloth, Koyata staggered to the street and then wandered the merchant district in search of a herbalist open at such an early hour. He found one, as expected, nearer the harbour, where the taverns started. Many a late night reveller queued up at the counter of old Nagayoshi.

The pharmacist took only one glance at Koyata's pained expression and bandaged head and reached for a well-worn cupboard. He took out a large square tablet of pressed brown powder.

"Break off a chunk and dissolve it in a cup of water – or saké, if you feel brave enough."

"I'm not drunk," the *doshin* said, weakly.

"It doesn't matter. This will deal with any pain."

"What is it?"

The pharmacist smiled. "For you, *doshin-sama*, this is sugar and rice flour." Koyata shrugged – he didn't care if it was Cursed Weed as long as it eased his ache. He took the tablet and reached for the money, but the pharmacist stopped his hand.

"On the house, *doshin-sama*."

I have to remember to check his warehouse one day, Koyata thought and winced. Even thinking was painful.

He returned home and lay on the floor, waiting for the brown powder to start working. He was in no shape to work today. Lately he was doing much more than was expected of him anyway. He had led several raids on the dens of the *rōnin* connected to the night attack on the Magistrate. He had been trying to discover where the grey-clad samurai had come from and gone to. He had investigated the rumours of the man in the purple cloak who had been asking many strange questions and then vanished without a trace.

He deserved rest. Perhaps it was the exhaustion that brought on the headache. Koyata was not young anymore. He reached for the basin he had brought near his bedding and changed the wet cloth on his forehead. The lightning strikes continued to pound mercilessly.

At length the medicine seemed to have started working. The ache lessened, but disturbingly, the flashes of light under his closed eyelids intensified. There seemed to be a pattern to them, a complicated design of red lines. Koyata opened his eyes and then closed them again. The pattern continued to flash, and now there was no doubt – he was beginning to see other vivid images, blinking bright against the black screen of his eyelids.

A dirt floor – a man crawling in his own blood – a stone watchtower concealed among pillars of black rock – a dark valley on a slope of jagged boulders – a fuming mountain overlooking the sea…

The images flashed in repeated succession and all the while the red pattern pulsed in the background. After what seemed like an hour, the pain started returning – the powder's effectiveness was subsiding. As his head began to throb again, the images under his eyelids melted away, replaced by the familiar lightning strikes.

He stood up abruptly; blood rushed from his head and he almost fainted, but he swayed to the cupboard and broke off another chunk of the brown tablet. This time he simply swallowed it. He had to know what the strange vision was. He had no power of prophecy like the priests – of that he was certain. It was almost as if somebody was sending him a signal…

He waited for the images to return. They were weaker this time, but since he was prepared, he could spot more details. The red pattern was drawn in blood on the dirt floor. The fuming mountain was scarred on the sea-ward slope. The man was tortured and beaten but alive and, beside him, lay another man with a face torn by a jagged scar. Koyata had seen this scar somewhere before.

The interpreter. And the other man – was he the wizard, Takashima?

He knew the mountain. His grandfather was a fireman in Shimabara and had died on that broken slope, rescuing villagers from the lava flow. It was far away, but he could reach it in a day, perhaps, if he made haste.

Koyata grabbed the brown tablet, thrust his *jute* truncheon into his sash beside the short *kodachi* sword and ran out.

"No, I don't care about your cousin's inn. We're not stopping at Kuchinotsu."

The old steersman snapped his toothless mouth shut and shook his head. The sky was turning dark and the waves grew higher on the evening breeze.

"*Kuso*! Here's a golden coin – do you recognise it? Have you seen so much money in your life?" Koyata shook the piece before the steersman's face. "This is what you will get if we reach Shimabara before night. And this," he said, tapping the truncheon's handle, "is what you will get if we won't."

The steersman's arms drooped. He turned the boat to the wind and raised the sail as high as he could. The boat picked up some speed but it wasn't enough.

When the evening star twinkled above the horizon, Koyata gave up at last.

"Just put us to shore wherever you can. I will walk the rest of the way."

When he reached a tavern on the outskirts of Shimabara it was past the Hour of the Rat and, at first, the landlord refused to let him in. Even calling on his authority helped little – this wasn't Kiyō, after all, and the people here had little respect for the city guards. At last, a mixture of pleading, threats and calling on the virtues of his grandfather, caused the door to slide open.

"All right, all right, you will wake up the guests! What have you been eating?" the landlord cried, waving his hand before his nose, "you reek!"

"Medicine – for my head. Please, I just need a roof to sleep under, I will be gone at dawn."

"So you've said – and trust me, I'll make sure of it."

Why is he so hostile? What is wrong with this place?

He bit off another chunk of the brown tablet and swallowed. The bitter taste no longer disturbed him; in fact, it was now sweetly pleasant. Soon the powder started working its magic and he was able to fall asleep.

It was dawn again when the boat wobbled up to one of the many piers of the Shimabara harbour. All through the night Master Tanaka had guided it around the crescent-shaped peninsula, following the blood beacon's weakening call, making notes, trying to determine with more precision where the signal was coming from.

"We will rest a while and then start on our way up the Unzen Mountain," he decided, upon consulting his notes and maps. His companion nodded silently.

What an odd fellow, thought Hisashige. Etō was, reputedly, one of the most trusted and skilled of *daimyo*

293

Naomasa's retainers, but his constant grim vigilance was most unnerving.

He knew the road to the top well. Mount Unzen was just across the narrow sea from Saga and he had often taken the trail. All along the winding path there were countless hot springs flowing from the volcanic rock, bringing relief to aching backs and limbs. If only they were not in such a hurry he would gladly soak his old weary body once again.

As they sat down to a quick breakfast, Hisashige noticed a familiar narrow face at another table. The flared nostrils were unmistakable, as were the triple dragon-scale markings of the Hōjō clan on his vest. The other samurai noticed them also and rose to greet them.

"Yokoi-*dono*!" Master Tanaka bowed, "what a timely meeting. What are you doing in Shimabara?"

"I'm on my way from Kiyō where I had some errands to run. You've met young Motoda, my pupil?" A barely adolescent man standing behind Yokoi bowed deeply, silently.

"Kiyō?" the old mechanician eyed him suspiciously. He knew Yokoi Tokiari was a mutual acquaintance, but he wasn't certain how much the man could be trusted.

The samurai leaned down and lowered his voice.

"Truth be told, I am investigating a disappearance of a certain *Rangakusha*."

"On whose authority?"

Why would Kumamoto be interested in the Takashimas?

294

"My own," replied Yokoi, straightening back. "Or rather, his heir."

"You've seen Satō-*sama?* Is the boy all right?"

The samurai nodded with a smile. "I see you know which family I'm talking about. He was fine when I last met him – although it was in the strangest of circumstances and I can't vouch for his safety now. I was hoping I could help in the search for his father, but alas, I could find no clues."

"Then what are you doing *here?*"

"What do you mean? I'm waiting for the ferry back to Kumamoto. My mission has failed."

"But – " Hisashige hesitated. He still wasn't sure how much the other man could be trusted. Then he remembered the divination. *The strength of allies...* " – but Takashima-*sama* is here!" he finished in a whisper, "on Mount Unzen."

Yokoi stared at him in amazement for a while then clapped his knee in joy.

"Good fortune brought us together! Tell me, tell me all, how come you know of this? But I will let you finish your breakfast first. We shall be waiting outside, pondering the twisted paths of Fate!"

Master Yokoi travelled in an elaborate, four-man palanquin and so, to keep up with him on the journey, Master Tanaka reluctantly had to rent one as well. His was a light, two-man piece, a little more than a cushioned chair with curtains. It allowed him to soak in the scenery of the mountain path and inhale the sulphur-infused air which he knew were good for his old lungs.

Etō refused a transport and instead walked at a hurried pace beside the two palanquins, ever watchful, as did young Motoda on the other side. The blood trail was now faint but it led them unmistakably straight up the mountain slope, a dome of black lava a few *ri* east of the main peak. The entire eastern mountain-side was sliced off as if with a great knife, a terrible mark left upon the earth by the devastating earthquake.

Master Yokoi loudly expressed his dissatisfaction with their chosen route, but had no choice but to follow. As the palanquins climbed up the path the wind whistled through the rocky outcrops and it seemed to Hisashige that the spirits of the thousands that perished in the Shimabara catastrophe still filled the land with their wails and despair. Even sixty years on, no plants grew upon the black, scarred stone. Past the huts of the quarry workers and poor farmers who struggled with their buckwheat and radishes on the hardy soil there were no settlements and the path seemed to end amid the rubble and outcrops of lava.

"Time to leave the palanquins," said Hisashige, climbing out of his vehicle. The wind dispersed the clouds and the sulphuric fumes and the pale sun was high up. He looked down, towards the harbour and the sea stretching to the azure horizon. Through some phenomenon of echoes the sound of the crashing waves reached his ears even here, mixed with the cries of the kites and the shouts of the fishermen.

"Are you certain of this, Tanaka-*sensei*?" Yokoi asked. He came up to the chunks of lava rock, perforated like a petrified sponge, piled across the path and searched for a way forward.

Hisashige focused on the beacon. He could barely sense it now, its power almost spent. He opened a small round box at his sash and looked at the geomantic compass inside. The needle wobbled and stabilised, pointing towards the peak of Mount Unzen.

"We're not far," he said.

Etō came up to them and said quietly: "I found a passage on the left side of the rubble. It's narrow, but we can make it."

They ordered young Motoda to stay with the increasingly uneasy porters and either wait until nightfall or follow if they could find another way. Then, one by one, they sneaked through an opening among two large boulders. Once past this obstacle, the path wound onwards, into an even more inhospitable land. There were no birds here bar a few carrion crows observing them curiously from the tops of the lava outcrops. The rock formations took on more fantastic shapes; sharp, jagged pillars and arches of black stone. Still they could see no trace of any place where the missing *Rangaku* scholar could be held captive.

The mountain top was within their sight and Master Tanaka was beginning to lose hope. What if Shūhan had only been carried through this dire place when he had sent his signal? He could be somewhere entirely different by now...

Just then, Etō discreetly tapped him on the shoulder.

"We are being followed," the samurai whispered.

"Are you sure?"

Etō looked offended for a brief moment, then nodded. "Let us hide around that next corner and wait," he said.

They referred the matter to Yokoi and all three hid behind a massive pillar of volcanic rubble. Etō drew his sword noiselessly and raised it above his head.

"Careful. It might not be an enemy," cautioned Hisashige, wary of his divinations.

A man walked slowly and carefully from around the pillar, holding one hand to his head with pained expression. Etō waited until they were certain the stranger was alone and then leapt out from the shadow, blade aimed at the man's chest.

"*Halt!* Who are you and why are you trailing us?"

"I could ask the same of you."

His hand reached for the handle of his truncheon but the fierce-looking samurai twitched the blade threateningly. Koyata tensed. He ran out of the brown powder some time ago and his head was beginning to thump again, though noticeably weaker than before.

"You could, but there's three of us and one of you," the samurai said coldly. "Besides, it's you who had been following us since Shimabara."

"I'm not following anyone. You are merely going in the same direction as me – it seems."

He could not decide whether they were friends or foes. They may have been allied with whoever was keeping Takashima captive, but one of the samurai wore the triple-scales of Hōjō and the other two bore the bamboo-shoots of Saga, the protectors of Kiyō. These were good credentials.

"I am following the red pattern," he said. "Perhaps you could explain to me what it is."

The oldest of the three stepped forward with an astonished expression. His head and beard were grey, almost silver, and his eyes were wise and well-meaning.

"You're a wizard?"

"I am *doshin* Koyata of the Kiyō town guards," he bowed low, "and although I know many *Rangaku* scholars, I am not one myself."

The grey-haired man whispered something to the other two. The one who bore the Hōjō markings nodded in agreement, but the other one remained unconvinced. At last he, too, lowered his sword.

"The pattern you seek is a beacon of help," explained Master Tanaka after they finished their introductions. "Sent by a friend of ours. Though why or how it reached you all the way in Kiyō, I cannot tell."

Koyata decided not to share with them the details of his investigation into the mystery of the Takashima mansion. He trusted them, but not much.

"Have you found the gorge of jagged stones yet?" he asked. They looked at him blankly.

"The black watchtower then?"

"We don't know what you mean," said Master Tanaka. "I was guiding us using divinations and geomancy."

"In fact, we were at a loss as to our direction," added Yokoi, "the path doesn't seem to go any farther."

Koyata looked around. The landscape was familiar; he had seen it before, flashing in his mind. He ran up to the next bend in the road and looked down.

"Over there," he said, pointing to a cluster of boulders with a lonely crippled pine struggling to take root in the cracks of the lava. "Follow me."

Past the boulders was a narrow gully which soon grew to the valley of jagged stones he had seen in his visions. He bade them crouch down and they made their way carefully between the rocks.

The lowest part of the gorge was green, overgrown with lichen and moss and a few gnarly trees. Water trickled from some spring in the mountainside, yellow and smelly. Beyond the spring rose a high tower of black stone, a square base with tapering walls supporting the slender second floor, reachable only by a ladder. The third level, rising above the edge of the gully, was built of cedar beams, once golden but now darkened with soot and smoke, underneath a triangular roof of black tiles.

Two spearmen in familiar grey uniforms guarded the entrance. A few more patrolled the valley, while a group of men and women worked behind the watchtower tending what looked like a very poor vegetable patch. There was one more building at the very end of the gorge – a living quarters for the guards and servants, guessed Koyata.

"The servants are here, but the master is away," said Master Tanaka, consulting his geomantic compass. "Can you smell the stench of blood?"

"I can smell nothing but brimstone," said Yokoi, shaking his head.

"It's faint, but it's there," agreed Koyata. "What does it mean?"

"I don't know. Evil things. But the needle is steady and I detect no more magic in this place than is present in an average *Rangaku* abode."

"Perhaps Takashima-*sama* is no longer here," said Yokoi.

"There's only one way to find out," said Koyata, drawing his short *kodachi* sword. He noticed the silent samurai, Etō, do the same with his weapon.

"There must be at least eight swordsmen in this valley," said Yokoi, "are you sure it's wise to just charge them like that? I mean, I can aid you with my blade but Tanaka-*sensei* here is, if you'll excuse me, past his prime…"

Hisashige's eyes glinted. "I would not insist on coming here if I thought I'd be a burden, Yokoi-*dono*."

"I did not mean…"

"Observe."

The mechanician took the lacquer sheath hanging by his belt and instead of drawing a sword he unscrewed the hilt and pulled out a short iron rod with copper wire coiled around it.

"*Teppō!*" gasped Yokoi.

"A Bataavian thunder gun," said Koyata studying the weapon. "I've read about them but never seen one. Are you a good shooter?"

"Good enough. But I reckon I can only charge this toy enough for one shot before the fight is over."

"Then make it count. I suggest the commander of that patrol on the right. He seems to me the toughest of the bunch."

They huddled behind a wall of piled rocks, waiting for the three-man patrol to come within range. Hisashige turned a gear on his gun and the copper coil lit up red. He aimed it carefully and pulled the trigger. The recoil almost threw the weapon from his hand, but the lightning hit the grey-clad swordsman straight in the chest, killing him instantly. Forking bolts grazed the other two men, throwing them into a daze.

Koyata and Etō leapt over the rocks and struck the other two *rōnin* down before they managed to recover from the stun. The *doshin* noticed that Yokoi stood back, only feigning a fight. *Two against six*, he counted quickly, *and they're not bad with swords, I bet. What was I thinking?*

Three more swordsmen ran up to them from the other side of the gorge. Koyata drew his *jutte* truncheon, trapped an enemy's sword in the hook protruding from the handle and pushed forward, tripping the grey-clad man's left leg. The swordsman fell down and never got up, a *kodachi* blade firmly embedded in his chest.

This felt nice. This was just like in the old days, fighting the smugglers and the bandits on the streets of Kiyō harbour. Koyata looked up – Etō fought two men at once, with three more running towards them. *Spears. Kuso. Doshin's* short weapons were no match against the pole arms. He turned to Yokoi, still waving the sword harmlessly at the back.

"Be useful!"

He grabbed the samurai by the sleeve and swung him around. Yokoi fell forwards, bumping into one of the grey uniforms. Etō did not waste the opportunity; one of his opponents was dead within seconds. Koyata finished the other one with a truncheon blow to the head.

"You fight well for a town guard," the samurai spoke, catching a quick breath.

"But now I'm afraid we've met our match," Koyata said, nodding towards the spearmen. Etō prepared himself, but his grim face twitched, betraying nervousness.

A sudden thunder echoed throughout the valley and one of the spearmen fell on his face with a cry. The other two halted and turned, looking for the owner of the gun. Etō yelled and jumped at the closest of them; Koyata followed, although he could only hope to distract his opponent. He dodged too late, tripped on a stone and the spearman thrust and pierced his side, almost pinning him to the rock. Koyata grabbed the shaft and struggled with the *ronin*, disregarding the pain.

A sword struck the bamboo shaft, splintering it in two. The spearman stumbled, losing his balance, falling straight onto the blade. Koyata rolled aside, letting the *rōnin* drop to the ground before finishing him off with the short sword.

"You're hurt!" Yokoi-*dono* helped him up. The *doshin* knelt on one knee, breathing hard, holding his bleeding side. As far as he could tell, his vital organs were still intact. All the enemies were dead. Etō was also bleeding from a cut, though not a severe one. Master Tanaka climbed out of his hiding place among the rocks, where he had crept during the fight, and helped to bandage the *doshin's* wound with a strap of cloth. Yokoi's nostrils were wider than ever, as were his eyes. His sword was bloodied. Koyata realised it was this blade that shattered the spear.

"Thank you, *tono*. And apologies for earlier. I was unspeakably rude."

"No, no, that's quite understandable. We were all fighting for life. But now we must hurry into the tower. I'm afraid the ladder…"

"It's fine. I'll keep watch."

The men and women tending to the garden had already disappeared into some nooks and crannies of the mountainside. The way to the tower lay open. Etō and Master Tanaka climbed the ladder first, followed by the ever cautious Yokoi-*dono*.

More sounds of battle came from inside the tower, followed by another thunder clap from Master Tanaka's gun. Soon the door opened from inside and Master Tanaka appeared carrying a bloodied, battered body. Yokoi climbed the ladder behind him, with another man in his arms. Last came Etō; his sword was broken and his right arm hung limply along his side. When the silent samurai reached the ground he staggered and fell to his knees.

"What now?" the *doshin* asked wearily. The make-shift bandage around his stomach was soaked through; he was badly in need of a doctor or a priest. "We'll never drag them back to the path. I'm struggling to stay up as it is."

"We won't have to," said Master Tanaka smiling. He pointed to the ridge of the valley where the young Motoda stood waving and shouting.

"It was madness," the *doshin* said, laughing quietly and wincing as the wound in his side twitched. The old priest taking care of the local shrine had barely enough power to stem the internal bleeding. "I would never have dreamed of charging a fortress like that with just four men."

"All my divinations confirmed my endeavour would succeed, but even I did not believe them in the end," said Master Tanaka, shaking his head.

They were sitting in the common room of the headman's house near the foot of the mountain. The porters managed to carry them down only to the first village; there the injured had to rest, waiting for the more skilled healers to arrive from Shimabara.

With Etō out cold in the headman's bedroom alongside the men they had brought from the watchtower, there were now just three of them left to decide the next important matter: what to do with the freed captives.

"I'm not sure I understand," said Master Tanaka when Yokoi-*dono* raised the question.

"Surely each of us had his reasons for coming here. Who of us will take the scholar back home with them?"

"Naomasa-*dono* has already prepared a house in which Takashima-*sama* will rest far from prying eyes," replied Tanaka.

"He could do the same in one of my Kumamoto villas," said the other man, "What about you, *doshin*? What were your orders?"

"I have no orders, *tono* – I told you, I came here of my own accord. The Magistrate officially announced the scholar dead. But if they ever found out he was alive and I helped him escape…"

"Do you have any family in Kiyō?" Master Tanaka asked.

"I don't – but I don't see what that's got to do – "

"My master's domain may be small, but Naomasa-*dono* has many connections in high places. He would gladly arrange a position for you somewhere else. A better position, in a more prestigious city."

Koyata noticed Yokoi-*dono*'s nostrils flare like two mountain caves. *He's started bargaining already. There's three of us and my vote decides. What can you offer, Hōjō clansman?*

He knew Master Tanaka's proposition was hard to beat. Hosokawa may have been a powerful *daimyo* here in the south, but he was one of the outer lords, with no access to the *Taikun*'s court. The lords of Saga, on the other hand, were welcomed even to the *Mikado*'s palace.

"The treasury of Kumamoto would be at your disposal," Hosokawa's retainer said uneasily.

A bribe, then. Not bad, but not good enough, either. Why was that injured scholar so important, anyway?

"I will have to think about it," Koyata said at last, standing up from the low table and bowing. "The wounded can't be moved until the priests arrive, so we're not in a hurry."

"Of course," both old men agreed eagerly.

"Oh, and what do you want me to do with the interpreter?" he asked.

"Who?"

"The other prisoner."

Yokoi-*dono* shrugged. "We didn't even know he was there, did we, Tanaka-*sama*? Is he of any interest to you?"

"I have a few questions to ask when he wakes."

Yokoi-*dono* waved his hand. "Do whatever you wish."

THE ISLANDS IN THE MIST

CHAPTER XVI

As the evening turned into night, the guards began to grow bored and restless.

In the north-western corner of the inner compound, a dirt path led through a small, simple gate deep into the forest. Once, it must have been built for transporting lumber for construction and repairs straight from the woods, but nowadays it was mostly used by those of the priests who went into the forest to gather herbs and mushrooms.

Apart from the gate leading towards the main courtyard, this was the only way in. Captain Kiyomasa, aware of the strategic value of this point, made sure to put a strong watch around it. Two of Hosokawa's retainers agreed to stand at the gate alongside several of Kiyomasa's own spearmen.

"Damn this fog," said the younger of the two, almost a boy, wearing striped *hakama* and blue kimono, "have you ever seen anything like it? It appeared so quickly, almost as if conjured."

"Hold your tongue," the other samurai reprimanded sharply, "you'll bring us bad luck with your superstitious talk. We should be glad the fog is here, nobody will attack in this kind of weather."

"Do you really think somebody would want to assault this shrine?"

"The Captain seems to think so, and that should be good enough. He's getting his orders directly from Hosokawa-*dono*, so we can't argue."

The younger guard scoffed.

"That upstart. I don't see why – "

"He's a good soldier. And he comes from a great family."

"A distant, impoverished offshoot. Thinks too much of himself, if you ask me."

"Good thing nobody asks you, then."

The younger samurai scowled and paced around the brazier to keep himself warm.

"There's nothing worth taking here," he said.

"I'm not so sure. Have you seen that great storehouse in the middle? There's three of our own posted in front of it and those mages keep coming in and out. I think there's some kind of barbarian weapon inside. You know what they say about those Satsuma folks."

The other retainer nodded. There was no need to add anything more, the Shimazu clan were well known in the South for their illicit contacts with the Westerners and it only made sense that there was some kind of device or magical treasure stored in the shrine that had something to do with the barbarians.

"I wonder how long we are supposed to endure this schedule," he said. "Night is for sleeping, not for standing outside in the fog."

"It shouldn't be more than a day or two; I think we're supposed to get some reinforcements from Kagoshima."

The guard in the striped *hakama* raised his eyebrows.

"Shimazu samurai are coming here? That should be interesting."

"I hope they will bring something to drink. This place is supposed to be famous for booze, but I haven't seen so much as a flask of saké since we've been stationed here!"

"What do you expect, it's a shrine. The only saké they have is the one on the sacrificial altar."

"Too bad Gensai-*sama* has gone with the princess. He always had something to wet one's lips."

The older guard started to laugh along with his companion, but the laughter died in his throat.

"Hark! Did you hear that?"

There was a strange, gurgling noise on the other side of the gate, where two of Kiyomasa's footmen stood guard. The old samurai stood up, grasping the hilt of his sword in anticipation.

"Everything all right over there?" he shouted. There was no response.

"Should we raise the alarm?" asked the other.

"Not until we know what's going on. You, man, go and see what's going on the other side."

Kiyomasa's spearmen, as ordered, opened a small wicket in the gate and peeped outside. A cry of terror froze in his throat.

In an instant, the gate burst open with a terrible force, showering the two samurai with shards and splinters of wood. Retainers drew their swords, ready for a fight. The soldiers stood alongside them, except one, who started running towards the alarm gong. The runaway was the first to die, slain by a dart thrown by an invisible enemy from within the mist.

"Who's there? Show yourself!" the older samurai cried, but there was nothing in front of them, only the milky white wall of the fog. A great spear blade cut through the air with a metallic whistle and one of the soldiers fell down without a sound, slashed almost in two. The blade struck again, but this time it clanged against the retainer's sword.

"Not so good against a real swordsman, eh?" the samurai boasted. "Come out and fight like a man, coward!"

A blood-curdling cackle rang out and the owner of the halberd moved into the light. It was no man, but a dark human-shaped shadow, hovering one foot above ground. It held the spear in its long, thin arms with confidence. Its head had no face, just a blank surface, but even without a mouth, it laughed.

The other retainer froze in panic and dropped his sword to the ground. The demon moved towards him in a flash and slashed his torso in two, then turned against the first one. The old samurai managed to parry another blow of the great spear, but he felt his shoulders stiffen with unearthly cold. *This is no match for a mortal man,* he thought briefly.

"Fall back to the storehouse!" he cried to the remaining soldiers. "Alert the priests!"

Before he could add anything more, the spear's blade pierced his chest. He slashed his sword at the ghostly shadow, but it went through the enemy as if through thin air.

With dying eyes, he saw the shadow move further into the mist and darkness in search of other prey. A human appeared in the gate, barely visible in his black *yamabushi* robes. He was leading two pairs of oxen by the reins. The animals were pulling a large, four-wheeled cart with a flat platform. The hermit looked down at the dying samurai with pity, then whistled. Immediately, six samurai appeared around him, dressed in identical grey uniforms.

The three guards posted at the storehouse huddled around a flaming tripod brazier. The day was warm but as night fell and the evening fog rose from the dewed grass, it got cold.

"I wanted to see today's *kagura,*" complained one of the samurai, sporting a large moustache in the fashion popular in the southern islands. It made him look older and more distinguished from the other two.

"Worthless rural circus tricks," scoffed another, shortest of the three, but wearing the most elaborate armour, old style, inherited from some belligerent ancestors. "I'm telling you, there's nothing like the Hakata theatre. These peasants don't know proper entertainment; it's just illusions and smoke for them."

"It would still be better than sitting here in this fog," replied the first one and sneezed, "only *shinobi* enjoy nights like this."

"There's no such thing as the *shinobi* anymore. The *Taikun* made sure of it."

Azumi scowled under her hood and clenched her fists. She was sitting a few yards away from the brazier, and had been observing the outpost for the last couple of hours, waiting for the signal to strike. They did not see her, of course; the *tengu*'s invisibility cloak was flawless.

"I know that! It's just a turn of phrase," the guard sneezed again.

"Here, have some of this," the third guard reached out to the first one with a gourd, "it's local, powerful stuff."

"Aaah, excellent! *Kanpai!*" the moustachioed samurai raised the gourd straight to his lips and took a great swig. "Enough!" laughed the owner of the gourd, "leave some for us."

"That hit the spot. Those Satsuma folk sure know how to brew!"

"Wait, did you hear that?" the armoured guard stood up, listening to something in the distance.

"I can't hear anything but the music and clapping from the stage."

It's enough that I heard it.

"It sounded like a cry coming from the lumber gate."

"Well, it's about time those lazy oafs announced their position. We should too, come to think of it," the moustachioed guard rose and cried out, "All clear at the store – !"

He didn't finish. A throwing dagger stuck into his throat. The other two jumped to their feet, swords drawn. "Attack! We're under attack!" cried the short samurai, slashing wildly into the air in front of him, searching for the shadowy attacker. Azumi observed this with slight bemusement, standing just a few feet away. *This is too easy.*

"Strike the gong!" the armoured guard cried. The other samurai leapt towards the alarm bell but before he could reach it, three sharp, small missiles whistled through the air and embedded themselves in his neck. Gurgling, he fell on his back. The remaining guard's eyes widened in fright as he recognized the star-shaped missiles for what they were.

"It's impossible… you have been vanquished! The *Taikun* had you all killed!"

"Not all of us," said Azumi, casting the hood of the *tengu's* cloak enough to reveal only her cold eyes. They were the last thing the guard saw before the swift sickle blade on a long iron chain bypassed his parry and slashed through his trachea. His spinal cord severed, he died in an instant.

The lid creaked open. Inside the plain lacquer box lay three slim vials of crystal glass, enclosed with porcelain stoppers. The contents of one was brown and murky, the other grass-yellow, like weak *sencha*. The third liquid was clear, transparent.

THE ISLANDS IN THE MIST

Brown was for sleep. Yellow was for waking. Clear was for death and glory.

Sugimoto took a gulp from the yellow vial. It was his time to join his brothers in the storehouse. The liquid itself was cool and bitter, but soon the familiar warmth and sweetness spread throughout his body. He felt his veins swell – this was the most unpleasant effect of taking the extract of the *maô* plant. This and the cramps that started wandering from his calf muscles to the shoulders. He shook his head and opened his eyes wide. He felt refreshed and fully wakened.

The earth wizard opened the door of the long, one-story building in which they had been settled and stepped outside, into the fog. Everything seemed bright and crisp. He knew the effects of the extract would soon subside and then he would have to take another sip to be able to stand through the night. And then another. The intervals between sips had been decreasing in an alarming manner.

His task was dull and dangerous, but he took pride in it. Master Heishichi had chosen Sugimoto and five other wizards from among many dozens. He deemed them most trustworthy, most reliable, and most skilled. Trained at the best of schools, by the best of teachers. Entrusted with the protection of Satsuma's greatest secret.

He stumbled over something in the mist. He looked down and saw, at his feet, the body of a dead samurai with a long, needle-thin blade sticking out of the neck.

"Look, there's somebody still alive!" the wizardess cried and, ignoring Bran's plea for caution, darted across the small courtyard in front of the warehouse towards a lonely figure, leaning its back against the pillar. The man raised his sword against them with a shaking hand.

"The pilgrims from the forest?"

"Captain Kiyomasa!"

"What are you doing here?"

Bran passed him by and ran up the short stair, through the burst open gate into the storehouse.

"It's gone," he cried from inside. "There're more bodies here."

He ran back out.

"You're too late," Kiyomasa said and started coughing.

"What happened?" Bran asked, looking at the five dead bodies.

"What does it look like? We were attacked by all sorts of enemies. *Shinobi*, ghosts, *rōnin*, you name it. The wizards came to help us and they're now fighting at the gate," the Captain said, pointing towards the fighting. The mist in the direction of the gate flashed with explosions and thunderclaps like clouds during a storm.

"Have you seen a man dressed in a crimson robe?"

"That I have not," the Captain replied and winced as blood spurted from the wound in his side. Nagomi knelt to examine it, but Bran stopped her.

"We don't have time for this, he'll be fine."

317

"I'm no use in a fight anyway," the priestess protested, shaking his hand off her shoulder. "Go on, I'll join you soon."

He hesitated for a moment, uncertain what to do. Satō made the decision for him.

"Come on, they're getting away!" she cried and pulled him into the mist.

The wheels of the oxcart squeaked away in the distance, accompanied by the shuffling of four pairs of hooves. The mist muffled the sounds.

"Wait," the *Daisen* commanded, stopping his students from pursuing the attackers. "Let Kiyomasa's men bleed them out first. We must act smart if we are to avenge our brothers."

Only Sugimoto and two others remained from the onslaught. Three mages lay dead inside the storehouse; the corpses made for a gruesome sight. They had no chance to defend themselves. The sudden assault disrupted the spell patterns and the backlash of magical energies destroyed their bodies even before the blades of the assassins reached them. That one of the grey-uniformed *rōnin* had also been caught in the torrent and torn apart was little consolation.

"Spread out," said the *Daisen*. "Ishida, go right, along the wall. Try to find out how they manage to control that damned *dorako* on their own." Somehow the enemy had succeeded in safely transporting the beast onto an oxcart. "Takano, help those soldiers out before they make a mess of themselves."

318

As the other two disappeared into the mist, the *Daisen* looked at Sugimoto and said:

"Stop that oxcart. At any cost."

The dense fog was no trouble for him; on the contrary – he could see the enemy without being seen himself. Sugimoto was adept at using the True Sight, a secret technique he had learned directly from a Bataavian tutor at Nansei. From a safe distance he was able to assess the situation and choose the best course of action undisturbed.

His attuned element was Earth. A rare, unpopular element, not as spectacular as Fire or Air. He could not bring down lightning or summon walls of flame like his brothers; but he felt comfortable and calm manipulating the slow, steady rhythms of the rock and sand, safe in the knowledge that, when the time came for action, he could be just as effective as the other wizards.

He knelt down on one knee and touched the ground with both hands, sensing the miniature ley lines like mole-tracks in the moist soil. He whispered the spell word and tugged at one of the invisible strings.

A ripple passed under the dirt like a giant earthworm and headed straight towards the oxcart surrounded by enemy soldiers. Several men fell down as the ground quaked beneath their feet. The wheels of the cart buckled and one of them snapped.

The earth so close to the magical nexus was pliable, yielding. With little effort the wizard turned the flow of the ripple against the bullocks pulling the cart. The animals lowed in panic as the earth beneath them started trembling and cracking. The man leading the oxen, a *yamabushi* in black robes, stopped and looked around, searching for the unseen enemy but Sugimoto was safely hidden in the thick, impenetrable mist.

The wizard was so concentrated on the task that he only noticed the shadowy demon behind him at the last moment. He turned around quickly to face the new danger. The spear's blade, aimed at his back, pierced the chest.

But Sugimoto was not one to go down easily. His dying hands grabbed the spear's pole. The grey shadow tried to wrestle it from the wizard, but his grip was strong. With freezing hands, he reached inside his sleeve and took out the third of the crystal vials. Pouring its contents down his throat, he felt a sudden surge of power. He knew the energies released would destroy him just like the mages in the storehouse, but it was too late to worry about it. With the last breath, with the last surge of power, Sugimoto cried the words of the most dreadful of his spells; the Earth Tomb.

"*Aardse Nor!*"

The earth opened beneath his feet and swallowed the wizard, the spear and the bewildered *yōkai*.

A jolt went through Ozun's body, and the *yamabushi* dropped to his knees, supporting himself on the staff. Azumi appeared at his side promptly, helping him up.

"What is it?"

"I lost the *yōkai* – the one from Honmyōji."

"Lost? How?"

"I don't know, but … it cost me dearly."

"Do you need help?"

"No." Ozun shook his head and wiped the trickle of blood from his nose. "Get back to the others. They need you now more than I do. I sense more danger coming."

She nodded and slipped back to the rear of the convoy.

He pulled on the reins strongly, forcing the oxen to press on. The animals lowed in protest, the broken wheel snapped away and the axle ground in the mud, but the cart moved slowly on. There was yet hope. The cart was their passage to freedom. The load had to be delivered to the Master; only then would he set them free from his service.

The ground around the cart was scorched, cratered and scarred with fire and lightning. The few remaining *rōnin* and Nanseians – masters of unarmed combat recruited from the southern islands – huddled behind a *kekkai* shield, helpless. The enemy wizards, out of range of any counterattack, were launching missile after missile against the weakening barrier.

"What happened to your other men?" Azumi asked the commander of the grey-shirts, a bulbous-eyed youth with big ears and a gloomy face. There should have been at least a dozen of his *rōnin* in the troop but she could see only half that number.

"We were ambushed by a bunch of samurai while you were flirting with your lover-boy," he snapped. "At least we got all of them."

"That shield won't hold for much longer," she said.

"You think I don't know that?" He ducked as another missile exploded a mere foot ahead of them.

"There's another wizard hiding in the fog; much more powerful than those two," explained one of the Nanseians. His bald head was covered with sweat and burn marks. "He keeps us in check whenever we try anything."

"Why don't you make yourself useful, *kunoichi*, and do something about it," said the grim-faced *rōnin*.

"Useless brawlers," she scoffed. She wrapped herself in the cloak of black feathers and disappeared into the shadows and fog.

From behind, the enemy wizard in glasses seemed almost unassuming. Thin, long-limbed, awkward in movements, a weakling by any measure. While Azumi approached him under cover of her magical garment, he performed a series of strange dance-like movements, waving arms in wide curves that left fiery traces in the air; a powerful incantation that even she, otherwise blind to magic, could sense through her quivering skin.

"Behind you!" a voice shouted a warning. The wizard turned around, losing focus; his incantation fizzled out in a noiseless flash.

Who dares?

Nobody should have spotted her. The black feather cloak was a powerful artefact – the old *tengu* fought long and hard defending it. Who could have peered through its magic?

She glanced to the side. Two youths ran, without stopping, towards the oxcart. One in *Rangakusha* clothes, paid her no attention. The other, in an indigo kimono, looked straight at her with a puzzled expression as he ran past. She recognized them in an instant.

Them! Here?

Was the red-haired girl somewhere here as well? She quickly shook off her surprise and started after them, forgetting all about the wizard.

He, however, would not let her go so easily.

"Show yourself, filth," the wizard cried and whirled his hands in half-circle, igniting the very air before him.

Her feather cloak caught fire.

THE ISLANDS IN THE MIST

CHAPTER XVII

The priestess tied the bandage and rose from her knees. Her hands felt warm on his cuts; blue light spread from her fingers and where she touched, the wounds closed.

"We need to help them," the girl said, ready to run after her friends.

"No, child," he said shaking his head. "Heishichi-*sama*'s wizards will hold out, and if they don't, we won't help them. But we can get help. Come with me."

He led her away from the battle, towards the outer court. As they got closer, the lights grew brighter and the cheerful din of crowds grew louder. The pilgrims were oblivious to the massacre in the inner compound and the Captain could almost forget about the fighting himself. The *kagura* dance entered its most frantic, loud and magical phase, the tale of *Mikado* Jimmu's battles with the Long-legged Man.

"Gather as many priests as you can," the Captain shouted over the noise, "and meet me back here. But don't take long."

"They… they may not hear me out," said the priestess.

"Tell them I sent you. Tell them it's about the Treasure."

The priestess nodded and her red hair disappeared into the crowd. Kiyōmasa himself ran to the Offertory Hall, where he was hoping to find the head priest and his retinue. If his suspicions were right, they would need all the holy hands they could find.

Near the gate the fog thinned out and Satō could see everything more clearly. It was a regular battle; the *Rangakusha* wizards, led by the lanky man in glasses, and Captain Kiyomasa's soldiers, strove against a few *rōnin* swordsmen in grey uniforms. There was a mage also among the enemies, some *onmyōji* who cast protective spells from behind, but she could not see him very well in the fog.

An oxcart was stuck in the middle of the lumber gate, one of its wheels shattered. The bullocks whined, trying to pull the broken wagon across the muddy road. On the cart's platform lay a large box-shaped container covered with a black cloth. The cargo was guarded only by two *rōnin*.

"Do you see the Crimson Robe anywhere?" asked Bran.

Satō shook her head.

"This is still sacred ground. He must be hiding somewhere outside."

"Can you take care of those two swordsmen?"

"Easily." She could feel the energies of the nexus surging through her. It made her dizzy and exhilarated at the same time. Even the headache disappeared. "Leave them to me."

She put on the leather glove and drew her sword. The gears whirred, the brass arrow reached half-way through the dial. She focused her power into the blade and the feedback, multiplied in the air sizzling with the energies of the nexus, made the sword jolt so hard she almost dropped it.

She had not been trained in using the True Sight, but even she could now faintly see the flow of energies around the blade; sparkling currents of blue and white light. When she drew the first frost rune, its image hovered for a moment in the air.

"*Bevries*," she whispered. The word thundered and echoed throughout the space between her and the *rōnin*. A wave of cold air spread from Satō's sword and froze both of the warriors into solid blocks of ice.

Such a powerful spell should have left her exhausted and spent, but she was barely tired, only a bit short of breath. She felt almost omnipotent. What would happen if she used blood magic here? *Would I even survive so much power?*

The box of the cart burst open in a flash which blinded her for a second. She laughed. Bran must have also discovered the ease with which magic worked in the shrine. Smouldering splinters and bits of molten iron showered the ground around her.

The oxcart was still moving, although even more slowly and laboriously than before. She saw Bran scramble off the ground, shake his head and jump onto the moving platform.

THE ISLANDS IN THE MIST

The boy struggled with the chains wrapped around some
large dirt-green metallic bulk lying on the cart. It had taken
Satō a long while to realise what she was looking at through
the mist and smoke. When she did, her heart skipped a beat.
The dragon, asleep, bound and famished, was a far more
magnificent sight than she could have imagined. No pictures
or description could have given it justice. Greater than any
animal she had ever seen, dwarfing the two oxen with its
immense girth; in its sleep it seemed more like a statue
carved of a single piece of jade, a pile of green jewels heaped
into the form of a beast. Moonlight shimmered off its scales
and black sickle-like claws. She knew she should feel the
onset of the dragon fear just looking at it, but all she could
feel now was awe.

Bran struggled with the chains and at last he managed
to burn them through, but the dragon still would not waken,
the leathery wings – *wings!* – still folded neatly along its sides.
The boy noticed something outside the gate, jumped off the
wagon and disappeared beyond the wooden fence.

The two *rōnin* in front of her were still encased in their
icy tombs – she wondered if they had already suffocated or
froze to death; for a moment she did not care. She could not
care about anything now that she had seen the dragon. But
there were more enemies to worry about, the other
swordsmen and Nanseians were busy with their own fight
somewhere in the fog – and she could now see more clearly
the mage standing behind the oxcart, casting shields and
deflecting the magical onslaught with a heavy iron mace.

She recognised the pattern of his magic first, then the
weapon, and then, as the smoke from another explosion
parted, she noticed that the mage had no head.

328

Pressing his hands and face to the scales, he felt the heat inside and smelled the faint brimstone of the dragon's breath. At last, after so many days, so many miles, so many misadventures they had been reunited. But even this close, he could no longer get through. His Farlink signals bounced off a powerful barrier; an envelope of strange, unfamiliar magic surrounded the dragon's mind and what little he could glimpse through the gaps in the barrier did not bode well. All he was getting was hunger, fury and confusion, the first symptoms of feralisation.

The spell maintained by the wizards inside the storehouse he could penetrate easily. But this was a new spell that no human could sustain alone. There had to be either a conclave of mages somewhere nearby or a focus artefact of immense power. Bran looked around quickly. Behind the oxcart the balance of the fierce battle of wizards and swordsmen was slowly tipping against the defenders of the shrine, but Bran had no time to worry about that. In front of the cart, holding the oxen reins, stood a man clad in black garb with a bell staff in his right hand. Their eyes met for a moment as the man struggled with the whining animals, forcing them to drag the vehicle despite a broken wheel. They were some twenty yards from a vermillion *torii* gate which stood further down the forest path, indicating a symbolic boundary of the holy ground. The driver was desperate to reach it, ignoring the fact that the cage and the box around the dragon was no more, ignoring even Bran who was standing at the platform with the sword drawn.

Looking further along the road, Bran saw somebody in the shadows of the trees, a silhouette ominously black with streaks of red light in the True Sight. In the stranger's hand an orb of dazzling white light shone like a tiny sun, a nexus of energies flowing around Emrys. Whatever spell held the dragon, this must have been its source.

With a yell, Bran leapt from the cart and started towards the *torii* gate; only now did the man in black let go of the reins and stood before Bran, the jingling staff raised like a lance in defence.

"Out of my way!"

Bran slashed wildly. His sword bounced off the staff with a loud clang and as he flung himself forward, the enemy swung around and suddenly appeared behind, grabbing him by the neck with the shaft of the staff and pulling him close.

"You're out of your league, child," he whispered "Get out of here while you still can."

Bran struggled but couldn't set himself free. He hit the enemy under the ribs with the pummel of his sword, but it was futile. *If it was my old sword, it would punch the breath out of him*, a thought flashed through his mind.

He grasped the arm of his captor and cried "*Rhew!*" The sleeve of the black robe lit up in flames. Its owner released Bran for a moment, but then caught the boy by the shoulder and spun him around. The last thing Bran saw was the butt of the staff heading for his face.

The oxcart was still lodged between the gate posts when they arrived. The battle seemed to have moved beyond it; the Captain Kiyōmasa could not see well through the smoke and mist, but he heard the clashing of the swords clearly. He did not know who was fighting whom. All his men, he had found dead. Of the wizards, the only one still standing was *Daisen* Heishichi, whom he discovered wounded and staggering by the side of the road. One of the priests healed his most threatening wounds and the *Daisen,* after gulping some of his life-giving extract, soon rejoined the fray.

The *dorako*! The priests halted seeing what lay on the oxcart. Only Nagomi kept on running.

"Come on! Look, a child is braver than you," the Captain shouted, prodding the priests onwards. Shaking off their fear, they grasped their weapons – long, iron-bound sticks – and followed the red-haired girl.

Bran came to seconds later, lying in the dirt of the road, his sword flung away from his hand. His nose was swelling up quickly and he was nauseated with dizziness. There was an odd buzzing in his head, a sort of murmur growing slowly from deep within. The man in the black robe was standing above him, putting out the flames on his sleeve.

"Ozun!" a strong, dark, commanding voice cried out of Bran's sight, "this is the rider! Bring him to me."

Ozun leaned over Bran and reached out to lift the helpless boy from the ground when a red shadow appeared behind him. He turned around; a sword flashed. Instinctively, he raised his left arm in a vain attempt to block the falling blade. The Matsubara sword cut through the forearm with ease, lodging itself deeply into the man's skull.

The severed hand dropped to the ground. The hermit threw his arms apart and fell backwards, without a sound.

Satō was standing in the middle of the road, her sword chipped and bloody. She was trembling and breathing hard. The man in black robes lay in the dirt beside Bran, his skull cleaved through. Blood and gore oozed from the crack onto the road. Bran scrambled to his feet hastily and tightened the satchel straps. He felt the acrid taste of vomit gathering in his throat.

He stepped over the dead body towards the girl and touched her on the shoulder. She raised her eyes to him, wide open, blank and black, but then shook her head and was almost back to normal; only her hands kept trembling. Looking down he noticed one of her hands, clad in a leather glove, was covered with fresh blood.

"You're hurt!"

"It's nothing. Bran, back there is the *onmyōji* – the one from the forest! I did all I could but he just won't die. I think the body must be animated by the Crimson Robe, he must be somewhere near – "

She stopped and narrowed her eyes looking past Bran's shoulder. He turned and saw the man behind the *torii* gate, now fully visible, standing in the middle of the road. His eyes gleamed golden in the gaunt, smooth face, his long black hair flowed gently over the shoulders draped in a robe of bloody crimson. The jewel in his head, an orange-sized orb, was also the colour of blood.

"*You…!*" Satō let out a hoarse cry, but before she could leap towards the Crimson Robe, out of the fog and shadows appeared a woman in a tight ashen-grey uniform. Her face and arms were burned, her eyes sweltering with fear and hatred. She saw the cleaved skull in the dirt and a wordless, feral howl escaped her lips. Madly she spun back towards Bran and Satō, flinging a deadly chain-and-sickle weapon towards them.

The wizardess barely managed to dodge the throw, more by instinct and luck than skill. The sickle's bronze blade grazed Bran's cheek, drawing blood. Weapon-less and struggling to keep focus required for spell-casting, he pulled back, knowing he would just get in Satō's way for the moment.

It was an equal match. The woman's skill with her weapon was far superior to Satō's swordsmanship, but the wizardess had her magic to rely on, flinging icy missiles and freezing the ground beneath her opponent's feet to catch her off balance. Bran had never seen anyone fight like that, so seamlessly matching magic and fencing. This must have been how the battle mages of old fought, in the Age of Unbridled Flame.

There was no time to admire the duel. Still more enemies ran towards them, as if answering to the unspoken summons of their master beyond the vermillion gate. Bran wondered briefly whether they had defeated everyone in the shrine already, or whether they chose him and Satō as the greater danger to their plans. The grey-clads and the unarmed warriors had gone past the oxcart and were almost upon them, but a greater danger loomed in the fog, slowly lumbering its way towards Bran. He could see it now without the need for True Sight – the headless, rotting body of the mage slain in the forest by Dōraku's twin blades.

Bran swooped underneath another flight of the sickle-chain, rolled and, jumping to a stand, summoned his Soul Lance. He hesitated. He could not strike a woman in the back, even in fierce combat. He shouted a challenge.

The woman produced a glass ball from her sleeve and shattered it on the ground. A cloud of smoke burst forth and by the time it cleared, she was gone.

Satō blinked and turned immediately towards the newly arrived enemies, clashing swords with the first of the grey-clad *rōnin*. Ice shards shattered around her, a cold wave covered the swordsman's arms with hoar. Bran looked around and, not seeing the woman in grey anywhere, joined the wizardess at her side, protecting them both with a front-facing *tarian*. His lance flickered worryingly. When did he lose so much energy? He had barely cast any spells…

Our last stana, he thought grimly, watching as more enemies arrived. *Where's Nagomi? Dia they get her as well?*

He caught a movement behind his back, to the right. He turned quickly, but not quickly enough. The sickle blade, hurled in a smooth, precise motion, flew towards Satō's back.

As in slow motion, Bran saw a white, blurry figure leap in between Satō and the blade, arms apart, red hair billowing. The bronze blade struck, wedging itself between ribs. Nagomi cried out and fell down.

Satō turned around, releasing the full power of her enchanted blade against the woman appearing from the shadows, cutting through the deadly weapon. The links shattered, the ice covered the rest of the chain and, through it, the assassin's entire arm.

The wizardess dropped to her knees beside Nagomi. The priestess gasped a few times and then collapsed limply into the arms of her friend.

Captain Kiyomasa arrived a mere few seconds too late. The little priestess lay dying in her friend's arms. And the boy... something strange was happening to the boy. He grew in stature, taller and broader than any man. Wings sprouted from his back, spreading across the width of the road. He roared like a tiger and spewed hot smoke and steam from his reptilian snout.

Even the ever stoic *Daisen* reeled from the monstrosity. The enemies pulled away. The creature made one giant leap towards a female assassin who was clutching the remnant of a chain and handle in half-frozen arms, and cast her aside like a rag doll. The woman hit a tree and collapsed to the ground. Several of the *rōnin* ran up to creature, trying to stop it, but the swords failed to penetrate the celadon scales, serving only to irritate the monster as it continued on towards the *torii* gate.

One more person stood in the creature's way. *No, not a person*, Kiyomasa realised. *A headless corpse.* By some unholy magic it still moved, casting all manner of spells against the approaching monster, waving a heavy iron mace threateningly.

The creature's clawed arm reached out and ripped the mace out of the corpse's hands, snapping it in two like a stick of bamboo. It then grabbed the animated body and in a swift move ripped it in two.

Kiyomasa did not even try to comprehend what he was seeing. The dragon, sleeping on the oxcart, would be enough to rid anyone of their senses. Now he observed a battle between a moving, headless corpse and a boy transformed into a giant lizard-like beast. He knew only one way to react.

He drew his sword and with a battle cry – "*Hosokawa!*" – he rushed towards the enemy swordsmen.

CHAPTER XVIII

Nagomi!

Something snapped within him. He cried and lunged forward in fury. There was nothing in his heart but hatred; hatred towards the woman who attacked his friends, towards the Crimson Robe, towards the men who had kept him chained in the cage for so long...

Wait, that's not me. That's Emrys.

Does it matter?

Pent-up energy surged within him; the dragon had plenty of it to spare. A grey-clad swordsman ran up to him – small and weak in Bran's eyes. One swipe of a clawed arm and the man fell down, blood spurting from a shattered hand. Another of the *rōnin* came up from behind; his sword broke on the scaled back. Bran turned with a fierce cry, which turned into a dragon's rumbling growl. He grasped the swordsman's head in his hand. The skull gave in with a satisfying crack.

These are not the men I want to fight. Where is the one with the spectacles?

He shook his head. *No, not that one either.* He turned again, towards the *torii* gate, where the creature in the crimson robe stood in the shadows, still calm, still smirking.

The demon stretched out a hand holding a large blood-red orb. His lips moved and the orb lit up with bright crimson light. Bran swayed as if some unseen force had hit him, but managed to swipe one of his claws and hit the enemy on its outstretched hand. The red jewel flew away. The smirk vanished from the demon's face. Another of Bran's swipes reached the face, leaving bloody claw-marks on its cheek.

The demon leapt back and drew his weapon, a giant, two-handed sword. Magic shimmered along the blade.

We don't want to fight it. Bran staggered away, trying to refocus. Emrys was growing stronger and, somewhere deeper, another will was stirring. *Shigemasa! If I have to balance all three inside me, I'll go crazy.*

The enemy. Concentrate on the enemy. But it was too late. In the crowd of clashing warriors, Emrys spotted the lanky man in the horn-rimmed spectacles. Bran tried to pull his attention back to the Crimson Robe, but the dragon's fury was too strong. He felt the beast's mind yank away and suddenly he was alone. The Farlink was broken.

A roar sounded behind Kiyomasa's back, a roar so tremendous it silenced all other noises. Even the sounds of the festival in the distance quietened down.

The Captain turned around and watched in terror as the green dragon rose, shook off the chains and spread its majestic wings. It roared again and in the wrath of its bellow the Captain heard the words of an ancient cry. He stood transfixed, unable to move or even blink.

"Down, fool!"

Daisen grabbed him to the ground and covered with his own body as the dragon lowered its head towards them and spewed a tongue of flame as hot as the Sun itself.

The dragon beat its wings twice, as if testing, before leaping off . It flew towards the shrine, fast like the wind, spewing flame and steam, setting fire to the thatched buildings of the inner compound, destroying everything in its path. In a few seconds, it was gone.

Bran's strength quickly waned. The Dragonform could no longer be sustained with Emrys awakened, away and unheeding his call. He was confused, lost, for the first time in long years not sensing the Farlink connection. He made a step towards the Crimson Robe. The red orb lay in the ferns by the roadside, shining with a pulsating light, making him dizzy and nauseated. Something was amiss, but he couldn't think straight enough to realise what it was.

The Crimson Robe scrambled towards the jewel. Bran tried to stop him but was too slow, too lumbering in his still transformed body. The demon rose, clutching the orb triumphantly. The gem beamed brightly and Bran swayed again under its spell. He felt tired and sleepy. Waves of negative energy flowed from the jewel. What little of the dragon power remained within him subsided; he could feel it seeping away.

The *Daisen* crawled off the Captain with a moan, holding his hands over his face. Kiyomasa scrambled to his feet, ready to fight again, but all around him was deadly quiet. Many of the priests and the grey-clad *rōnin* lay dead, scorched by the dragon's breath; the others were afraid to get up.

In this silence, the Captain watched the boy-turned-beast sway aimlessly to and fro, disoriented. He seemed to be shrinking in size. A long-haired man clad in a dark red robe emerged from the shadows of the *torii* carrying a great *nodachi,* a horse-slaying sword, effortlessly in one hand, and an orb of red crystal in the other. The man stuck his weapon into the ground, reached with the freed hand inside the folds of his garment and drew a bunch of white paper dolls. He scattered them on the ground under his feet.

"Ozun!" the man spoke with a voice that sounded like death itself. "I have not yet released thee from my service. *Fight for me!*"

At this signal a dark, sinister spirit rose from the dead man's body. It grabbed the bell staff and stomped it one-two-three times. In answer to the summons, the spirits of all who had been slain until now also abandoned their bodies and appeared, hovering above ground, holding ghostly, translucent weapons.

"Abomination!" cried the Head Priest. The surviving acolytes and the samurai picked themselves off the ground, ready to continue the fight. "These spirits must be put to rest!"

The battle broke out anew around the oxcart. Magic, holy power, ghostly energies and steel blades clashed in deadly strife. Wherever a man fell, the jingling staff brought him back to life. But whenever a ghost was slain, either by cold blade or by a priest's exorcism, one of the paper dolls at the Crimson Robe's feet burned out.

Somebody was calling Bran's name. A despairing voice slowly made its way through to his brain, muddled with fury, bloodlust and confusion. *Satō...* She was still kneeling on the road, clutching the priestess in her arms. Blood trickled slow and thick from the wound in Nagomi's chest. The priestess was pale, her lips blue, her chest no longer rising in frantic gasps.

"*We need to run, boy,*" a familiar voice in Bran's head broke through the dizziness.

"Shigemasa! Where have *you* been?"

"*No time to explain now! Trust me, I've seen many battles in my life, and this one's already lost. We'll be slaughtered if we stay here.*"

"But there's ...nowhere to go."

They were now cut off from the shrine by the heat of the fighting. Even the female assassin was getting back up, ready to attack again. In the opposite direction stood the Crimson Robe, the orb in his hand shining with cold red flame.

A few men led by Captain Kiyomasa broke through towards Bran. They all stopped between him and the

Crimson Robe, but for one youngster who charged at the demon.

The Crimson Robe's great sword flashed forward, cutting right through the man. Black fangs dug deep into the priest's neck. The man died with a gurgling cry and the demon cast him aside.

Bran stared at the dead body which shrivelled and shrunk, like a quickly drying piece of meat. The Captain's voice broke him out of the stupor.

"I don't know who or what you are or what you want, but I won't have a priestess's death on my conscience. If she's still alive, save the girl and yourself," said Kiyomasa. "We'll guard your retreat. *Run!*"

Bran cast a final look at the oxcart and the remnants of the chains. Emrys was lost from him, a dot of green flame in the night sky, flying westwards first, then turning north in a blind rage.

"I'll come for you," he sent a thought through the Farlink, without a hope of an answer. "I'll find you again."

"*You'll find your death in a moment,*" a nagging voice in his head urged him on. Having a little of the Dragonform strength still left in his arms, Bran lifted the unconscious priestess gently from the road, nodded at Satō to follow him and darted into the deep forest.

The right sleeve of her kimono felt wet. Surprised, she looked down – it was soaked with her own blood. At some point in the heat of the battle, either the assassin's sickle or one of the grey-clad swordsmen's blades must have reached her.

Though Nagomi was dying, she was not dead yet, and Bran – if it was still him under the dragon-like disguise – was carrying her off into darkness, into safety. She noticed a sword lying on the road, and a leather satchel with a broken strap. She picked them up, thrust the weapon into her sash alongside the Matsubara sword and, clutching the bleeding arm, she followed the transformed boy, crying with pain.

The Crimson Robe noticed the escape and tried to follow, but she did not let him. She now had no need for the glove's needle; she had plenty of fresh blood to spare. She put her left palm on her right arm, and the right hand on the trunk of a nearby cedar tree, discharging all the power she had left and could yet summon. A web of thick ice spread from tree to tree, halting the demon's pursuit.

The release made her tremble with ecstasy. She gasped. *So much power! If only I could wield it all of the time…*

She heard the sound of a bugle conch in the distance, but there was no time to wonder what it meant. Bran was already out of sight. She forced herself to run.

The dense forest muffled the noise of the battle and suppressed the lights from the blazing shrine. She was running in silence and darkness now, up the hill, along animal paths and lumberjack cuttings. The Westerner in front of her grew smaller. She was too exhausted to wonder at what had happened to Bran. His monstrous form now all but subdued, he looked almost human again. He seemed to barely have enough strength remaining to carry Nagomi's body over the gnarled roots and wet, mossy stones.

"Are they… following us?" he asked, breathing heavily. His voice was croaking, guttural.

"They must be – but I don't see anyone yet."

"I… have to… rest."

They halted by a large rocky outcrop, a wall of sheer black basalt. Bran laid Nagomi down. Part of the assassin's sickle blade, snapped off by the ice, was still sticking out from her breast, as they were afraid to remove it without a way to stem the resulting bleeding. The priestess was pale like a sheet of paper but she was still breathing.

"I can't run with her anymore," Bran explained feebly. "My strength is gone."

"We'll just have to carry – no! They're already here!"

A glimpse of crimson appeared among the trees in the light of the moon. The pursuit was almost upon them.

"Young *tono*! Over here!"

Satō looked at where the voice was coming from. A girl was crouching on top of the outcrop, her hands reaching down towards them, touching about blindly.

"Yōko! How did you…"

"Please hurry!"

The wizardess pulled herself up the ridge and, together with the servant girl, took Nagomi's limp body from Bran, who soon followed to the top.

"It's no use, he'll find us here," said Bran quietly, as the Crimson Robe appeared at the glade, accompanied by the ashen-clad assassin and a bald Nanseian warrior.

"Please come," Yōko whispered and led them, crouching, into a small niche in the rock. The nook seemed barely large enough to fit one person, but turned out to be an entrance to a long cave. When they were all inside, Bran lit a flamespark. They were in a tunnel.

"What is this place?"

"I do not know," Yōko replied, "but there are tunnels like this all over t' mountain. As old as Gods, some say. This one will lead you to safety. Please hurry."

"How did you know we'd be here?" Satō asked. They were now running down the damp corridor lined with limestone flags. Bran was still carrying the priestess, but he was now only his normal height and strength, and could barely keep up the pace.

"I – 'tis a curse," the girl said shyly. "Sometimes I have visions of t'future… sometimes I can see things others can't. Like the samurai inside you, *tono*," she said. "This is how I learn'd about them tunnels in the mountains. I saw terrible danger befalling you all, and I jus' had to try and help."

"And with a gift like that, you are still just a kitchen servant?"

"T'priests say there is no *kami* presence about me and that only a demon could grant such powers. It is a grace that they allow me to stay at t'shrine at all."

It was obvious to Satō that the girl had latent magical powers and, with proper training, could grow into a great wizardess. *The priests must have known it, too. They keep her hidden from Shimazu…*

"This is the end of t'tunnel," Yōko pushed open a wall in front of them. There was nothing but darkness and silence outside. "You are far from t'shrine, and from your enemies. I hope yer' not too far from help," she said.

"What about you?" asked Satō. The girl smiled.

"My place is in t'shrine. The priests will need all help they can get."

The girl rummaged for a while in the clump of tall ferns.

"'ere, take this."

She handed them a small, shallow clay vessel and a bundle of grey cloth.

"What is this?"

"It's a holy light that the priests carry 'round. Your friend will need it."

"These are my things!" Satō said astonished, checking the inside of the cloth bundle. "My books, my notes!"

"Thank you," Bran put the vessel into his satchel. "A day will come when we will repay our gratitude properly.

"Please, just let me sister know I am well, young *tono*."

"I will, Yōko," said Satō.

The hatch closed behind the girl and the tunnel exit blended into a rock wall. They were in the middle of the cedar forest, somewhere high up on the slopes of Mount Takachiho. Bran laid Nagomi's body on the damp ground and lit a faint flamespark. Satō knelt beside the priestess to assess her injuries. Around them, the wood was dark and deadly quiet.

Satō took out a dagger and cut through Nagomi's sash. He turned his eyes away as she parted the priestess's robe to reveal the pale, soft skin underneath.

"Don't be so squeamish," the wizardess said, misunderstanding his embarrassment. "Can you still do magic? I am spent."

He nodded. "It's fading away without my dragon, but I still have a little left…"

"I need you to cauterise the wound."

She guided his hand. "Here." Bran produced a small, hot flame from his fingers at the same moment when Satō pulled out the sickle shard. Nagomi stirred in pain, but the wound bled only for a second. Pink dribble trickled out of the corner of the priestess's mouth.

"We need to find some help," said Bran, "or find a way back to the town."

"The Crimson Robe must have his men all over that place. Besides, I don't even know how to get back. I lost my orientation in that winding tunnel."

She tore a strip off her sleeve and prepared a makeshift bandage.

"There must be *something* around here," she added, looking around. "Why else would a tunnel lead into the middle of the forest?"

"I'll go look for some shelter. It's starting to rain. Will you manage on your own?"

"I may not be a spirit healer, but I've observed Ine and Itō-*sama* at work many times. I'll do what I can."

He returned a few minutes later. The rain was beating on the leaves above, but not much of it was yet getting through the canopy.

"How is she?"

"I don't know. She's still breathing... barely... she may be bleeding inside – there's no way to tell. Have you found something?"

"There's a cave nearby. But the path is slippery. We need to be careful."

They wrapped Nagomi in her robe and carried her slowly along an old, long-overgrown path leading up the hill. The priestess seemed fragile, as if her body was made of fine china. She moaned and whimpered quietly a few times when Satō or Bran tripped on the slippery stones.

Using his sword like a machete, Bran cut through the vines, ferns and bracken to clear the way. The path wound for a few hundred feet over slick outcrops and lichen-covered boughs. At last it reached a large cave, carved by a trickling waterfall in the volcanic rock of Mount Takachiho.

Bran's faint flamespark could not light all of it, but he could see the remains of a camp on the floor.

Hunters or poachers, he thought, seeing remnants of traps, bits of rotten rope and broken-off shards of spearheads and harpoons.

"It smells," Satō wrinkled her nose.

Somewhere at the back there had to be a fissure leading to the depths of the volcano, from which seeped the fumes, filling the cave with the faint stench of brimstone – but also making it drier and warmer than it at first seemed.

"It's a shelter. And look, there's water," Bran said, pointing to a waterfall trickling away in the corner. "Lay her here, I'll start a fire."

He gathered all the bits and pieces of wood scattered around the cave floor, brought in some of the drier deadwood from the forest and set the shoddy campfire aflame. It burned fast, bright yellow in the sulphur-infused air.

Satō crouched over her unconscious friend, washing the wound with the pitiful amount of water she managed to bring from the waterfall in the clay beaker the servant girl had given them – the only container they had.. Her movements became automatic, rigid, as she struggled to cope with pain, exhaustion, and the shock of battle.

"You're hurt as well," Bran said, touching Satō's shoulder gently where the enemy blade had cut the deepest. The silk of her kimono was soaked red.

She shook her head.

"It's nothing. I've had worse at swordplay trainings."

"It still needs to be looked after…"

"Not until we find help for Nagomi."

"Will she make it through the night like that?"

"We can but pray."

Gently, but forcefully, he sat her down away from the priestess. She had neither strength nor will to oppose him.

"You can do no more now," he said. "In the morning it will be easier to look for help."

"Yes," she answered feebly. "What about you…?" She raised her hand to his face.

Now that the battle rush in his veins had gone, he was feeling the dumb ache in his broken nose again, and the stinging on the cheek where the assassin's blade cut him.

"I got lucky," he said with a forced smile. "Scars only make a man more handsome."

That's what my mother used to say about my father. Am I too going to be covered in scars when I'm old?

He took the clay beaker from Satō's trembling hands.

If I ever manage to grow old…

"What do we do with this?" he asked.

"I don't know…"

Bran put the vessel into Nagomi's hands. A tiny orange wisp of light appeared inside the shallow bowl, flickering weakly. It seemed the priestess's face became more peaceful and relaxed, but it may have been just a trick of the dancing light.

"Look there, by the waterfall."

As if in answer to the holy flame, a tiny sparkling dot appeared above the stream, then another, and another. A cloud of fireflies danced in the shadows like a school of fairies.

"So beautiful," whispered Bran, but Satō rose, picked up a stone and threw it at the fireflies.

"No! Get away!"

The dancing lights vanished.

"What are you doing?"

"It's the souls of the dead coming for Nagomi! I won't let them!"

She threw another stone and then slumped down to the ground, exhausted and dejected. Bran reached his hand towards her.

"We must rest. I'm sure in the morning everything will work out – somehow."

They lay down on the damp, rocky floor. The flames of the campfire illuminated the cave walls, casting strange, trembling shadows. They did not even have blankets to cover themselves from the cold of the night; they had used both their cloaks to wrap up the priestess.

"What was that… charm you were under?" Satō asked.

"Dragonform, the last resort of a rider... I was channelling Emrys's raw magic power – at least for as long as I had contact with it."

"I'm sorry you lost your *dorako*... again."

Bran did not reply. He was trying to remember his actions under the spell's power.

Did I... did I kill somebody?

"I have seen it," said Satō. "Up close. It was magnificent, even bound and locked like that. And then when it rose and spewed the flames... I could feel its power – it was immense."

"Emrys is yet small and not fully grown. You should've seen my father's dragon..."

She sneaked closer to him in the darkness, shivering from cold. He reached his arm around and embraced her.

"Tell me something about it," she urged.

In the darkness he could hear her laboured breathing.

He spoke at last. "Nine years ago my father took me to the hatchery by the Pont-y-Pair Falls on River Llugwy, to let me choose my first dragon."

"You were seven and you were given a *dorako?*"

"I would not get to own it for three more years, while it grew in the hatchery. And it hadn't even hatched yet when we arrived. There were just three eggs to choose from, the baby dragons ready to break out. While we watched, two green heads emerged from the eggs. Viridians of Gwydyr Forest, proud, stout beasts of ancient lineage. Father liked one of them immediately. *Take this one, son,"* he said, *"look at how bright its eyes are."*

"Was it Emrys?"

"No!" Bran said with a quiet chuckle. "Emrys started hatching last. Its egg was smaller, less shiny. As soon as it came out, the hatchmaster wanted to take it away and drown it."

"Why?"

"It was a swamp wyrm. We knew it immediately by the smell. A poor, cheap breed that must have got mixed up with the others. Nobody would offer one of these to the son of Dylan ab Ifor. It would have been an insult."

"What happened?"

"It fought back. It bit the hatchmaster's hand and leapt towards us – it couldn't fly yet. My father wanted to kill it, but I stopped him. The dragon jumped on my lap. It stank of the swamp – it still does – but I didn't mind. It snuggled up to me, seeking protection. I knew then that I never wanted another dragon. Since then, it never threw me off, never bolted, and although I've had it for six years now, it never showed any signs of going feral – until we got here. And now… it is lost."

He fell silent. Satō had stopped paying attention to his story a while ago, dozing off between the sentences with her head resting against his chest.

I lost everything. Emrys, Nagomi, a chance to go home – I couldn't even keep the ring…

It was his last thought before he fell into an exhausted, dreamless sleep.

CHAPTER XIX

The forest air was unpleasantly hot and humid; the wind machine had spluttered and died as soon as they had left Kirishima. With the wizards gone, nobody in her escort knew how to fix it. Atsuko opened the shutters of her palanquin to let the air in, but it did not help much. She yearned for some rain. This year the beginning of the rainy season was remarkably dry.

There will be drought, she thought, *and poor harvest again.* Her heart went out to peasants, striving against bad weather. Satsuma would survive – her adoptive father was a good administrator and made sure there was always enough surplus rice in the villages. But other provinces might not be so lucky, especially if the drought repeated itself the next year, as it often did.

She hoped there would be no famine, like in the year after her birth. People still told dreadful tales of the time. It hit the Northern provinces worst, but Chinzei had been affected by a flood of refugees. It had taken years for the samurai and merchant families to recover from the crisis.

The princess looked around and noticed something amiss about her escort. She motioned to an officer walking nearby.

"Sergeant, where is Captain Kiyomasa?"

"I'm sorry, *hime*, but he received urgent orders from Hosokawa-*dono*."

Atsu quickly counted the samurai surrounding her palanquin.

"Did he also have to take half of my escort with him?"

The officer avoided her gaze, staring at his sandals uneasily. "Yes, *hime*. Those were the orders."

"And is he going to catch up to us eventually?"

"I'm afraid I don't know. But there is nothing to worry about," the sergeant raised his head, "we are safe."

"That's not what I heard. I heard there are bandits in this part of the mountains."

"Merely rumours, *hime*. Besides, the escort is still strong. No bandits would dare attack a troop of samurai!"

"I hope you're right. And I hope your master has good enough reason for ridding me of half the guard. I will have to report to my father about this, of course."

"Of course," the sergeant stared at his sandals again.

"When do you expect us to leave these stuffy forests behind?"

"Tomorrow we descend onto the plains of Hyūga. The winds there blow from the Eastern Sea, so the weather should be more pleasant. Do you need anything, *hime*?"

"Bring me some more water, Sergeant."

"Right away *hime*."

The inn and the small village that grew around it were both perched on the edge of a mountain spur reaching east, deep into the valley of Oyodo River. These were the last vestiges of the great cedar forests. One of the windows in Atsuko's room looked out onto the valley and the vast plain of the Hyūga Province. The Sergeant was right – even here, so many *ri* from the coast, the breeze speeding up the river carried with it the memory of the sea, the promise of the rolling waves and the crying of the kites.

She tried not to think of the journey ahead of her. In a week or so they would reach Akae Harbour and from there embark on a month-long sail to Edo. A month at sea! Stopping for the nights, of course, and with longer interludes along the way in Naniwa and Chūbu; still – she could hardly imagine a voyage so long.

She touched the *obidame*. She had resolved to wear it on her sash at times; it was pretty enough, even with the stone missing, and it reminded her of the green-eyed boy she would never see again. She wondered if his quest had succeeded… *He would have laughed at my fears*. He must have spent months out in the open ocean, suffering storms and typhoons – and maybe even sea monsters… And if he managed to endure all this, what right had she to complain of her little escapade? *No*, she decided, *I will not moan. My father expects me to do my duty and nothing else.*

She heard a horse outside, galloping at first then coming to a stop. She looked out the west window at the road before the inn. A messenger from Kumamoto. What did he want? Was it to take away even more of her escort?

The courier did not dismount. A samurai came out to greet him – Atsuko recognised Kawakami Gensai's thick topknot. The two men exchanged a few quick words and then Kawakami handed the messenger some small item, a piece of jewellery. Sunlight glinted briefly off its azure surface. The messenger hid it in a lacquer container at his waist, nodded and galloped away.

She had little time to wonder what she had just witnessed. As soon as the courier disappeared into the forest, another commotion drew her attention. Cries rose from the direction of the village. Commoners appeared, running down the road, panicking. The patrons poured from the inn, pointing at something and shouting.

Atsuko tried to see what everyone was so agitated about, but the west window was barred with bamboo poles and she could see nothing beyond the stretch of the road in front of the inn.

There was a knock on the door.

"*Hime!* We must be on our way," the servant said.

"What is going on?"

"I don't know. The locals are saying something about the mountain being… on fire. Kawakami-*sama* insists on us leaving immediately."

Eruption? Atsuko shuddered. No volcano had erupted on Chinzei within her lifetime, but she had heard enough terrible stories to fear any mention of the "mountain on fire".

"I will get myself ready."

In a few minutes she was guided by the servants to the courtyard where the black-and-gold palanquin awaited her. Before going inside she stopped and looked up towards the peaks of the Kirishima ridge.

Far away, near the top of one of the conical summits, a long, narrow patch of a dark, hazy wood had been set ablaze. This did not look like an eruption, rather, a strangely regular forest fire. Suddenly, as she was looking, another patch of the forest burst into flames in a straight line going sideways across the mountain slope.

"*Hime,*" the servant girl insisted. Her eyes were full of terror, but in Atsuko's heart curiosity replaced fear. What was going on over there?

She shaded her eyes and looked towards the peak one last time. She thought she could see a dark dot soaring over the mountains, like an eagle but much, much larger. But then it disappeared in the haze and she was no longer sure whether it was just a trick of the eyes.

With a sigh, she climbed into the palanquin and closed the shutters, sealing herself from the world outside.

THE END

APPENDICES

GLOSSARY OF TERMS

(Bat.) — Bataavian

(Yam.) — Yamato

(Pryd.) — Prydain

(Seax.) — Seaxe

aardse nor *(Bat.)* spell word, "Earth Tomb"

amazake *(Yam.)* a traditional sweet drink from fermented rice

ardian *(Seax.)* the Commander of a Regiment in the Royal Marines

banneret *(Seax.)* the Commander of a Banner in the Royal Marines

bento *(Yam.)* a boxed lunch, usually made of rice, fish and pickled vegetables

bevries *(Bat.)* spell word, "Freeze"

biwa *(Yam.)* fruit of loquat tree

blodeuyn *(Pryd.)* spell word, "Flowers"

bugyo *(Yam.)* chief magistrate of an autonomous city

bwcler *(Pryd.)* magical shield covering a fighter's arm, a buckler

cha *(Yam.)* green tea

chwalu *(Pryd.)* spell word, "Unravel"

Corianiaid *(Pryd.)* a race of red-haired dwarves from Rheged

cwrw *(Pryd.)* beer

dab *(Pryd.)* creature, thing or a person

daimyo *(Yam.)* feudal lord of a province

daisen *(Yam.)* chief wizard

dap *(Pryd.)* the same size and shape as something

dengaku *(Yam.)* a meal of grilled tofu or vegetables topped with sauce

denka, —denka *(Yam.)* honorific, referring to the member of the royal family

derwydd *(Pryd.)* druid

dōjō *(Yam.)* school of martial arts or fencing

dono, —dono *(Yam.)* honorific, referring to a noble man of a higher level

doraco *(Yam.)* Western dragon

doshin *(Yam.)* chief of Police

dōtanuki *(Yam.)* a type of katana, longer and heavier than usual

draca hiw *(Seax.)* spell word, "Dragon Form"

draigg *(Pryd.)* a dragon

duw *(Pryd.)* a swearword

dwt *(Pryd.)* a young child

egungun (Yoruba) a holy spirit, also a shaman dancer representing Egungun

enenra *(Yam.)* a spirit born of smoke

faeder *(Seax.)* father

fudai *(Yam.)* an "inner circle" clan; one of the vassals of the Tokugawa Taikun before the battle of Sekigahara

futon *(Yam.)* a roll-out mattress filled with rice husks

gaikokujin *(Yam.)* a foreigner, non-Yamato person

genoeg *(Bat.)* spell word, "Enough" (to mark the end of a continuous spell)

gornestau *(Pryd.)* magical duel

graddio *(Pryd.)* school graduation ceremony

gwrthyrru *(Pryd.)* spell word, "Repel"

hakama *(Yam.)* split trousers

hamon *(Yam.)* visual effect created on the blade through hardening process

haori *(Yam.)* a type of outer jacket

hatamoto *(Yam.)* the Taikun's retainer, samurai in direct service to the Taikun

hime, —hime *(Yam.)* honorific, referring to women of high position

igo *(Yam.)* a board game for two players, using identical black and white tokens

ijslaag *(Bat.)* spell word, "Ice Layer"

inro *(Yam.)* a wooden container for holding small objects, hanging from a sash

inugami *(Yam.)* a dog spirit

jawch *(Pryd.)* a swearword

jutte *(Yam.)* police truncheon

kabuki *(Yam.)* a form of classical dance theater

kagura *(Yam.)* a type of theatrical dance with religious themes

kakka *(Yam.)* honorific, referring to lords of the province or heads of the clans

kambe *(Yam.)* a shrine servant taken from an adjacent village

kami *(Yam.)* God or Spirit in Yamato mythology

kanpai *(Yam.)* Cheers!

kappa *(Yam.)* a water sprite, reptilian humanoid

katana *(Yam.)* the main Yamato sword, over 60cm in length

kaya *(Yam.)* a bright yellow wood used for making igo boards

kekkai *(Yam.)* a magical shield, similar to tarian

364

kimono *(Yam.)* official layered robe of the noble class

kirin *(Yam.)* a chimerical creature of Qin, body of a deer and the head of a dragon with a large single horn

kodachi *(Yam.)* a short Yamato sword, less than 60cm in length

koenig *(Seax.)* the monarch of the Varyaga Khaganate

kosode *(Yam.)* basic, loose fitting robe for both men and women

kun, —kun *(Yam.)* honorific, referring to young persons of the same social status

kunoichi *(Yam.)* a female shinobi assassin

kuso *(Yam.)* a swearword

lloegr *(Pryd.)* Dracaland east of the Dyke

llwch *(Pryd.)* spell word, "Dust"

long (Qin) Qin dragon

mam *(Pryd.)* mother

mamgu *(Pryd.)* grandmother

Matsubara *(Yam.)* the family of katana swordsmiths

metsuke *(Yam.)* inspector representative of the Taikun

mikado *(Yam.)* the divine Emperor of Yamato

mikan *(Yam.)* fruit of tangerine tree

mithraeum (Latin) temple of Mithras

mitorashita *(Yam.)* worshippers of Mithras

mochi *(Yam.)* a sweet made of rice gluten

mogelijkheid *(Bat.)* magical potential

monpe *(Yam.)* workman's trousers

naginata *(Yam.)* a polearm formed of a katana blade set in a bamboo shaft

nodachi *(Yam.)* a large, two-handed sword, over 120cm in length

noren *(Yam.)* a curtain hanging over the shop entrance, with the logo of the establishment

oba (Yoruba) chieftain

obi *(Yam.)* a silk sash wrapped around the waist

obidame *(Yam.)* a buckle for tying the obi sash

oden *(Yam.)* a type of stew

omikuji *(Yam.)* fortunes written on a strip of paper

onmyōji *(Yam.)* a practitioner of traditional Yamato magic

onmyōdō *(Yam.)* traditional Yamato magic

oppertovenaar *(Bat.)* overwizard of Dejima

pilipala *(Pryd.)* spell word, "butterfly"

proost *(Bat.)* Cheers!

rangaku *(Yam.)* "Western Sciences", study of Western magic and technology

rangakusha *(Yam.)* a practitioner of Western magic

reeve *(Seax.)* the Staff Sergeant in the Royal Marines

rhew *(Pryd.)* spell word, "frost"

ri *(Yam.)* measure of distance, approx. 4 km

rōnin *(Yam.)* a masterless samurai

ryū *(Yam.)* a Yamato dragon

Saesneg *(Pryd.)* (slur) Seaxe

sakaki *(Yam.)* a flowering evergreen tree, used to produce **sacred** paraphernalia

sama, —sama *(Yam.)* honorific, referring to peers of the same social status

sencha *(Yam.)* popular kind of tea

sensei, —sensei *(Yam.)* honorific, referring to teachers and doctors

shamisen *(Yam.)* a three-stringed musical instrument

shinobi *(Yam.)* assassin

shōchū *(Yam.)* strong liquor (25-35% proof)

shōgi *(Yam.)* strategic board game similar to chess

shukubo *(Yam.)* accommodation for temple pilgrims

sokukamibutsu *(Yam.)* a self-mummified monk

stadtholder *(Bat.)* the ruler of Bataavia

swyfen *(Seax.)* a swearword

tabako *(Yam.)* tobacco

tadcu *(Pryd.)* grandfather

tafarn *(Pryd.)* tavern, inn

tafl *(Pryd.)* strategic board game, played on a checkered board

taid *(Pryd.)* grandfather

taikun *(Yam.)* military ruler of Yamato

taipan (Qin) leader of a trading company

Taishō *(Yam.)* field marshal, commander-in-chief of all the forces in the field

tarian *(Pryd.)* magical shield surrounding entire body

tengu *(Yam.)* a forest goblin

tenpura *(Yam.)* small fish and vegetables fried in batter

teppo *(Yam.)* a "thunder gun" — hand-held lightning thrower

terauke *(Yam.)* a passport produced by an affiliate temple

tono, —dono *(Yam.)* honorific, referring to a noble man of a higher level

torii *(Yam.)* wooden or stone gate to the shrine

tozama *(Yam.)* an "outer circle" clan that was forced to become the vassal of the Tokugawa Taikun after the battle of Sekigahara

tsuba *(Yam.)* a handguard of the katana

twinkelbal *(Bat.)* sparkleball; a stone used for thaumaturgy practice

twp *(Pryd.)* insult, "stupid, simple"

tylwyth teg *(Pryd.)* Faer Folk, a race of tall, silver- or golden-haired humanoids

waelisc *(Seax.)* (slur) Prydain

wakashu *(Yam.)* an "unbroken" youth, a virgin

wakizashi *(Yam.)* a short sword used as a side arm, 30-60cm in length

xiexie *(Qin)* "thank you"

y ddraig goch *(Pryd.)* Red Dragon

yamabushi *(Yam.)* an ascetic mountain hermit

yōkai *(Yam.)* evil spirit, demon

yukata *(Yam.)* casual summer clothing, simple light robe

GLOSSARY OF CHARACTERS

G<small>WYNEDD</small>

CANTRE'R GWAELOD

DYLAN AB IFOR o Cantre'r Gwaelod

b. 2566 a.u.c. Ardian of the Second Dragoons Regiment of the Royal Marines. Married to Rhian ferch Rhys.

Mount: Highland Silver, Afreolus (*Unruly*)

BRAN AP DYLAN o Cantre'r Gwaelod

b. 2590 a.u.c. A graduate of Dracology at the Llambed Academy of Mystic Arts.

Mount: Rhos Jade, Emrys (*Ambrosius*)

ROYAL MARINES

EDERN mab Gwyn

b. 2526 a.u.c. Banneret of the Second Dragoons Regiment of the Royal Marines. A Tylwyth Teg.

Mount: Highland Silver, Nodwydd (*Needle*)

GWENLLIAN ferch Harri

b. 2577 a.u.c. Reeve of the Second Dragoons Regiment of the Royal Marines.

Mount: Highland Silver, Tywyll (*Dark*)

WULFHERE of WARWICK

b. 2589 a.u.c. Ensign of the Twelfth Light Dragoons, descendant of Richard Warwick the Kingmaker.

Mount: Highland Azure, Eolhsand (*Amber*)

HYWEL AP CADELL o Llyn

b. 2590 a.u.c. Flight-Leader of the Twelfth Light Dragoons

Mount: Eryni Ruby, Taran Goch (*Red Thunder*)

BROUGHTON REYNOLDS

b. 2542 a.u.c. Rear Admiral of East Bharata and Qin Station

QIN

TSENG KUO-FAN "BOHAN"

b.2564 a.u.c. An eminent Qin official, general and scholar, commander of the Eastern Army.

LI HUNG-CHANG

b. 2576 a.u.c. A scholar, officer and translator. Personal aide to Tseng Kuo-Fan.

<u>YAMATO</u>

KIYŌ

MIZUNO TADANORI

b. 2563 a.u.c. *Bugyō* – Magistrate of Kiyō. *Hatamoto* retainer of the Taikun.

KOYATA JŪMONJI

b. 2570 a.u.c. *Doshin* – chief of police – of the Merchant's District in Kiyō

ISHIDA TAKUYA

b. 2566 a.u.c. Lieutenant of *Doshin* Koyata

HIRATA MITSUYU

b. 2574 a.u.c. Lieutenant of *Doshin* Koyata

TSUKINARI SHIGEZAEMON

b. 2578 a.u.c. Captain of the guards of Kiyō Magistrate

BLACK RAVEN SOMERLED

b. 2577 a.u.c. Cast-away, teacher of Dracalish

TAKASHIMA

TAKASHIMA SHŪHAN

b. 2544 a.u.c. A *Rangaku* scholar, head of the Takashima School of Wizardry.

TAKASHIMA SATŌ

b. 2589 a.u.c. Heir of Takashima School of Wizardry.

SUWA SHRINE

HOSOKI KAZUKO

b. 2567 a.u.c. High Priestess of Suwa Shrine.

NAMIKOSHI TOKOJIRO

b. 2581 a.u.c. An interpreter of Dracalish language.

ITŌ NAGOMI

b. 2591 a.u.c. An apprentice at the Suwa Shrine.

IKŌ

A servant girl at the Suwa Shrine

374

SAKUMA

SAKUMA ZŌZAN

b. 2564 a.u.c. A scholar of *Rangaku*.

SAKUMA KEINOSUKE

b. 2594 a.u.c. A student at the Takashima School of Wizardry.

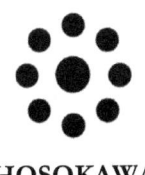

HOSOKAWA

HOSOKAWA NARIMORI

b. 2557 a.u.c. Daimyo of Kumamoto domain, tenth lord of Kumamoto Castle.

SATSUMA

SHIMAZU NARIAKIRA

b.2562 a.u.c. Daimyō of the province of Satsuma, lord of Kagoshima Castle.

SHIMAZU ATSU

b. 2589 a.u.c. Adopted daughter of Shimazu Nariakira, princess of Satsuma.

TORII HEISHICHI

b. 2557 a.u.c. *Daisen,* Arch-wizard of Satsuma.

KOMATSU KIYOKADO

b. 2588 a.u.c. A samurai of Satsuma.

ŌKUBO MINEKO

b. 2591 a.u.c. A court servant girl in the court of Satsuma.

SUGIMOTO YOSHIO

b. 2566 a.u.c. An earth-wizard from Satsuma, student of Torii Heishichi.

KUMAMOTO

MAGONOJO ITSUNEN

b. 2579 a.u.c. A monk at Honmyōji temple, host of *shukubo*.

MOTOMENOSUKE INGEN

b. 2570 a.u.c. A monk at Honmyōji temple, cook of *shukubo*.

IPPONIN

b. 2538 a.u.c., d. 2606 a.u.c. Previous abbot of Honmyōji temple

CHIZONIN

b. 2565 a.u.c. Current abbot of Honmyōji temple

SOZAEMON FURUHASHI

b. 2567 a.u.c. Fifteenth abbot of the Unganzenji Temple

KATŌ KIYOMASA (I)

b. 2315, d. 2364 Founder of Kumamoto Castle, general, one of the *Seven Spears of Shizugatake*

KATŌ KIYOMASA (II)

b. 2570 Captain of the Guards Regiment at Kumamoto Castle.

GENSAI KAWAKAMI

b. 2577 A retainer of the Kumamoto Domain. Master swordsman.

THE ISLANDS IN THE MIST

HŌJŌ

YOKOI SHŌNAN (TOKIARI)

b. 2562 a.u.c. A scholar and reformer at the Hosokawa's court in Kumamoto.

MOTODA NAGAZANE

b. 2571 a.u.c. A student of Yokoi Shonan.

ITAKURA

ITAKURA SHIGEMASA

b. 2341, d. 2391 a.u.c. Daimyo of Fukōzu Han in Mikawa Province, commander of Taikun`s forces during Shimabara Rebellion.

TOKUGAWA

KAYAMA YEZAIMON

b. 2547 a.u.c. Daimyo of Uraga, commander of coastal defences of Edo Bay

MORIYAMA EINOSUKE

b. 2573 a.u.c. Interpreter of Dracalish at Edo court, school friend of Tokojiro Namikoshi

MASAHIRO ABE

b. 2572 a.u.c. Chief Senior Councillor in the Taikun's government

HOTTA NAOSUKE

b. 2568 a.u.c. Senior Councillor in the Taikun's government

MAKINO TADAMASA

b. 2552 a.u.c. Senior Councillor in the Taikun's government, chief of Edo defences.

KUZE HIROCHIKA

b. 2572 a.u.c. Senior Councillor in the Taikun's government.

MATSUDAIRA

MATSUDAIRA NOBUTSUNA

b. 2349 a.u.c. – d. 2415 Commander of the Taikun's forces in the final victory over the Shimabara Rebellion.

MATSUDAIRA TADAKATA

b. 2565 a.u.c. Senior Councillor in the Taikun's government.

MATSUDAIRA NORIYASU

b. 2548 a.u.c. Senior Councillor in the Taikun's government.

MITO

AIZAWA SEISHISAI

b. 2534 a.u.c. A scholar and a thinker of the Mito School.

NOBUMITSU AOYAMA

b. 2560 a.u.c. A student, later scholar at Mito School

TENKŌ TOYODA

b. 2558 a.u.c. A student, later scholar at Mito School

SAGA

NABESHIMA NAOMASA

b. 2568 a.u.c. *Daimyo* of the Saga Domain.

SHINPEI ETŌ

b. 2587 a.u.c. Retainer of the Saga Domain.

TANAKA

TANAKA HISASHIGE
b. 2552 a.u.c. A scholar of *Rangaku* magic, mechanician and thaumaturgist.

TANAKA DAIKICHI
b. 2598 a.u.c. Heir and apprentice of Hisashige Tanaka.

EIGHT-HEADED SERPENT

OZUN

b. 2581 a.u.c. A renegade Yamabushi priest

AZUMI

b. 2585 a.u.c. The last of the line of shinobi assassins of Koga

VARYAGA KHAGANATE

FRIDRIK OTTERSON

b. 2568 a.u.c. Varyagan admiral, Captain of the *Diana*.

MAGNUS INGVARSSON

b. 2549 a.u.c. The ship's doctor on *Diana*.

HJALMAR NOBELIUS

b. 2554 a.u.c. Varyagan inventor and thaumaturgist, creator of the *Diana*.

Thank you for reading *The Islands in the Mist*
If you enjoyed it, why not leave a comment on Amazon or
Goodreads?

The Year of the Dragon cycle contains the following volumes:

The Shadow of Black Wings

The Warrior's Soul

The Islands in the Mist

The Rising Tide

The Year of the Dragon: Books 1-4 Delux Edition

THE RISING TIDE

PROLOGUE

The grounds of the Imperial Palace of the Divine *Mikado* were as tranquil as the blue, cloudless sky above. Noble men shuffled along gravel paths in silence. Thrushes sang softly in the gingko trees. Water trickled in the canals along the avenues into the ponds where frogs croaked the coming of the evening.

Crown Prince Mutsuhito sat down on the springy grass beside one such pond, looking at the great white wall stretching all around the palace gardens. Beyond lay the bustle of Heian, the Imperial Capital. The streets of the city he had seen only once, when as a child he had to run from a fire to the Shimogamo Shrine across the river.

"Trapped in a palace like *Butsu-sama* himself," he said quietly. Nobody heard him beyond the silk curtain. Since he'd been three years old and could express himself formally, the Crown Prince had insisted on having his path concealed from the outside world wherever he went on foot. Nobody protested, of course; nobody questioned. The word of the imperial heir was a command of the God.

"How is my Divine Father doing today?" he asked louder.

"His Imperial Majesty is busy writing another letter," an unnamed servant answered from beyond the curtain. All his servants were noble lords themselves, of course, coming only from the finest aristocratic families.

"He is angry, then," the prince guessed. He imagined his father's jowls shaking with fury. *Mikado* Kōmei was often angry, and when he was angry, he wrote letters.

"There are... disturbing news from the Taikun's court."

"Oh?"

"I am not sure, *denka*. We did not have an official report yet, so we must rely on rumours."

"What is it, then?"

"There is a rumour of – unspeakable as it sounds – the barbarians landing in Edo."

"Invasion?"

The prince stood up abruptly. A frightened frog leapt from under his feet.

"A scouting party, perhaps... I believe if it was indeed an invasion, we would have more news about it by now."

But how? The Divine Winds were supposed to be impenetrable... have the Bataavians betrayed us?

"Prepare the curtain," Mutsuhito ordered, "I think I shall visit my Father."

An acrid, unpleasant smell filled the imperial chambers; the stench of alcohol and women. Mutsuhito covered his nose with a handkerchief and entered his father's study.

The *Mikado* ordered the woman away. The Prince recognised her – one of the ladies-in-waiting. The woman picked up her kimono, giggled and disappeared through the back door.

"I thought you were writing letters, Father-*sama*."

The *Mikado* tried to rose with dignity, but swayed back onto the silk cushions. His face was purple.

"I was! I am! Look, here it is. It's almost ready."

Mutsuhito reached for the scroll and browsed through. Despite his state, his father's writing remained calm and dignified. It was a missive reminding the *Taikun* of his duties to the protection of the Divine Land and the need of expulsion of any barbarians who dared to stand on it.

"What happened in Edo?" the Prince asked.

"The barbarians have set up a camp south of the city and demand to speak to the *Taikun*. Why have they not yet been annihilated or how did they even get so far inland, I don't know. They are not telling me everything – but I *will* find out. I have my own ways."

The barbarians, Mutsuhito thought, *what were they like?* They were not all bad – he touched the burned-out circle of skin on his arm where he had been secretly vaccinated against the pox by a red-haired physician. Not even his father knew about it – all Western medicine was forbidden in the palace.

"I like the toys the Westerners make," he said, "the dolls that move of their own accord, the birds that sing when you turn the key..."

"Mere tricks to gain our confidence!" the *Mikado* cried. "I will order these toys burned!"

The prince said nothing, not risking his father's wrath turning against him. There would always be more toys sent from the south.

"I can see you are busy, Father-*sama*," he said, glancing towards the back door. "I will leave you to your... duties."

The *Mikado*'s lips wobbled. He raised his hand feebly, holding the wooden sceptre, the symbol of his power.

"It's all my fault," he said.

"What is?"

"If the land suffers it means the sovereign is to blame. It's the punishment of Heavens. The fires, the earthquakes and now this... I have been frail and I have neglected my duty as the Divine Father."

"There has never been a more dutiful *Mikado* than you."

His father hid his face in his hands and started sobbing. Mutsuhito felt it best to leave him alone.

The Prince studied his reflection in the round bronze mirror. He untied the ribbons holding his long black tresses in place and the hair fell down his shoulders, clad in the red ceremonial robe.

His fingers smelled of fish, despite frequent washing. It was customary to present the Crown Prince with fresh sea fish on any occasion, these having been of old an item of luxury in the landlocked capital city. There were neither jewels nor gold adorning his room. The Imperial Family lived in traditional austerity, dependant on gifts from the courtiers and a meagre yearly stipend.

There were some more gifts coming his way, and slightly more opulent. His Coming of Age day was swiftly approaching. Soon his long boyish hair would be cut off and his plain robes replaced with the clothes of an adult.

It seemed to him ominous to have such an important ceremony in such a critical time. There were more news of the barbarians coming from Edo and none of it served to calm Mutsuhito's father down. The *Mikado* had ordered prayers for Yamato's prosperity in the seven shrines and seven temples of the capital and then sat down to write another angry missive to the *Taikun*.

Mutsuhito wondered if anyone ever read the letters. *Probably not.* Why would the all-powerful overlord and commander of all of Yamato armies care what the Imperial Puppet had to say on matters of state? The *Mikado* represented a symbolic and spiritual power, without any real influence. It was said that all the healing power of the shrine priests depended on the *Mikado*'s well-being, but Mutsuhito suspected this was just a story made up by the chroniclers in the ancient times to justify the need for the existence of the Imperial Family. His father had only very limited command over the spirits. His biological mother, he remembered, a daughter of a noble family from Chinzei, had become a skilled healer, but only once she had retired to a temple in the mountains.

A tiny bell rang out, signifying the water had reached the desired temperature. He stepped towards the bath, untied the silk sash and dropped his red robe. Nobody attended his baths, not even the chamber maids. This was a breach of the custom but, again, nobody dared to question his command. They just assumed it was one of his divine whims.

But there was another, much more important reason for his seclusion. One that only his mother and his physician knew about. At first – they told him – it was just a small spot of infarction on his upper thigh, a bit of hard, dead skin. But as the prince had grown, so had the blemish and by now it covered most of his thigh, descending below the knee in places.

It didn't hurt or itch. In fact, somehow it felt even more natural than his human skin. He sat on the bath's edge and scratched the thigh absentmindedly; the soft light green scales shimmered in the candle light.